The Witch, the Baker, and the Curse Maker

COLLEEN DELANEY

The Witch, the Baker, and the Curse Maker

COLLEEN DELANEY

CITY OWL
PRESS

This book is a work of fiction. Names, characters, places, and incidents either are products of the author's imagination or are used fictitiously. Any resemblance to actual events or locales or persons, living or dead, is entirely coincidental and not intended by the author.

THE WITCH, THE BAKER, AND THE CURSE MAKER
The Witches of Star Island, Book 5

CITY OWL PRESS
www.cityowlpress.com

Cover Design by MiblArt. All stock photos licensed appropriately.

Edited by Tee Tate.

For information on subsidiary rights, please contact the publisher at info@cityowlpress.com.

Print Edition ISBN: 978-1-64898-583-6

Digital Edition ISBN: 978-1-64898-584-3

Printed in the United States of America

To Mom

Thank you for instilling a love of gardening and writing in me.
I only wish I had inherited your uncanny ability to rhyme at a moment's notice.

Praise for Colleen Delaney

"Delaney casts a spell with the first in *The Witches of Star Island* paranormal series. The love story is endearing and the supernatural twists propel the story forward at an exciting clip. The ending leaves many questions unanswered... but Delaney's sturdy worldbuilding ensures this series has plenty of places to go. This is a strong start." — *Publisher's Weekly*

"Family relationships, soulmate relationships, past lives, and incredibly well done magical elements keep you turning the pages of this one." — *HJ Reviews*

"*Finding His Mate* is an interesting story in a dystopian future where different paranormal creatures rule the world. The characters are so damaged and so resilient, and the next book promises more of the same. Highly recommend for fans of shifter romance with fated mates, especially if darker backstories are your thing." —*Jaycee Jarvis, author of The Hands of Destin series*

"The Hedge Witch is a fast-paced and delightful read with a heavy dash of spice as well. I recommend this to fans of a good witchy romance, particularly if you enjoy a suspenseful plot to go along with it." — *Your Book Friend Blog*

Also by Colleen Delaney

THE WOLVES OF LUVEN

Finding His Mate

Waiting for His Mate

Stealing His Mate

Protecting His Mate

Aching for His Mate

THE WITCHES OF STAR ISLAND

The Hedge Witch

Bewitching Rosemary

Hauntings and House Witchery

Warlocks Get Witched

The Witch, the Baker, and the Curse Maker

Chapter One

October first arrived with a sense of unease on the wind.

It was officially the last month of the prophecy. Thirty-one more days until the tide turned. Since last May, the Bay sisters had been visited by dangerous witches and warlocks out to steal their powers and had met adoring soulmates from lifetimes ago.

Lavender had had enough of both at this point.

All four of her younger sisters were currently in serious relationships with their soulmates. Rosemary and Asher bought a house by the sea, Laurel and Owen were renting an apartment while they built a house, Verbena had moved into Luke's cabin, and Sage and Will were cohabitating in the ancestral Bay cottage.

Which left Lavender living in an apartment by herself for the first time in her life at thirty-four.

A loud meow echoing in the bathroom reminded her she wasn't actually alone. Erie, her new kitten, was her roommate now. He was a bit of a slow learner and didn't quite understand what it meant to be a witch's cat, but Lavender had high hopes that before the year was out, the little guy would be well on his way to becoming her familiar.

Lavender took quick stock of her new apartment. The kitchen was completely unpacked and lived in, with her measuring cup collection permanently littering a corner of one of the countertops. The living room, on the other hand...it needed work. She had a small wall of boxes pushed into one corner, containing everything from winter coats and seasonal decor to extra towels, books, and her throw blankets. All things that needed to be unpacked and settled sooner rather than later.

This week, she resolved to finish moving into her apartment. Maybe she would even ask Verbena to help, but that might be more of a headache. Oh! Maybe she would ask Verbena to do it for her while she was at work. That would be worth it. Nothing like a house witch setting up your apartment. The vibes would be immaculate.

Her phone buzzed on the countertop, shaking Lavender out of her daze. It was four forty-five. Time to go to work.

There were a few positives to moving to an apartment in town. Biggest of all, she could walk to work. Her fifteen-minute drive was now a three-minute brisk walk down the street. Which at four forty-five in the morning in July was downright beautiful. Now that autumn was firmly seated on Star Island, it was getting pretty chilly. She tried not to think about four forty-five in January.

Lavender wrapped her burnt orange scarf around her neck twice, added her camel pea coat, slipped on her ankle boots, and was out the door after blowing Erie a kiss goodbye and reminding him to behave.

A few moments later, she unlocked the backdoor to the Immortal Cupcake, flipped on the kitchen lights, and unbundled herself.

She loved her bakery.

Twenty-year-old Lavender never would have believed that fourteen years later she'd own a bakery on Star Island. Becoming a sudden guardian to three of her four sisters had nearly broken her. Doing it all basically alone—Rosemary tried, but eighteen-year-old Rosemary was still a child at heart—seemed insurmountable. She became a parent overnight, moved halfway across the country, and did it all with minimal help from anyone.

But here she was. Thirty-four, a business owner, with four relatively normal and well-adjusted sisters.

She did the best she could. And it had turned out okay.

Lavender pulled out the trays of bread dough from under their towels and stuck them into the oven. Then she got to work on cookies, sweet breads, cakes, and muffins. It was officially October, and the residents of Star Island would expect nothing less than perfection from their baker.

"I can't believe you would take the zucchini chocolate chip muffins off the menu. Especially without telling me. I have one every morning." Mr. Sherman rapped his knuckles against the counter. "They are a staple in my diet!"

"I am so sorry you are disappointed," Lavender began, eyeing the line forming behind him, "but those are a seasonal offering. We only have them from July until September. Every year. Since I opened the store."

"That cannot be true." He looked flustered now. Damn, Lavender hated disappointing customers.

"Can I recommend a morning glory muffin? Carrots, apples, cinnamon. They are really good."

"I don't know if I'll like it..."

"How about I give you this one for free." She handed him one in a paper bag. "And if you love it, just tell everyone you meet. If you hate it, not a big deal."

His eyes brightened. "Really?"

"Yup." Lavender could hear Hazel coming in through the back door. She turned her head away from Mr. Sherman. "Hazel, we're swamped out here."

"Washing my hands!" she called back.

"You really are," Mr. Sherman said as he lowered his voice, "a very kind woman. No matter what the gossip is about your sisters."

She plastered a practiced smile on her face. "Thank you."

Eight hours later, Lavender slid the last batch of portioned-out salted caramel cookie dough into the fridge to chill and shook out her hands. She was tired. It was autumn, so her body naturally began to slide into the "why aren't you sitting by a fire enjoying the fruits of the harvest you worked so hard this summer to prepare?" feeling. But this was more. She was constantly on edge—either the bakery was swamped, or she got a huge order for a party just around the corner, or a chaos warlock was trying to kill one of her sisters.

Miloslav Stoch.

Lavender had recognized him the second she saw him. That asshole from her past. Of course, *of course,* he had to come back to her in this life. And worse than that, he was even more connected to Sage. Lavender wondered if there was another Stoch waiting in the wings who had it out for her. Sure, when Miloslav was Charles he'd been responsible for the deaths of basically everyone she loved, but...

But it was war. It didn't feel like he had a personal vendetta against her. Hell, Sage had killed Miloslav in three different lifetimes. Laurel had cursed Morana to live without happiness for centuries. Rosemary had broken off her betrothal with Ivan, and Verbena...well, Verbena had been a comely servant girl who'd ruined a lord's plans for his nephew.

But Lavender and Miloslav? Their connection was flimsy at best. Sure, he was a double agent and caused a great number of casualties to the Allied forces, but it wasn't the same. Lavender knew him, a bit, as the jerk patient she had to deal with. But beyond that? He was just some guy.

If only she'd thought, as she'd lain dying after his betrayal, to curse him. That would have been helpful right about now.

"I was thinking," Hazel interrupted her thoughts. "You are probably ready now, right?"

Lavender looked up from the cookie dough at Hazel, who currently wrestled a giant gray scarf into a cute knot.

"Ready for what?"

"Lavy. To date! For the past ten years, every time I tried to set you up with someone—some very good catches I might add—you've always said, I can't, my sisters. Well," Hazel added, waggling her eyebrows, "Rosemary is shacked up with Sheriff—excuse me, former Sheriff Evans, Laurel has that big-eyed man following her around like a puppy, Verbena and Luke finally got together, and don't pretend like I don't know that Sage is with that bookish guy. Which honestly shocks me."

"Why would that shock you?"

"I always thought Sage would end up with a strong farmer, you know?" Hazel shrugged.

Lavender barked a laugh. "Sage is a strong farmer. She doesn't need one."

"Touché. But to the point, you don't have any excuses left. Your sisters are all paired off. All over eighteen. All living separately from you. You can finally date."

"Haze," Lavender began.

"What? Would you like a woman? My cousin Mirie is smoking hot. Legs for days. Recently single. Loves baked goods and can change a car tire. I should know. Before I moved here, I called her anytime I had car trouble."

"Thank you for the offer. I am not into women."

"Good news for you, I have an insane number of cousins. What about Andy? Accountant in Boston. Very nice man if you can get past his fleece vests. Thirty-eight, never married. Handsome. From now on, assume all my cousins are good looking. They are related to me after all."

"Again, thank you for the offer. I don't want to date anyone."

"Aren't you lonely?"

Lavender shook her head. Hazel didn't know. She could never know. Lavender would be hard-pressed to say something along the lines of "Oh, I've already met my soulmate. But we left each other after a spell gone wrong, and he disappeared from my life completely. And even though I am aching for companionship, I know that no one except him could ever, ever make me whole."

Instead, she said, "It's nice to have some quiet finally. I haven't been alone since I was twenty."

"Suit yourself. But the moment you change your mind, there will be a cousin dressed up and ready to take you on a date."

"Thank you, Haze. Really."

"I'll see you tomorrow. You sure you'll be okay closing by yourself?"

"Yup." The next day was Monday, and now that the North Atlantic was getting choppier, tourists only flooded the bakery on weekends. By the end of October, barely anyone would be heading out this far into the ocean. In November, the ferry would switch to every other day, and then twice a week for January and February.

"I'm off, then. Joey is making chili tonight and sent me a picture of it bubbling already. Can't wait." With that, Hazel was out the door and Lavender was alone.

She eyed the kitchen one last time, tucking dirty dishcloths into the laundry bin and eyeing the dough in the fridge, then left. Two years earlier, she'd finally made enough money to hire a nighttime cleaner, which made her life so much easier. Spending all morning baking, then all day working at the bakery, and then all night cleaning had nearly driven her to a mental breakdown. Now she took her nights off, didn't work on Tuesdays, and took off Wednesday afternoons and Thursday mornings. It was a better way to live.

She pulled her scarf a bit tighter as the wind picked up outside. It was dusk, a gorgeous golden light spilling down the street on the back of a wind, reminding her winter was coming soon. Before she knew it, she'd be walking home in the dark, trying not to slip on ice.

Lavender unlocked her apartment and found Erie curled up on the couch. She sighed, hung up her coat, scarf, and purse, then collapsed beside him.

"I'm not lonely, right? You and I are going to be okay. Just the two of us." Erie rewarded her by jumping off the couch and darting into her bedroom and under the bed.

She huffed and sank deeper into the couch, closing her eyes as she tipped her head backward.

"I..." She cleared her throat and started again. "I am going to pretend you are here. And that you are in a listening mood and not a talking mood." She smiled to herself. "I don't know why I am telling *you* this, *you* can't really hear me. And I don't need your permission to have an imaginary conversation with you." She sighed and settled her arms across her waist. "I don't know if I can handle this. I've been taking care of my sisters, all of them, for so long I barely remember who I was before that. And they've all been adults for six years now, but that doesn't just turn off. I don't stop worrying because of some arbitrary birthday that tells me my duties as guardian are over." She paused and noticed a slight weight coming off her shoulders. "Charles is back. Now he's called Miloslav Stoch. He's as charming as you remember. If you still remember. There's this curse and it's such a mess and all I keep thinking is...what if I gave up? I'm so tired. And this fight...I don't know if I can win it. He's a chaos warlock. He's not just connected to me but Sage too. And his sister is looped with Laurel, his brother with Rosemary, and his uncle with Verbena. It's like the fates put us in a perfect line for him to take down, and I can't help but wonder, what if we are supposed to fall? Is this supposed to be the end of the Bay line?" She let those words settle in the air. "No. It can't be. But hell. I don't know if I can win this fight." She rolled onto her side and squeezed her eyes shut as hard as she could, attempting to conjure the scent of him next to her. Freshly baked bread and frost on a winter wind surrounded her.

"I miss you. I love you. I'll see you on our next chance."

Chapter Two

Another September gone. Another year with nothing to show for it.

Gavin sat at his desk, closing every browser, exiting out of documents he wouldn't open until September first the next year. Grief washed over him like a wave. It was harder every year. He started Septembers with such hope. This was the time. He would stumble on *something*—some clue he hadn't noticed. Or she would finally use social media. Be added to some company's website. Anything.

Where was she?

He collected his loose papers from when they were first separated. Her parents' obituary, the listing of their house in Ohio. A printout of her class schedule for the spring semester that never came.

He tucked everything away for another year, then left his apartment for the night. He needed food, as much as he hated the thought of doing anything but wallowing in his sadness.

Gavin lived in the Wicker Park neighborhood of Chicago. He'd moved there for one reason and one reason only: they'd talked about moving there after graduation. They were going to open a restaurant together, be written up in every food blog. It was going to be called Oak and Beam and it was going to revolutionize the restaurant scene.

A lot had changed in the last thirteen years, and it wasn't the restaurant scene. Gavin worked at Radka as head chef when he wasn't researching the whereabouts of his college girlfriend. He had no plans beyond that, no life. He cooked, he spent one month a year looking for the love of his life, and he ran. He ran because it was all he could do to keep himself from going insane. But, he was thirty-five now. His knees had about five years left until four marathons a year would become undoable. Maybe he needed to switch to swimming. It was supposed to be better for the joints. But he loved the rush of air in his ears when he ran. It was the only time he felt like his head went quiet.

The only time he could forget.

He pushed into the diner at the end of his block and grabbed a seat at the counter. He wasn't looking for anything fancy, just something to make sure he didn't get sick from hunger, and a diner like this was the perfect place for that. The decor hadn't changed since the 1970s, the cushions were a little sticky, and there was a man in his nineties sitting in a booth with a newspaper spread over the entirety of the table.

"What'll you have?" The waitress behind the counter asked, pen and pad in hand.

"Cup of coffee and whatever you would order for yourself."

"'Scuse me?"

He managed a small grin. "You know what's the best. I'll take what you get when you're on break."

"Grilled cheese and tomato soup with a slice of banana cream pie."

"Not pumpkin?"

"Nah, our pumpkin pie is terrible."

"I appreciate your honesty. A grilled cheese, tomato soup, and slice of banana cream pie it is."

She nodded and took his menu, then disappeared into the kitchen.

Gavin buried his face in his hands. He heard the clink of a mug set in front of him and the soothing pour of coffee that followed.

What the fuck was he going to do? He'd been looking for her for thirteen years. She didn't want to be found. He needed to take that to heart and accept it. He was never going to find his girl.

But how could he give up? He knew what they were, what they meant to each other. It would be impossible to let her go forever.

"Gavin? Gavin Murphy?"

He slowly pulled his hands away from his face and turned to look at a very smiley blonde woman.

"Hi?" he said slowly. Part of his brain niggled, reaching for where he knew her from. But her name stayed just out of reach.

"It's Rebecca! Rebecca Anton? From DePaul?"

"Oh, Rebecca." He stood up and awkwardly hugged a girl he'd spent a lot of nights drunk with fifteen years ago when his roommate had dated her. "How are you?"

"I'm great! You know. Living in Chicago. Obviously. How are you?"

"Good, good," he lied. "Also living in Chicago."

"Oh my God, this is so crazy running into you! Like the universe is messing with me." She laughed loudly.

"How is the universe messing with you?"

"I mean, just this Labor Day, I went on vacation and saw Lavender! It's like my frosh year is following me around."

Gavin felt all the blood drain from his face.

"Wait, what did you just say?"

"Uh, I saw Lavender? Remember? Lavender Bay, the girl you dated—"

"No, I remember her." Play it cool, he chided himself. "Where did you see her?"

"Star Island. It was the cutest little island near Massachusetts. We had such a good time. I have two kids now, it was a family trip."

"Wow. How weird you were both on vacation at the same time."

"Oh, no. She lives there. I walked into a bakery to grab a coffee and some doughnuts for my kids, and she was right there, standing behind the counter! And now I run into you! I wonder who else from freshman year is going to be thrown in my path." She giggled, then dropped her smile. "Crap. Definitely a few people I hope I don't run into. Well, it was good to see you." She lifted the takeout bag in her hand. "I need to get dinner home."

"Good to see you too," Gavin mumbled, but he was already going for his phone.

Already opening his browser and typing in "bakery star island."

Already opening the page for the Immortal Cupcake and going to the "About Us" tab.

. . .

Six years ago, LB bought the former Sweets Shop and revamped the space into the Immortal Cupcake.

LB. Lavender Bay.

Gavin's hands started shaking. A bakery on an island in the Atlantic. It sounded like something she would do. He quickly opened a new tab and typed in "Bay Star Island Massachusetts." The results populated with a listing for Laurel Bay reading tarot cards.

Lavender had a little sister named Laurel.

Holy shit. He'd found her.

"One grilled cheese and one tomato soup."

"Thanks," Gavin answered without looking up. He'd eat and leave a hefty tip, but his mind wasn't in the diner anymore. It was miles away, years away, wrapped up in every memory of Lavender. Jumping to what he would say the moment he saw her again.

Hell, he was going to see Lavender again.

He shot off a text to his boss. He needed time off, serious time. This wasn't going to be a long weekend. Gavin hadn't taken a vacation in years. It was time to call in on all the late nights he'd worked, all the Christmases and New Year's Eves, all the Sunday mornings and Saturday nights. Every birthday he'd worked in favor of spending it alone. It had all been worth it now. She was within his grasp.

He was finally going to see Lavender.

Chapter Three

Moonbeam.

His mouth had pressed against the back of her neck, lips had moved against her skin like silk. One hand buried in her hair, the other slipped over her ribs to hold her.

"Never leave you. Never ever. Promise. I promise on everything I am. I'm yours."

"Don't make promises," she had said, like she'd already known in a month they'd be apart, in a year completely separate. In ten, she would swear she'd forgotten the sound of his voice, the smell of his skin in the morning. He would be a shadow from another life, a happier, easier version of the one she ended up living.

Like that other life, but somehow still sharp, no matter how much time and space slid between them.

"I can't help it. When I'm with you, I want to swear every bit of my soul over to yours."

She had laughed against him, had smiled when she had turned toward him. He had been so warm, so right. Everything had felt good. She had kissed his jaw, had sighed just before she whispered, "Promises made in the middle of the night are the easiest to breathe and the easiest to break."

Goddess, they'd been barely older than children, but she'd loved him.

Loved him more than she'd ever dreamed possible. He was half her soul, half her breath, half her life. When they were together, Lavender was whole, something complete and right. Something unbreakable.

Lavender blinked awake. The pale sun of an autumn morning streaked across her room and directly into her eyes.

She hated those dreams.

They felt great when she was in the midst of them, tangled up in memories and his arms. But even then, there was also a cast of sadness over them. Her dreams could only do so much. They couldn't erase the heaviness she carried since they'd separated.

And she always woke up, always remembered. She'd been so prideful, so sure of her powers and their love. She'd thought they'd survive anything.

She had been wrong.

Goddess, she didn't even recognize the little girl in those dreams. Going to college, partying on the weekends, living in Chicago hundreds of miles away from her family. That wasn't Lavender anymore. She'd morphed into the person she was now out of necessity, and there was no shaking off her new persona.

She checked her phone: nine-fifteen. Everyone should be up. Well, everyone except Laurel, but Owen did a good job answering for the two of them as a couple on the family text.

LAVENDER: Everyone good? No run-ins with Stochs overnight?

VERBENA: All good at the Bay/Karnes household!

ASHER: Rosemary is still sleeping, but it's all fine here.

OWEN: Laurel is also still sleeping but nothing is going on.

SAGE: As far as I know, Will is working and I am fine harvesting pumpkins in the back. Speaking of, does anyone want acorn squash? I have more than I can sell this week. Probably more than I can sell this month.

VERBENA: I'll take a couple!

. . .

Lavender set her phone back on her nightstand and stared at the ceiling. At least they'd all made it through the night.

Miloslav would be back. A soul like that wouldn't give up easily. Plus, he had a weird obsession with Sage. When Lavender had been someone else... well, Miloslav hadn't been interested her in the same way.

She pushed her blankets off and climbed out of bed, nearly stepping on Erie's tail.

"Ah! Erie!" Lavender shouted as her cat darted under the bed. "On my bed or on your bed! Not a good sleeping spot." She steadied herself, then headed to the bathroom. She may have had the morning off, but there was always stuff to do.

Not her entire list, but the most pressing to-do was how on earth she was going to handle the chaos warlock and company who were terrorizing her family. Related to that, there was a generational blood curse over her line. The two were of course connected, as Miloslav Stoch had helped lay the curse in a previous lifetime, and now wanted to make good on the promises. He'd tracked down all the living Bay Witches. Now he just needed all of their blood.

He had a bit of Laurel's, but then again so did his sister, Morana. Neither of them seemed particularly like people who wanted to share power.

But Miloslav had managed a bit of Sage's too. So, he was only three Bay sisters away from a completed curse.

In short, the other three Bay sisters needed to steer clear of a chaos warlock who knew where they lived. It wasn't an ideal situation.

Lavender had faith in the gods, as much as any witch did. She understood that good didn't always win over evil, and that witches who dabbled in darkness had patrons as well as those who bathed themselves in light. There were no guarantees to happiness, soulmates broke up, parents died, and bloodlines ended. Life wasn't fair. Not this one, or any previous one.

"Pull it together," she chided herself as she marched into the bathroom. She couldn't afford an existential breakdown right now. She had four hours until she needed to be at work, and in those four hours, Lavender was going to attempt to break a generational curse and test out a new recipe for a pie she was tentatively calling "The Chocolate Peanut Butter Dream Team." Her time was in high demand.

So, just like many oldest children before her with too much on their plate, Lavender pushed all her feelings deep into the pit of her stomach and got ready for the day.

"Lavender? There's a line," Cece called from the front.

"Shit!" Lavender hissed. She'd burned the batch of salted caramel cookies. She didn't usually make another batch this late in the day, but after the third customer asked if there were any in the back, she took it as a sign. But now that stupid sign had her with a tray of burned, unsellable cookies and an overwhelmed employee.

"I'll be right there!" She scraped the cookies off the baking sheet and into the garbage, then quickly rinsed the sheet with water so the caramel didn't immediately harden. She rushed through the swinging door as she wiped her hands on her apron and immediately banged into Cece.

"Ow!" she shouted.

"I'm sorry! I should have yelled door." Lavender quickly moved past her to tend to the line. "Can I help who's next?"

The bakery was packed, but her eyes went straight to the next customer. Ice blond hair. Smirk that could freeze her heart. Her stomach dropped as Miloslav Stoch stepped toward her.

"Hi, Ruby. Heard this is the best place on Star Island for a treat."

"Don't call me that." Beneath the counter, Lavender quickly traced circles around her wrists, a protection spell Verbena had taught her. "We're in public. Unless you are here to order a cookie, get out of my place of business." She kept her voice low, and the bakery's din managed to keep any other customers from staring at them.

"Hm...should I call you another name?" He grinned wickedly. "I'll take a chocolate chip cookie."

"Don't have 'em. Read the menu, there's a line."

He smirked and made a show of looking above her head. "Well. All looks good. Nothing blood-themed though. For Halloween, I mean." He leaned in close. "I bet you cut yourself in that kitchen all the time, Ruby. All it takes is one glistening drop. Don't you think it would feel good to let it all go?

Give it all up. I'm going to win anyway. Fate isn't on your side. Wasn't last time, isn't this time."

Lavender's vision started to go hazy on the sides, like an ocular migraine. Chaos magic. Hell, was he going to attack her right here in front of all her customers? She tried to retrace the circles on her wrist, but her hands felt uncontrollable, like she was extremely drowsy. She swayed where she stood, fighting to stay on her feet.

She'd never been in so much pain in her life...the cabinet on top of her, the medical tent in shambles. Did anyone survive? She could see Arthur. She stretched her one free arm toward him. If she could just touch him, he'd be fine. He had to be fine...

"Dude! Order or get the hell out of the line! I have an entire soccer team waiting for their cookies!" Beth Goodman, the woman standing behind Miloslav, gave him a nudge with her elbow. "Tourists! I swear to God, you people are the worst! You do not walk into the Immortal Cupcake without knowing your order. And having a backup. I cannot wait for the weather to turn so we don't have to deal with you lot."

A few other people joined in, hassling him to make a choice, to the point that when Miloslav looked back at Lavender, his magic had completely dissipated.

"Sir, you can order right now, or you can go to the end of the line."

"I'll be back," he huffed, then stomped out of the store.

Lavender sagged against the counter, her palms nearly slipping off the surface due to how sweaty they were. Hell, that was strong magic. It was like she was in France again, experiencing dying for a third time.

Miloslav was back. She should have known it wouldn't be long. What would she have done if Beth hadn't broken the spell? She needed stronger wards at the bakery.

"What a weirdo. Blood cookies?" Beth started. "All right, I need six oatmeal frosted, six snickerdoodles, four French toast bars, and have you started making that mulled wine cake yet?"

"Uh, no. Not until November."

"Bummer. Make it five French toast bars. I definitely deserve a treat after that game."

She nodded and mindlessly began filling a bag with the treats. As soon as she handed Beth her order, another customer stepped up. And then another. Lavender switched into autopilot, smile plastered on her face, even though she was riding a wave of nausea.

Miloslav was here, had come into the Immortal Cupcake with no issues, and used magic on her in front of an audience. She was screwed.

At five minutes to five, the store was empty. Cece had left, the counters were wiped down, the leftovers wrapped for the day-old basket tomorrow. Lavender pulled out her phone and tapped out a quick message to her sisters.

LAVENDER: Miloslav is back on Star Island. He was alone. I am okay.

She slipped her phone back into her pocket and tried to ignore the buzzing against her thigh.

Was she okay? Would she ever be okay? It hadn't mattered for so long. It had been thirteen years of simply trying to survive. Honestly, she didn't know if she was up to one more task. A chaos warlock, and not just any. A man whose soul she knew to be a rotten one. He'd cursed witches, the worst thing a warlock could do. His soul was not one that could be reformed.

How was she supposed to fight that?

The door jingled opened.

"I'm sorry. We're closing. I should have locked the door."

"Hey, Moonbeam."

Lavender dropped the stack of receipts in her hand.

No no no no no no!

Not him. Not now.

She slowly turned around, afraid of who would stand before her. A trick by a chaos warlock? Or something worse?

"Lavender," he whispered, his voice awash with relief. "I found you."

Gavin.

Lavender fell to her knees.

Chapter Four

"I found you," he said. God, she was beautiful. He hadn't forgotten her, not one part of her soul, but she was a little different now. Her hair was darker, her shoulders softer than he remembered. He wanted to run to her, kiss her, twirl her in the air, tell her just how much he had missed her and wanted to—

Lavender fell to the ground behind the counter.

"Lavender!" he yelled, then dashed around the glass display case and to her side. She was on her hands and knees, hyperventilating. They locked eyes as he slid down to the floor. She looked like a rabbit in fight-or-flight mode.

But she was here. She wasn't running. At least, not yet.

"Shit, put your arms over your head." He arranged her to sit against the wall, then guided her arms over her head. She didn't shirk from his hands and did as he asked.

"Slow breaths. In through your nose, out through your mouth." He kept his hands on hers and breathed with her. Lavender closed her eyes and leaned her head back. "I've got you," he said slowly. "You're okay. I'm sorry I scared you."

She nodded but still hadn't slowed her breathing. Damn, was she going to faint?

Gavin moved his hand down her arm, gently tracing circles just below the inside of her elbow. He used to do that when she was stressed about exams, and it usually led to her falling into a sound sleep. He kept up the rhythm, featherlight, figure eights.

"You remembered," she gasped. She still sounded panicked though. It wasn't so simple that a few touches would soothe her.

He should have called, emailed the bakery. Eased her into it. But he couldn't. A small part of him thought that if he gave her the chance, she would have disappeared again. Selfishly, he wanted to be the only one who knew where the other was. He couldn't give it up. Thirteen years of looking...and now he was looking at her.

"I remember. Don't try to talk," he added. "We'll sit here until you feel better." Gavin settled to sit against the wall beside her. He took her hand in his and continued running his other fingertips over her skin. "This is a beautiful bakery. I would know it was yours even if you weren't here. Even smells like you in here."

"That's cinnamon." She huffed a laugh. Her voice sounded a little steadier now. "Only smells like that in here from September until January first."

"And then it probably smells like bright citrus. Mint in the spring. And then in June, I bet you can smell sugary strawberries down the street." He could picture her here now—baking her masterpieces, bringing so much joy to this little island. Flour on her hands, brilliant ideas in her head. His perfect Moonbeam.

God, thirteen whole years and he was still completely in love with her. One glance, and it was like no time had passed at all.

He sat beside her, basking in the joy of her skin under his hand, and smiled. It was all going to be okay now.

"Gavin." Her heaving stopped, her fear-stricken face melted into something more familiar. "What are you doing here?"

"I needed to see you." It was as simple as that. He *needed* to see her. He had needed to see her every single day since he'd last seen her. He needed a thousand other things—to spend every day with her, to make her happier than she'd ever been—but for now, one thing was enough.

"You shouldn't be here," she said slowly, her voice catching on the end. "I'm sorry."

All the anticipation and hope he had for this moment slowly deflated.

She didn't want him here.

He should have known better. Hell. She had been hiding for thirteen years. She made a conscious decision to be unfindable.

But...Lavender believed in fate and the universe pushing people together.

"I'm going to pretend for a minute that we haven't had a thirteen-year break in seeing each other. I'm going to pretend I can talk to you like you're still my girlfriend, like we told each other 'I love you' before we went to sleep last night, and there's no need to hide anything from you. I've wanted to find you since the last time I saw you. Rebecca Anton walked into a diner I was sitting at a few nights ago, mentioned she saw you here. It was a sign. She told me exactly where you were. Even if you don't want to see me, some part of the universe wanted me to see you. Even if it was just my last chance to look at you." Gavin squeezed her hand, then let it go.

He'd known there was a possibility of this. She could tell him to leave, that she was over him and that was that. If that happened...he would go. But God. He didn't want that.

A small smile escaped from Lavender's mouth. "When I saw her...I thought something like that might happen. No one from Chicago comes here on vacation." She paused. "Do you still live in Chicago?"

He nodded. "Wicker Park."

Her brow creased and her eyes softened. "What's it like?"

"Different without you." He paused. "But good. It's changed a lot since we were in college. More families, less tattoo parlors, but I think you would still like it. I haven't been priced out just yet."

"Gavin, I—" The front door burst open so forcefully, it hit the wall.

"Lavender!" Someone screamed.

"I'm here. I'm okay." She pushed herself up to stand, so Gavin followed suit.

"Shit, do not text that and then ignore me! I was worried that Milosl—" Lavender's sister Rosemary caught a sight of him and stopped talking. "Holy fuck! Gavin?" If he'd thought Lavender looked shocked to see him, Rosemary looked downright dumbfounded. Her eyes quickly darted between the two of them.

"Oh, my goddess. Oh, my goddess. Lavender! What...wha..."

"I had a similar reaction," she admitted. "Gavin's here. On Star Island."

Rosemary nodded, her eyes staying the size of dinner plates. "Whelp. Gavin's here. Shit. And Miloslav's here. Okay. Okay. Um. Should I go? I should probably go, right? Ash is on his way here right now. Just in case he needed to jump between me and mortal danger."

Gavin had spent enough time with Rosemary when she would come visit for the weekend to know that her speech patterns leaned a little crazy.

"I think Gavin and I should talk. Preferably without you." Lavender turned toward him. "Would you mind if we went to my apartment? I should lock up here. And if we leave the lights on, someone is bound to knock and hope they can convince me to open for them."

"Yeah. That's fine." His palms started sweating like he was nineteen again, going home to her dorm for the first time.

Rosemary blew out a breath, looked between the two of them, then turned to go, leaving Gavin and Lavender alone in the bakery.

God, he wanted to wrap his arms around her. Pull her close and bury his face against her hair. It had been mostly blonde in college, but this darker brown suited her. It was softer and made her blue eyes even more stunning.

Those thoughts were all ridiculous. She'd fallen to the ground when she saw him. He was lucky she wasn't kicking him out this instant.

"Gavin?" she prompted, taking a few steps toward the door.

"I'm coming."

He'd follow her off the edge of a cliff, into the churning ocean...He'd follow her to another lifetime when he'd loved her so dearly and lost her so terribly. He'd always follow. Even if it destroyed him, body and soul.

Lavender stepped out of the door and waited for him to cross the threshold. She looked wildly down the street both ways, then locked the door quickly.

"Let's get off the street. It's just a block away."

Gavin nodded and turned with her, staring at the darkened sky. She didn't want to be seen with him. That was fine.

No matter what happened from here on out, he had found her. His life's mission was complete.

Chapter Five

Gavin Murphy coming to not only Star Island but also to her apartment wasn't something Lavender had ever thought would happen. Sure, she'd fantasized, dreamed, and even feared it, but deep in her soul, she never saw it actually happening.

Yet here he was, walking down the streets of Solaris beside her.

Damn. He looked really good. He was the same, yet so different. His hair was longer, brown curls tickled his ears and the nape of his neck. In college he'd always kept it buzzed. He added facial hair too. Lavender remembered mornings with patchy growth, teasing him about his stubble against her cheeks, but now Gavin sported a lush brown beard. But his eyes were the same. His hands were the same. The rumble of his laugh, the way he called her Moonbeam as if he'd been whispering it every day for the last thirteen years...

Hell. She was in trouble.

Stop it. You are going to talk to him for a few minutes, explain that he needs to leave, and move on. You've been apart for your entire adult life. This doesn't change anything.

"This is my building," she said quickly, trying to focus. She slipped her hand into her purse, produced her keys, and tried to keep from shaking.

"I never would have thought a place like this had regular-looking apartment buildings," Gavin said as he followed her up the stairs. "Figured everyone here lived in a seaside cottage or something."

Lavender hummed a laugh. "It has that vibe."

"Can you see the ocean from your window?"

"A little sliver. And only from the bedroom. And it's too dark anyway right now." She felt her cheeks redden after that comment. Why did she bring up her bedroom? Gavin Murphy was *not* allowed in her bedroom. No matter how much she wanted to forget the past hurt, with the present danger of losing herself to him again and the constant danger of a Stoch showing up, falling into bed with Gavin wasn't the distraction she needed. This could not happen.

"This is me." She unlocked and pushed through the door. "I have a new cat around here somewhere. His name is Erie, but he might be staying hidden. He's only met my sisters."

Gavin stepped over her threshold and Lavender felt the atmosphere shift. The unfamiliar, distinctly new feeling faded away in a breath and was replaced with the unmistakable atmosphere of home. The lights were warmer, the couch looked lived in and in its proper place. Even the empty coffee mug Lavender had left next to the sink looked correct. It was like being hugged by a place, finally.

It made sense, Gavin was her soulmate, and now that he was here, this new apartment could shift into a home. She didn't know how to tell the apartment that he wouldn't be staying.

"Your sisters? Do more of them live close by?" Gavin shrugged out of his coat and set it on the back of the couch. "I was pretty surprised to see Rosemary here. Figured you were all spread out across the country."

Lavender sighed. What was she doing? Having small talk with the man who broke her heart?

"Gavin. You're on Star Island. And by the lack of shock on your face, I think you were probably looking for me before Rebecca told you where I was, right?"

He nodded.

"We have...a past and I don't particularly want to hash it all out right now, okay?"

He looked like he was going to protest so she quickly added, "Let's make dinner. Together. We can talk, while we're cooking."

"Like old times?"

"Yeah. A lot has happened since..."

"Since that September," Gavin finished for her. "Probably be good to have a task to complete while we're talking."

"Yup." The last thing she needed was to fight hugging him the entire time they caught up. That's all this was going to be. They were going to catch up, and Lavender would send him on his way. She could handle this. It would be an hour, at most, and then he would leave. If things settled down, well, maybe she'd call him in a month or so. But not now.

"How hungry are you?" Gavin asked as he washed his hands.

"Um. Pretty hungry, I guess."

"So, nothing that takes too long." He opened her fridge and took stock of the contents. She smirked a little. No one had a fridge like she did.

"Holy shit, are you having a party tomorrow?"

"No."

"Is that a three-layer cake? And look at all that produce! It's enough to feed a party of twelve."

"I always have a lot of fresh produce." Lavender slid between him and the fridge, trying to contain herself as her hip brushed against his. She pulled out some chicken thighs, two zucchinis, a hunk of fresh Parmesan, and a bunch of spinach. "Lemons are in the bowl next to the stove, onions by the sink. You want to do the meat or the veggies?"

"It's your kitchen, chef. Put me where you want me." Gavin ticked his eyebrow up as he fell into their old game.

"All right, tone it down," she answered. "Get chopping, Murphy."

"Yes, chef."

"I can't believe Baby Sage has a soulmate. And she's living with him. Shit, does he need to be talked to? Make sure he's a good guy who isn't going to trifle with her heart?"

Lavender chuckled over her glass of pinot grigio. "Sage is fine. If anything, someone should talk to her about not trifling with him."

"I remember her being such a shy little kid."

"She's definitely shifted from shy to stoic. And Will is a very nice young man. Plus, he's a warlock so it isn't like he didn't know what he was getting into."

Gavin looked down at his plate for a moment, then looked back at her. "Lucky guy."

"I didn't mean...well. You know what I meant."

He nodded and leaned back in his chair. "How'd you pick Star Island?"

"Ooof." She twisted the stem of her wineglass between her fingers. "I'm sure you heard my parents died."

"I did. I tried to—"

She put her hand up to silence him. There was no use going through all of that right now. Not if she wanted to make it through dinner in one piece.

"After we had the funeral and everything, I was able to gain custody of Laurel, Verbena, and Sage. My parents had a mortgage on their house still, and even if they hadn't." She shrugged. "We needed a fresh start. My great-aunt June left the five of us a house here a few years before my parents died. Thirteen years ago, the cost of living on Star Island was pretty low. I made an executive decision for us to move here. New schools, new lives. We were outsiders for a while, but the bills were low. We made it work."

"Must have been really hard."

"It was. Still is."

"You gave up a lot."

Lavender tried to cover a sigh with a laugh. "You know, I really love my sisters. Sure, they can be assholes and do absolutely batshit crazy and stupid things, but I love them deep in my bones. I couldn't..." She paused and took a breath. She owed him this much. "Look, the other option was my mom's brother. And they live a completely unmagical life. I couldn't make Laurel and Verbena and Sage go through that. They couldn't suddenly be forced to hide who they are, in their own home. I made the decision to raise them. Yes, it was hard as hell. I was exhausted for years, probably still am a bit sleep-deprived. But it was the right decision. I made the right choice." She knew she was right. No matter what his argument would be, she knew that life had unfolded how it was supposed to.

Gavin sat there in silence, tracing his fingers around the edge of his fork. "You didn't want a partner?"

"Don't," she said harshly.

"What?"

"Don't dredge up the past like that. Not right now. It fell the way it was meant to. We weren't...it was a long time ago. We were basically kids. And it was my decision to make. Myself." Hell, she'd wanted longer with him before he brought it up. It was a fantasy, really. To think that she and Gavin could have a night without hashing everything from the past. She couldn't do that tonight, not with her mind so crowded with everything else, so this had to be the end. "It's not really a good time for me to reconnect with you. Dinner was nice, but we should plan to meet up after the holidays."

"I'm sorry, what?" Gavin leaned forward in his chair. "Are you kicking me out of your apartment?"

"No. But I can't...I can't deal with all of this right now. My life is pretty crazy at the moment."

"What, the bakery? I understand how busy the holidays can be. I'm not asking you to quit working to hang out with me. Hell, I have to go home at some point."

"It's not the bakery," she mumbled as she stood and took her plate to the sink.

"What is it then?"

She hesitated. She wanted so badly to spill all her secrets, all her fears, to ask Gavin to hold her while she fell apart in fear of what could be coming.

But that wasn't who they were anymore. He was her...ex-boyfriend. Her college sweetheart. He didn't know her anymore, not really. And she didn't know him. Thirteen years was a long time. They were now in their mid-thirties. People changed. Their love was in the past, and for now, it needed to stay there.

"It's nothing you need to worry about," she finally settled on. "I'm dealing with it. My sisters are dealing with it. You don't have to—"

Gavin stood abruptly from the table, nearly knocking his chair to the ground. "Please don't. Don't give me the whole...I'm doing this alone."

Lavender chewed on the inside of her lips trying to still her tongue... trying to hold back.

She failed.

"Why? I've always done it all alone."

"Yeah. Because you chose to."

"I chose to?" She took a deep breath and tried to settle the fire building in her to no avail. "All right." Lavender crossed her arms over her chest and faced him. "I called you forty-two times. In two weeks. Forty. Two. Times. You didn't think that warranted picking up? That there might have been something wrong? Some sort of emergency?"

"I asked you for some space. I didn't know what happened."

"You thought I wouldn't respect your boundary. You thought I was calling to beg you to come back. Of course, that must have been it. Me ignoring your request. Not me begging my boyfriend—the love of my damn life, my stupid soulmate—to come back to me when I was suddenly parentless with four younger sisters."

"Lavender, I didn't know! You didn't leave one message. Didn't send one text. Just hang up after hang up. And when I found out I called. I called and called and called. You got rid of your number! Fuck, I drove to Ohio to try to find you. Do you have any idea how long I've been looking for you? How many hours, days, fucking years, I have spent trying to find you?"

Lavender shook her head. She didn't want to hear it. It was so much easier when he had simply disappeared from her life.

"The alumni office hates me. Same with your high school. Every person you ever talked to in college. I have alerts on your name online. I have been trying to find you since the last time I saw you."

"You left me," she spat. "I needed you so badly, and you weren't there for me."

"You're right. I did leave you. But I came back. And you didn't leave. You disappeared. You wiped out your existence. You stopped talking to every single person from DePaul, every single one of your neighbors in Ohio. No forwarding address. Not even a state. LB? Who on earth has ever called you LB? Yet that's the only thing it says on your business website. You were hiding from me. And you did a good job for a long time. Well, the fate you so preciously hang onto led me here. After thirteen miserable years, I am here. And I am not going back to Chicago until..."

"Until what? Until you force me to be with you?" She knew it sounded like a dare, one he would never take.

Gavin snorted. "I would never have to force you." He took two steps around the table closer to her. "All that witchy stuff you talked about in college...I know it's true. I know most men would get over their college sweetheart and move along with their lives. I can't. I won't. I've seen our past right beside you. I know your soul is intertwined with mine forever." He lifted his hand to her chin and tipped her face upward. "I can't fight it. I know you can't either. You may have done better when we were separated... but now that I'm here? You really want to test your resolve?"

Lavender let out a shaky breath. He was so close to her...she could wrap her arms around his neck, drag his mouth to hers, without taking more than a step.

Hell, she wanted him. Wanted him so badly her body ached. It would be so easy to fall back into his arms. Take him to her bedroom. Give in to every fantasy she'd had since she last saw him. Being with Gavin would be like riding a bike. They'd been together so many amazing times...she could almost taste his mouth on hers.

No.

"I think you should go," she muttered and took a step back, his hand falling from her face.

"I'm not leaving Star Island."

"I didn't say Star Island. I think you should leave my apartment." She picked up his plate and walked into the kitchen. "Do you have a place to stay?"

"No. I can find one, though."

She nodded furiously, keeping her back to him. "The hotel will love to have a customer. It's only a couple blocks east of here. Toward the harbor."

"I'll find it." She heard him walk to the door and open it. "I'm not leaving this time, Moonbeam. I'm not letting you go again."

Lavender turned to face him, but he was already shutting the door.

And just like that, she was alone again.

It was what she needed. What she deserved. Things with Gavin...it wasn't the time. She had too much to do.

It might never be the time for them. Lavender had made her peace with that years ago. This might not be the life she got to have with Gavin. And as awful as that was, she didn't have time to wallow in her grief.

Lavender rolled her sleeves up and started on the sink full of dishes. She needed to push Gavin out of her mind before she attempted to work on the Fortworth curse. Because as much as she wanted to sit and sulk about everything that had just transpired, she didn't have time for it.

Chapter Six

Gavin stomped down the stairs, his backpack bumping against his shoulders.

What had he expected? That the past would be forgotten and they'd fall into bliss immediately? No. Now that the ache of missing her was somewhat placated, he was still pretty angry at her for keeping them apart for thirteen years. And clearly, she hadn't forgiven him.

He pushed out of the building with a guttural growl and turned to find the hotel.

"What's up?"

Gavin jumped back startled. Rosemary leaned against the building in front of him.

"Oh. Hi." He looked back at the door and then at her again. "Are you waiting for me to go so you can go talk to Lavender? If yes, have at it. I've been asked to leave."

"No, I'm waiting for you." She motioned to a car parked on the street. "Come on, I'll give you a ride."

"To the hotel?"

"Hotel? Hell, no. You are staying with Asher and I. Asher's my soulmate. We haven't made the relationship legal yet, but you know how it is. We just moved into a big house and there are a lot of empty rooms perfect for a Bay sister's soulmate to stay in while she figures out her emotions."

Courtesy said he should refuse the offer and get a room at the hotel, but Rosemary was the one of Lavender's sisters he actually felt like he knew. "Thanks."

"Course." They both climbed into the car and Rosemary pulled away from the curb. "I still owe you one. I don't forget someone who picked me up when I was about to make a terrible decision."

Gavin furrowed his brow for a moment before it dawned on him. "Oh shit. The Wolf Den. I forgot about that."

"I did not. It isn't every day that a high school senior sweet talks a bouncer to let her join the bar top performance. I didn't even have a fake ID."

"That guy totally thought he was going to sleep with you."

"I know. And you and Lavender showed up at the exact right moment."

"How so?"

"I already had three hundred dollars in my pocket from the gentlemen watching me dance, and I didn't have to deal with that bouncer wanting to sleep with me and being disappointed. Or worse. Saved me a lot of trouble when the two of you started shouting that I was only seventeen and the police should be called." Rosemary sighed. "I wish I still had those leather pants. They ripped a couple years later. I looked amazing in them." She giggled. "Those were the days. So. How's life? You in Chicago?"

"Yeah. Stayed there after graduation. Wanted to be easy to find."

"That was considerate. You know..." She paused like she was choosing her words carefully. "You can be as pissed as you want. I don't know what happened. She never told me. Lavender keeps things pretty close to her heart. It's like wringing out a dry rag to get her to open up. With the exception of me, none of the sisters know about you."

"She didn't tell her family about me?" Wow, that hurt. They had dated for two years.

"No, she said she had a boyfriend at DePaul. But I'm the only one who knows you are her soulmate. She didn't even tell me. It's part of my, you know." She waved her hand in the air. "Gift."

"So, you believe in soulmates?"

"Dude. It's not a belief for me. It's a fact. Hell, Asher and I died pretty spectacularly in ancient Norway. I know he's my person. He knows he's mine. I'm also pretty sure you aren't going to question the fact that I know about a past life."

"Yeah," he said softly.

"Lavender always kept that spell pretty quiet. Something she cooked up in college. But I figure she had to have tried it on someone, and who better than herself? So. Who knows what you both saw back then and how it changed things."

"I...messed up. I didn't take the spell well."

"You were a kid. I didn't take the spell well and I knew exactly what I was getting myself into."

"I don't like to think about it." He paused. "That life. It's not as fresh as it was, but I associate it with losing Lavender, so it keeps the pain pretty sharp."

"I understand. I still have a hard time when I think about what Asher and I went through before. What we lost."

"I lost everything." Gavin swallowed hard. "And it was so scary. Living through war, the injuries, the atrocities. I didn't know how to handle it. I ended up screwing up the best thing of any life I've had."

She drove out of the city, and the roads suddenly became very dark. The thick clouds moved quickly across the sky, obscuring the moon and stars from view. "I'm sorry you two met so young. It's hard. Same thing happened to Verbena. It's easier when you're settled. Though it's never easy. And Lavender had the added heartache of losing her parents."

"When did you meet Asher?"

"Oh. This June. And Laurel met Owen in May... Sage met Will in September."

"All this year?"

"Yeah. There's this prophecy. Lavender was convinced, because the two of you had already met, that she was exempt, but that isn't how prophecies work. You gotta do the whole thing. Even the shitty parts."

"What's shitty about being with your soulmate?"

"Well. It wasn't just about the soulmates. There are these other people. Warlocks and a witch. They aren't...good. You and Lavender can talk about that tomorrow. She should give you her point of view before you get mine. New subject. How's your dad? Your stepmom?"

"Um. Sheila died two years ago."

"Oh, Gavin! I am so sorry. Are you okay? Is your dad okay?"

"We are both, you know, doing our best. My dad moved down to Florida last year. His brother is in Tampa, and he was sick of Wisconsin winters. It's good for him with me being in Chicago. Plus, I think it was hard for him to stay in the house."

"I get that. Sometimes it's easier to live without the ghosts. Even if they aren't actually there." Rosemary pulled down a wooded road. "We're here."

"Is there a house at the end of this forest? Or did you tell Lavender you'd take care of me?" He laughed, half-joking.

"Please. I would never get in the way of two souls getting the chance of happiness. Too many of our lives end in misery."

A beautiful white farmhouse came into view and Gavin relaxed considerably. Rosemary pulled up beside the porch and shut the car off.

"Hey," he asked before climbing out of his seat. "Did Lavender tell you? About...why we split?"

"No. But...you were suddenly not there. After she wouldn't shut up about you for years. I asked her, you know, why you weren't at the funeral, and she couldn't even speak about it. It took her months. Maybe even a year? And then one night when it was just the two of us, she told me that you guys had broken up." She shrugged. "Your secrets are your own, and I would never demand them. But I'm guessing being in your twenties and away from family isn't the ideal time to meet your soulmate. Especially not knowing that life as we knew it was about to change completely." Rosemary grabbed her purse. "Come on. You need to meet Asher."

Within thirty minutes of arriving, Rosemary had set up the spare bedroom for Gavin, opened a bottle of wine, did some sort of cleansing ritual over him, and then insisted he get to know Asher.

"Thanks for letting me stay here. Especially since I barely know Rosemary anymore."

"It's cool. No one can hurt her when I'm around." Asher chuckled. "Didn't mean for that to sound ominous. You know, right, about all the magic stuff?"

"I have a general understanding that spells and stuff work."

"Cool. I'm a Guardian. Rosemary is who I guard."

"Nice. I'm a chef." Gavin was beginning to wonder if the hotel might have been a better idea.

"Rosemary gave me a very brief overview of your past with Lavender."

"Thirteen years apart and now I'm here to try and heal that."

"Do you have a plan?"

"My plan was to get here and talk to Lavender and hopefully figure out how it all went wrong, apologize to each other, and go from there. I can't just move here tomorrow. I have an apartment full of stuff in Chicago and a job there. I don't want her to disappear again though. I'm not leaving until I'm confident she won't."

"I wish you the best of luck. There's a lot going on right now, with the Bay sisters. It seems to go hand in hand with them finding their soulmates. But if you meet anyone named Miloslav, Ivan, or Morana, run."

"Who the hell are Miloslav, Ivan, and Morana?"

"They are a big problem." He clapped his hand on his knee and stood. "I have to run. Went back to school and have a shit ton of homework. But maybe make a better plan for tomorrow?"

A better plan.

He probably should have come up with one of those before he left Chicago. But he couldn't risk Lavender slipping through his fingers again.

Gavin pulled out his phone to call his dad then stopped. He'd been a strong proponent that Gavin needed to forget about Lavender. To the point that Gavin had kept the fact he'd still been looking for her a secret for the past ten years. It was one thing for a twenty-four-year-old to still be hung up about someone he dated two years earlier, but a thirty-five-year-old holding out for someone from thirteen years ago? He knew that sounded insane.

It had been a long couple of days, and an even longer evening. It was probably time for him to hit the hay, even if it was only nine his time.

Gavin walked upstairs to the room Rosemary had deemed his for the week and shut the door behind him. There was a twin bed with a worn multicolored quilt and small bedside table. There was also an enormous ficus that was brushing against the ceiling and a framed poster of a nude woman reclining on a bed of roses and a blurry photograph of two naked people who looked suspiciously like Rosemary and Asher running along the coast.

Staying with Rosemary was going to be an experience.

Chapter Seven

"I think I am going to marry you," Gavin teased. His mouth was a breath away from her skin, so close she could feel the heat coming off him.

"You think? Glad I am being considered as your life partner." Lavender cuddled against him and threw her leg over his.

"I think I have to. No part of me ever wants to get out of this bed. We'll have to have the wedding here, of course." He moved his hand to her hair, pushing it back from her face a few times before settling and smiling.

"On the third floor of LeCompte?" She looked around her single dorm room. "Might be hard to fit even our families in here."

"True. Maybe someone can drag the bed outside. That way I could stay in bed with you forever." He buried his face against her neck. "Don't make me get a job and leave the comfort of you."

"You're making it sound like the only thing you like about me is my body."

"First of all, I love your body." He squeezed her thigh. "Big fan. But I also love your brain. Your heart. Your soul. Your baking abilities. The way your voice gets serious when one of your sisters calls. You could say I love everything about you."

"Even when I leave my used tissues on my bedside table in the middle of the night?"

"It's not a deal-breaker." He laughed. "It's the one flaw so I know you aren't a spy sent to seduce me into giving up my secrets."

"Secrets? What secrets? Oh, my goddess, do you work for some sort of government agency as a spy? Quick, tell me all your secrets!" She tickled him for a moment until he flipped her to her back and spread his body over hers. She wrapped her legs around his waist and sighed.

"If I were a spy, you would have gotten them all already."

Lavender punched her pillow a few times and kicked her blankets off. She needed to stop thinking about college, about Gavin. Her mind was racing, memory after memory assaulting her every time she closed her eyes. She didn't want to think about happy times. Even memories laced with fear from when they were Arthur and Ruby wouldn't stop crowding her brain.

Around three in the morning, Lavender resigned herself to the fact that she wasn't going to sleep. Which sucked. Work started in less than two hours, and she felt like absolute crap. If emotions had hangovers, she had the worst one of her life.

Why did Gavin come now? Why, why, why? She was already at her wits' end with the Stochs and the curse and losing the simple life she had with her sisters before all of this started.

She knew the reason, and it was fate. Fate was back again to screw with her. To make sure every damn thing that could go wrong, did go wrong. The same forces that had her trying out that past-life spell for the first time two weeks before the worst thing could happen. The same forces who made sure that when she needed Gavin most, he was gone.

Lavender hadn't done the past life spell more than once. After Gavin left, there was no reason. It would have been really shitty for her to force him to live through it all again with no warning. But it also meant she hadn't seen an ending for her and Gavin that didn't end in heartbreak, and as far as she was concerned, there probably wasn't one. They were fated to fall in love, passionately and all-consuming, but it wouldn't last. Something horrible would happen. A war. A car accident. A spell. There was always something.

She headed to the kitchen and turned on the overhead lights before boiling water for tea. If sleep eluded her, she would use her time more wisely. Lying in bed staring at the ceiling and reminiscing about Gavin would do her no good. She had some serious spell work to figure out.

So far, breaking the generational curse set by the Fortworths in the eighteenth century had been akin to banging her head against a wall. Nothing worked. She'd tried unbinding spells, unweaving spells, good old-fashioned breaking spells. It was like nothing she had ever come in contact with before.

Instead of breaking the curse, Lavender decided she would deal with the more pressing problem.

Miloslav Stoch.

He was a rotten warlock through and through, and unluckily for them, was the reincarnated soul of Jonas Fortworth. It didn't help things that Sage had killed him multiple times in other lives, and Lavender...well, it wasn't her first time meeting him. She still remembered the day that soul walked into her life: February 10th, 1943. She would never forget it because it was the same day Arthur walked into Ruby's life. A group of badly injured soldiers pulled from the front and deposited in her temporary medical tent in France.

But unlike Sage, who had an intimate knowledge of Miloslav in every previous life, Charles and Ruby weren't really connected. Yes, he'd been the double agent whose information had killed Ruby and Arthur, but she didn't really have contact with him otherwise. He was sort of a weird guy with a shattered forearm, nothing else.

But he was here again, so they were connected. And she couldn't continue having her soul knotted to his. But more than that, Sage couldn't. It was seriously dangerous to have their two souls alive at the same time.

Lavender opened her pantry door and pulled out her favorite herbs. Basil, dill, knotgrass...between those three, she should be able to make an unbinding spell. But trying to get Miloslav to eat it? Especially if it tasted like grass? That would be another thing.

"Cake it is," she mumbled, pulling out flour, sugar, baking powder, and salt. "Oooh. Maybe a rich chocolate? That might mask it." With cocoa powder, a bar of 86 percent cacao dark chocolate, butter, and milk, Lavender began concocting her recipe.

Lavender had woven hundreds of spells into baked goods. She'd baked solace into funeral cakes, joy into birthday cupcakes, gratitude into Thanksgiving pies. She'd mended broken hearts with muffins and steeped forgiveness into cups of tea. Her whole life had been leading up to the moment in which she needed to do extremely powerful magic...in the form of a chocolate cake.

In no time, her kitchen counters were covered in mixing bowls, measuring cups, discarded herbs, and splashes of milk. Whenever baking and spell work went hand in hand, Lavender shut the rest of the world out. She got into a zone she couldn't explain. Her sense of hearing went fuzzy, and it was like she was wearing blinders. She became her spell work.

Today, she focused on severing. Unbinding. Breaking souls apart, not curses. She needed to deal with Miloslav this time, not wait for another life for him to intrude on. Especially if he succeeded.

No. She couldn't let that happen. No matter what happened, her sisters would be okay. They would all retain their power. They were on this path and it was treacherous, but they would prevail. Lavender could not lose hope. Not when the outcome was so unknown.

If Miloslav managed to steal their power would they survive it? She doubted it. A witch without her power...it was a scary thought. And even if they did survive, they would be completely vulnerable to the Stochs. Lavender couldn't let that happen.

An hour later, her kitchen was a disaster and she was no closer to creating a baked good that would banish Miloslav's soul from the path of hers. Damn, she missed living with Verbena. She used to be able to destroy the kitchen, and her house witch sister would have it shining in no time, all with a smile on her face. Now Luke was enjoying that chipper little cleaning machine and probably had no idea how good he had it.

Lavender got to work putting away all the ingredients first. Dishes were something she could leave soaking in the sink if it came to it. She scraped the remnants of the failed cake into the garbage, tucked her spices back into the pantry, and cleaned up the eggshells.

It was so damn quiet here.

"Erie?" she called softly, hoping her kitten might offer her a bit of company, but so far, she'd noticed he was a pretty heavy sleeper, especially in the dark mornings.

She missed home. Not the Bay cottage, *home.* She missed the loud mornings with her sisters. She missed knocking over a deck of tarot cards accidentally or finding Rosemary and Sage bringing in fifteen new houseplants. She missed running out of hot water on the weekend, driving Laurel to bachelorette parties, putting a huge pot of soup on the stove, and then cozying up with bowls around the table with her sisters.

She missed her family.

Lavender wasn't stupid; she'd always known this would happen. Hell, even if they weren't witches, it would have happened. People grew up, they moved on. Sisters make their own families. It was never going to stay how it had been. The sooner she could accept that her life was in a new season, and that season might be lonely, the faster it would feel normal.

There were full years in her early twenties Lavender cried herself to sleep wanting this. An apartment by herself, a quiet kitchen. She had wanted to cook for one, spend her nights reading or on spell work instead of signing permission slips and trying to remember how to do trigonometry. She had begged for some silence. Now she was surrounded by it.

"Stop wallowing," she chided and dove into the dirty dishes. She had fifteen minutes until she had to leave for work, and while that wasn't enough time to get it all done, she'd make a dent. That was better than returning to a sink overflowing with mess.

Just as she was elbow deep in suds and finally getting her cake pan to shine, her phone rang. At four forty-five.

"Shit." She grabbed a towel and scrubbed herself dry, then answered.

"Everything okay?" she asked whoever was on the other end.

"Yes!" Verbena answered. "I'm fine, don't worry. I knew you'd be up."

Relief crashed over her.

"I was thinking," Verbena continued, "we need different wards at the bakery and the florist. Because you and Rosemary have permanent places of employment, Miloslav or any of the other Stochs can find you really easily. I think I can block anyone of their bloodline from both places."

"Really? That's super specific."

"Yeah. It might mean that Luke and Danny wouldn't be able to go into either shop, but once this is dealt with, I'll just lift the ward. I'm not sure at what point in the genetic line this spell will stop." Verbena's soulmate and his cousin were both distantly related to the Stochs through a great-grandmother. "I think it's our safest bet. Miloslav not only came to the bakery but he used magic on you. That's insane. He isn't afraid to use magic in public. We can't take any chances."

"Yeah," Lavender answered quietly. "What time do you want to come lay the wards?"

"I'm already at the Immortal Cupcake. I used my spare key."

"Verbena! You shouldn't go in without me being there." Lavender cradled the phone between her shoulder and her ear and pulled on her boots. "What if Miloslav had been waiting for me?"

"Then he would have had to contend with an alchemist. I'm sure his chaos magic is strong, but I'm also pretty sure I could change his bones into, I don't know, jelly for a second or two to scare the shit out of him."

"V,"—Lavender grabbed her purse and her keys—"that is very unethical. Do not do that."

"My ethics end when someone is trying to hurt my family. Miloslav already attacked Laurel and Sage. I consider that an aggression that can be answered with magic. Plus, I should probably practice it on someone before I actually need to use it. A man who has attacked my sisters is a good volunteer."

"Fine," she huffed. "But wait until I get there before you do any magic. I want to see what's happening to my shop before it happens."

"Deal."

Lavender shoved her phone in her purse and ran down the stairs, out the door, and down the block. If Miloslav was out there watching for her, well, he was going to have to catch a slow to medium-paced runner.

Chapter Eight

With fresh wards laid, Lavender could relax. Verbena only stayed long enough to put her magic down, then hurried to do the same at the florist. Hopefully Therese, Rosemary's boss, didn't have an alarm system.

Lavender pulled the cinnamon muffins out of the oven, stacked the loaves of bread for the day, and double-checked her espresso machines. She put on a fresh apron and unlocked the front door.

Opening at six past September 30th wasn't truly needed. There were only three customers who came in before seven: Jolene, who taught fifth grade at the elementary school, Ray the mechanic, and Stephanie. Stephanie was Laurel's age and recently had her fourth child in as many years. If only for Stephanie, Lavender would stay open that extra hour. Plus, she liked the quiet.

In the summer, when the island was flush with tourists and the sun came up before five in the morning, there'd be a line at six. She wouldn't be able to handle the crowd by herself, and she had to make four times as many baked goods as she did now. Once January hit, she'd halve her daily quantity again, and even then, the day-old basket would be pretty full at the start of every morning.

Lavender brought her four loaves of pumpkin bread to the front and sliced the first two, then wrapped the next two in foil. She wanted customers who showed up before eight to have the option of a "fresh out of the oven" warm slice of deliciousness without needing to warm it in the microwave. She arranged the sliced bread in the display case, then hurried into the back to bring out the cookies of the day: salted caramel, snickerdoodle, double chocolate chunk, and oatmeal frosted. Cookies weren't usually a hit until after one, but she never knew when someone would come in absolutely needing one. She'd done her best to sprinkle today's offerings with joy, which everyone on the island could use once the sun slid farther and farther away. The dark and cold were coming, and there was no escaping them on an island in the ocean.

The bell on the front door chimed, and Lavender hurried from the back with her last tray of snickerdoodles expecting to see Stephanie or Jolene. It was still a little early for Ray.

"Morning, Moonbeam," Gavin greeted her. "Those look good."

Lavender opened her mouth to respond but instead ended up standing there like a fish waiting for a hook.

"Why are you here?" she said when her brain finally caught up with her mouth. This was her job. He'd already showed up once when she was closing and thrown her into a panic attack. He could not be here when actual customers could walk through the door, and she needed to serve them.

"Figured not many people would be coming in when it's this early, this cold, and this dark." His instincts had been correct. "And I wanted to talk to you without bombarding you at your apartment."

Lavender walked to the display case and slid the cookies on the top shelf. "Go ahead."

"I'm not leaving. That's the end of it. I'm not leaving you again. I left you once, it ruined the next thirteen years of my life. I'm not doing it again. I'm not going to stalk you or harass you or anything. If you ask, I'll never come inside this shop again. But I am staying on Star Island. End of discussion."

"Uh, wasn't much of a discussion. You made a decision and I have to live with it," she pointed out. "That would be like me saying, you're leaving because I say so."

"True. But I'm also a thirty-five-year-old man, and if I want to live on Star Island, I can."

"What are you going to do for work?" she countered.

"I have barely spent any money the last thirteen years. I'll be fine if I take some time off. Eventually, I'm sure the owners at Convito's down the street would give me a couple of shifts. I'm great at Italian food."

"You can't stay in the hotel long-term. If nothing else, that will bankrupt you." She was reaching now. Didn't Gavin understand that they shouldn't do this? It would only end in heartbreak. Again and again.

"I'm not staying at the hotel. I've been gifted a room in someone's house."

"Who?" she asked, shocked. Lavender couldn't imagine anyone on Star Island simply asking him to stay. They were friendly, but not insane.

"Rosemary and Asher. The three of us had a lovely time last night. Rosemary reminded me that she still owed me one from her escapade at The Wolf Den."

Lavender fumed. Rosemary! She was supposed to be on her side, not Gavin's. And here she was, offering sanctuary to the very man she needed to get off Star Island. "I will be having some words with her." She took a steadying breath. "It's not a good idea for you to be here right now," she began. She needed him to understand that there was a curse, a chaos warlock, and a ticking clock without actually telling him any of those things. Because even though it had been years, Lavender knew Gavin, and he'd never leave if he thought she was in danger.

Gavin walked around the back of the counter so he was less than two feet away from Lavender, her back pressed against the wall. "Mhm. And when will it be a good time for me to be here? A week? A month? A year? Another decade? I've come to the conclusion that you might not be the best judge of when we should be together."

"Gav," she began, her voice barely above a whisper. "The last time...we hurt each other. Worse than I ever thought possible. Jumping back where we left off isn't a good idea. This goes beyond bad timing." She closed her eyes for a moment and tried to collect her thoughts. She wanted him safe, away from Miloslav, away from the curse on her line. All she wanted was for Gavin to be okay in this life. She couldn't save him last time...she couldn't go through losing him again. Even if it was only for a few hours before she inevitably followed him into the ether.

"Listen. You can tell me to fuck off, or you can tell me to stay away from you, and I'm going to do exactly what you say. But I'm not leaving Star Island. I'll be here until you figure out that we should be together. Got it?"

Lavender didn't get emotional. She kept it all bottled up until it eventually dissipated. She didn't have outbursts or cry in front of people. Lavender Bay was capable of keeping it together.

But not with Gavin. Never with Gavin.

He had an innate ability to drag down her walls and make her express her feelings. It was basically a magic trick. Lavender never let anyone see her cards. Except Gavin.

So, while she should have told him to fuck off, told him to stay away from her, she couldn't. She could only look at him and think...

Goddess, I want that man.

She grabbed his waist and crashed his body against her, pinning herself against the wall. He looked at her—both wildly and shocked—then cupped her face and turned her chin up to him.

They stood like that, inches apart, chests heaving in unison, their eyes locked on the other. It was like nothing else existed in the world but this moment.

Lavender was in Gavin's arms.

She'd dreamed of this. No matter how much she told herself she wouldn't think of him, wouldn't let herself imagine being with him, she could not control her dreams. And Gavin came to her at night.

But nothing—no dream, no wish, no passing memory—was as sweet as finally holding him again.

Goddesses, what was she doing? This was the exact opposite of what needed to happen. She should let go of him, calmly tell him to come back to Star Island in a month or so. Promise not to disappear again and hope he believed her.

This wasn't the right time.

But then...had it ever been the right time for them?

"Tell me to leave," he murmured as he stroked her cheek slowly. "If you don't want this, you have to tell me."

"I..." Lavender's voice caught in her throat. She needed to tell him to leave. She needed to let him go. But...

But she was so tired of being alone. She was so tired of never doing what she needed and always doing what was right.

She'd left him. Built a life without him to raise her sisters. She'd been a good little guardian for over a decade. It was time Lavender Bay let herself have a moment of reprieve.

"Gavin Murphy. Kiss your soulmate."

As his mouth crashed against hers, the invisible wall between them fell.

He was her soulmate. They'd shared lives and losses. They'd shared a bed, their bodies, and secrets.

They'd broken each other's hearts.

But there was no denying their connection. Their souls were woven together, life after life, body after body. And Lavender wanted him. She wanted him even when she shouldn't. Even when being with him put them both in danger, she couldn't stop wanting him.

Gavin thrust his hand into her hair until he cradled the base of her skull, molding her against him. He tasted...

He tasted like he always did. A mix of mint, coffee, and chocolate. He'd been a mocha drinker in college and she wasn't sure if he'd made one at Rosemary's house or if that was how he naturally tasted, but she'd craved the burst of bittersweet his mouth brought.

"I missed you so much," he breathed as his lips trailed off her mouth. He kissed her cheeks, her neck, the tip of her nose, behind her ear. He buried his face against her hair as he wrapped his arms tightly around her waist. "I'll never leave you again."

The door jingled and, in an instant, Lavender had two hands against Gavin and pushed him away from her as she jumped three feet in the opposite direction.

Stephanie bounded into the bakery with a baby strapped to her chest, a toddler in each hand, and her five-year-old trailing behind.

"Morning! Last night was H-E-L-L. I need a large Americano and...oh, the cookies are out! Three snickerdoodles for the kids. That should get us to morning nap time." She finally looked up and noticed Gavin standing behind the counter. "Hey! New employee? I'm Stephanie. If you work mornings, you'll be seeing a lot of this little army."

"Oh," Gavin stammered and looked at Lavender for guidance.

"He's not a new employee. He's a chef friend from school. Came to see the bakery." Lavender busied herself with stuffing the cookies into a paper bag, then grabbed a cup to make the Americano.

"Oh, welcome to Star Island! And definitely take notes. The Immortal Cupcake is my saving grace. Especially on these cold mornings." Just as Stephanie handed Lavender her credit card to pay, the door jingled again and Ray and Jolene walked in and formed a line.

Lavender threw Gavin a look. As much as that morning kiss had been an absolute dream...she had customers. She couldn't have Gavin distracting her. And if he was still here when Hazel got in, Lavender would never hear the end of it. Plus there were a million other reasons they shouldn't be together, and at the top of that list was a chaos warlock who had separated them before.

"I'll go. You have a lot to do. But I'm coming back."

"Got it," she answered quickly, hoping her cheeks weren't red. If anyone other than Stephanie had been the first customer, rumors of Lavender making out with some man in the bakery at six-twenty in the morning would abound. Thankfully, Stephanie was far too distracted by her small brood to notice.

Gavin threw the customers a smile, then ducked out of the bakery.

Lavender shook her shoulders, took Jolene's order, and pushed Gavin out of her mind.

She'd made out with him in her place of work. Damn. She was in trouble.

Chapter Nine

G*avin Murphy. Kiss your soulmate.*

Lavender's voice echoed in his ears as he walked out of the bakery. In the very dim light of nearly breaking dawn, the world finally seemed friendly. Gavin was with Lavender. She didn't push him away, didn't tell him to go or that she never wanted to see him again. She kissed him. *Really* kissed him. Kissed him like she had hundreds of times before. Nothing in the world mattered but the two of them, forever entwined.

Gavin took off running, his first time since getting to Star Island. He felt amazing. Like he could run a marathon right this minute without breathing heavily. His heart soared. He flew down the streets, running circles around town. He found the restaurants and the park, saw a few people pulling up to retail shops with their keys ready to open for the day, and a group of teachers outside the preschool laughing as they chatted.

He continued running down the street toward the harbor. He could run back to Rosemary and Asher's but he wasn't sure if he remembered the way. Plus, he'd begged a ride from Asher this morning, who had happened to be awake quite early, but didn't feel comfortable asking him to come get him so quickly. He would just enjoy the morning walking down the streets of Solaris and let himself bask in the glory of Lavender.

He slowed to a walk as he got close to the water. The harbor was quiet.

He could imagine it in the summer, when floods of tourists crashed onto the coastal island. The streets crowded with people, a line outside the Immortal Cupcake. He liked it like this—undisturbed. As if, like the world, Star Island was heading to sleep for a season.

The air off the water had a bite to it, the salt mixed with a touch of frost. Gavin pulled the sleeves of his jacket down to cover his hands and walked on.

There was another man at the harbor, walking as well. He had a familiarity about him Gavin couldn't place. He couldn't imagine there was another person he'd known before on Star Island—simply finding Lavender was magical enough—but he couldn't take his eyes off him. It was almost... as if...

"Charles," he breathed.

Charles was in front of him. On Star Island.

It all rushed back. That other life, that stingingly painful other life. Watching Ruby... It was Charles's fault. All his fault.

We were brothers in arms... We dragged him out of battle, unconscious and bleeding, saved his goddamn life, and how did he repay us? Gave our position to the Germans. Killed Ruby. Ruined my life...

Gavin set his jaw. Prepared to give him a piece of his mind. To tell him—

Stop. That man probably had no idea who he'd been before. What he'd done. Without that past life spell, they were all ignorant to what the past held, whatever atrocities were committed. That didn't stop Gavin from wanting to lay him out.

But...right before Gavin turned on his heels and left the harbor, that man turned to him. He barked a laugh like he recognized Gavin. But that was impossible.

"Arthur," the man called, nodding his head and waving. "Thought I might see you."

"Charles," Gavin seethed in return. "How..."

Charles shrugged. "Doesn't really matter how, does it? Who would have thought it? You, me, Ruby? All together on Star Island. Almost like it's fate." His voice had a serpentine quality this morning. How had he never noticed that before when they were fighting beside each other?

"Stay away from us."

"Come on, I was a different person then!" He smirked. "Can't blame me for something that happened before I was born."

"You were a traitor to your country. You were the worst type of person around then. You killed...everyone."

"Technically, *I* didn't kill anyone. Sure, my information may have led to some strategic bombing, but what can I say? It was war."

"You left us all there to die. After what we did for you? We could have left you behind. They wouldn't have known who you were to them. They would have killed you the moment the line was crossed. You deserved to be shot for your crimes."

Charles laughed now, deep and loud. "Oh, don't you worry. I was. Not for my crimes, but war is war. Very few of us got out unscathed. I was definitely shot, more than once." He chuckled a bit more and lifted his arm. "That first one was just a taste. It's hard to remember exactly how many times I was shot before the end of that life. Maybe seven? I don't know, it's all a blur to me."

"It's not a blur to me."

"Of course not. You're with a Bay witch. They all take the past life stuff to heart. People change, you know."

"I think if you were changed you wouldn't be taking this so lightly." Gavin did his best to bite back his rage.

"What do you want, an apology? For something that happened in 1942? Sorry, I'm all out of past-life apologies. And I've yet to get one from the person who's the shadow on my soul." He paused, looking angry for a moment, then replaced it with a smirk. "Maybe the whole lot of the boys will show up! We could have a little reunion. Bobby, Dunk, Timmy. And who was that redhead nurse Ruby was friendly with? The one with the deep dimples...Dorothy. Woo, I'd like to see her again sometime. Legs for days. Wonder if she still looks the same. Pretty little thing."

Heat rose up Gavin's neck to his face. How could this man speak to him with such irreverence? They'd been friends, they had all been friends. Brothers in arms. And he'd killed them all. He was a monster.

"You...I never want to see you again. You put us all through..."

"Hell? Yes. That was the point. War is hell. It always is. For both sides. Doesn't matter if you are a loyal little soldier or an opportunist. It's all hell." He clapped Gavin on the shoulder. "Now let me ask. Did you know she was a witch back then? In the 40s? Do you know she's a witch now? A wicked little witch with a very wicked little sister."

A pit formed in Gavin's stomach. This was wrong...he shouldn't know that about Lavender. Why would she tell Charles of all people? He was a monster. She had to remember him. Unless...

Unless Charles was magical too.

Suddenly, the empty harbor didn't feel safe. The quiet was sinister instead of soothing. He glanced around, hoping a crowd was forming somewhere, but there was only the lone light in the ticket shack. It could have been on all night for all Gavin knew.

"Ah, so you do know. Interesting." Charles leaned in and sniffed deeply. "You smell the same though. Nothing...unnatural about you."

"But if I could smell you, I'm sure it'd be unnatural."

"Watch it. I don't see a Bay witch here to save you."

Gavin felt oddly calm. This man—this soul—had ruined his life last time. And in seeing it, Gavin had ruined this life for a long time. He should have been terrified and running. Instead, he looked at him with renewed interest. Icy blond hair, piercing blue eyes. Charles had been gingery with teeth a little too big for his mouth. Not uncommon in a time when imperfect smiles were all over London.

There was no reason Gavin should recognize him. It was a little worrisome. Was Charles here to ruin this lifetime as well? He suddenly wanted to see Lavender.

"What's your name?" he asked.

"Charles, you know that."

"I mean this time around. I'm obviously not called Arthur again."

"Too bad. I always thought that name suited you. Stern. No fun. Never wanting to join me when I enjoyed the local women."

"Never felt the need to terrorize a bunch of French teenagers for a laugh," Gavin bit back. "And I had Ruby willingly."

"Pretty Ruby. With lips to match her name. Back then, you know, I wasn't as sharp in that lifetime. Missed a lot. Not like this time. But I always wondered what made her choose you over all of us. Injured, scared to go back to the front. There were a hundred men coming and going in that field hospital. Braver ones, richer ones, ones that could have given her a good life after the war."

"No one could have given her a good life after the war. You made sure of that."

"I did, didn't I?" He grinned. "The soulmates. Always wound together. But we're something too, you know? I'm right behind you, like a predator you can't outrun. Lifetime after lifetime, I'll follow you. And if you're there, so is she. Ruby, Lavender, whatever you call her, she's there. And I'm a breath away from her."

"Stay away from Lavender." Gavin clenched his fists at his side.

"Or what? You think a human can stop me from doing anything? If I wanted to, I could make you drown yourself right now."

"Then why haven't you?" Gavin tested.

Charles shrugged. "Witches are interesting. When they are backed into a corner, they can do really unexpected things with their magic. Better to let them keep thinking they have a way out. Even if they don't." Charles smirked. A car noisily barreled down the street toward the harbor, catching Gavin's eye. "That's my cue to leave. I'll see you around, Arthur. I think I'll keep calling you that. Cowardly Arthur. Shell-shocked Arthur." Charles mock saluted him, then ducked into the shadows and disappeared.

"Gavin!" Rosemary shouted from the window of her car. "Get in!"

He jogged over and threw open the door. "What? Is Lavender okay?"

"Are you? That was Miloslav Stoch you were talking to. Did he hurt you? Or use magic on you?"

"I...I don't think so."

"You two were just chatting?"

Gavin climbed into the front seat and pulled the door shut. "No. We sort of know each other. From before."

"Ah. That makes sense." Rosemary pulled away and headed out of town. "I was hoping Lavender would have told you this, but for your own safety, I will right now. Stay away from him. He's an extremely dangerous warlock, particularly to the Bays and anyone connected to them. You shouldn't be wandering around Star Island alone while he is here."

"Yeah, he wasn't a good person when I knew him before."

"I'm going to take you home. My house is warded pretty heavily. You should be safe from him there."

"You're going to keep me prisoner in your house?"

"For a day or two. It's only a matter of time before Lavender has you moving into her apartment."

"I don't think Lavender is inviting me to stay anytime soon." Sure, they'd had a great kiss less than two hours earlier, but that didn't mean she was ready for anything more. Gavin felt like he was approaching a skittish animal caught in a trap. He didn't want to scare her, but he knew she needed his help.

"Sure, sure. We all tried to fight our soulmates and we were all living with them in under a month. Speaking of which, make sure when everything calms down that you two move outside the city. Nothing wrong with Solaris, but a witch needs wide-open spaces. It's where we thrive."

Gavin sighed and settled into his seat. Rosemary might have high hopes that he and Lavender would be moving quickly, but now that Charles was here and dangerous? Everything became a lot more complicated in the blink of an eye.

Chapter Ten

Lavender locked up after a day full of steady work, nothing out of the ordinary. Miloslav hadn't shown up, none of her sisters had been attacked. She should be calling or texting Gavin, or driving straight to Rosemary's to find him.

But instead, she walked home alone. Slipped off her boots and coat at the front door.

What was she doing? Kissing Gavin Murphy like...

Like he'd never left her. Never broken her heart. Never forced her to face the worst moments of her life without him.

As if Miloslav Stoch was a stranger on the street, and she didn't know what he was capable of. As if he didn't already have Laurel and Sage's blood.

She fell to the couch and pulled her phone out, then opened the sisters-only text. She wanted...

She wanted her sisters. Even if she'd always been in charge, been the adult in the situation, there was something unexplainably comfortable about slipping back into that role. The problems of thirteen years ago...they were so sharp and heartbreaking. But she knew her role then. She was the oldest sister. The guardian. The problem-solver. She was the homework helper and the parent-teacher conference attendee. She made sure the house had toilet paper and tampons and milk and stuff to make school lunches. She had allergies memorized…even now, ten years after she needed to know it, she could recite Laurel's Social Security number. She wanted to nestle herself back in that life. There had been no time for thoughts of Gavin. There had been no time to marinate in her heartbreak or even turn her mind to it for more than a moment or two. There had always been something to do. A meal to cook, a room to clean, an appointment to make. There was work, her sisters, her magic, and there wasn't room for anything else.

Now she was blown open. Her sisters gone from her care. She set her phone on the coffee table. What was she even going to say? Ask if they were okay? They were. If they weren't, one of their soulmates would let her know.

Lavender looked at the kitchen. She was bone tired and the last thing she wanted to do right now was bake. But the Stochs needed to be dealt with. She could make an unbinding cake, she knew she could. Hell, in college she'd made a past-life bread so powerful it nearly ruined her life. This had to be easier.

She pulled her hair back and pushed up her sleeves. Five minutes was enough wallowing. There was always work to be done.

There were four white mixing bowls Lavender liked more than any. They weren't non-slip or particularly great for stirring. Her hands were a little small for them. They couldn't be transferred straight into the oven and they were too wobbly to go into the fridge. But Lavender used them for everything important.

They were the last gift she received from her parents. A set of mixing bowls for her twentieth birthday. Her mom had teased that she was going to get her a KitchenAid mixer when she graduated from college. She was the only one in their family asking for an appliance as a present.

But the mixing bowls were the last thing. When Lavender went through all their possessions, stacks and stacks of dishes and books and towels and blankets in their house in Ohio, deciding what they should pack, what else they needed to say goodbye to far before any of them thought they would have to, she had clung to those bowls like a talisman.

Even now, when Lavender added chopped herbs and whispered spells that sounded more like pleas, she could feel her parents there. They were always *there*, just on the periphery of her eyesight. When she hadn't known what to do when Sage's freshman year math teacher told her she wasn't a fit guardian, when a pipe had burst at three in the morning in January the first year they'd lived on Star Island, when they'd all gotten the flu and Lavender had cried in her bed, wanting someone to take care of her—she'd caught glimpses, almost like a prism against a window. It felt like them. She could hear her dad's joking tone, her mom's soothing voice, telling her she was doing a good job, call the emergency plumber, take some painkillers and get the grocery store to deliver soup, crackers, and liquids.

She sprinkled sugar over the chopped thyme and mint. "I know," she began, "we aren't always in the right. We've done bad things. We've deceived and cast spells on the unknowing, we've damned and cursed and killed. I do not ask for forgiveness. The Bay line doesn't beg for absolution. I simply want us to be split from their souls. Unweave the threads of fate that bind Sage and Will, Gavin and I to Miloslav. That bind Laurel and Owen to Morana. That bind Rosemary and Asher to Ivan. That bind Verbena and Luke and Danny to Boris. Let us go. Let them go. Break the bonds and with it, all of us may find some peace." Lavender closed her eyes and worked her hands through the herbs and sugar, massaging the leaves until the entire apartment was as fragrant as a late spring morning in the herb garden at Bay cottage. She waited. Waited to see if something shifted, if magic wafted off the mixture. She reached out, seeking something more than sugar and herbs and found...

Nothing.

"Damn it." She brushed her hands off into the bowl. She walked to the sink and flicked on the water. One of these had to work. It had to. She couldn't believe—

Her phone dinged. Then dinged again. And again.

"Shit," she mumbled and grabbed a towel as she ran to it.

. . .

LUKE: A man grabbed Verbena outside The Muse. He scratched her, bad. Drew blood. She didn't get a good look but I think it was Miloslav. It's a nasty scratch. I'm taking her to the hospital.

ROSEMARY: Oh, my goddess. Asher and I are on our way. We'll meet you there.

LAUREL: Owen isn't home and has the truck. Can anyone grab me on the way to the hospital?

SAGE: Will and I can. I am going to fucking murder Miloslav.

"No, no, no," Lavender whimpered. Miloslav now had three sisters' blood. She and Rosemary were the only two left...he was getting too close.

She grabbed her jacket and jammed her feet into her boots.

LAVENDER: On my way. Be there in five minutes.

She dashed out of her apartment and raced down the stairs. She needed to put eyes on Verbena, make sure the scratch wasn't worse than Luke was letting on. A scratch? Hell, with Laurel he'd bit her neck. With Sage he'd bit her so hard she was in bed for hours. But now a scratch?

Lavender skidded to a stop before pushing outside. He could be waiting. She quickly drew circles around her joints and stuck her keys between her fingers for good measure. Miloslav Stoch might be a chaos warlock, but keys to the jugular did a lot of damage no matter what.

She stepped outside, whipping her head from side to side. It was eerily quiet. It wasn't like Lavender lived on a bustling street, it was Solaris after all, but at this time of night, usually someone was out.

Her car was on the other side of the street, half a block down. Moments like this, Lavender missed her personal driveway. But there was nothing she could do about it now. She clutched her keys so hard they dug into her palm and sprinted to her car.

"It's my fault. I wasn't paying attention," Verbena explained as the Bay family crowded around her. "I don't know what I was thinking. All I needed to do was step inside The Muse and I would have been fine. The anti-violence spell would have protected me."

"Even though it was just a scratch?" Lavender asked. She fought the urge to brush Verbena's hair back and check her forehead for a fever. Verbena was twenty-six. Luke was beside her with his arm around her. A doctor would be here shortly to stitch her arm up. She didn't need her older sister checking her forehead like she was a child.

"Yeah. Nothing with ill-intent can be done inside The Muse." Verbena shook her head. "Two steps inside was all I needed. I'm so sorry."

"Do not apologize," Lavender told her sternly. "You are not at fault for being less than hypervigilant for a moment at six in the evening on the street in Solaris."

Sage crossed her arms over her chest. "Maybe I should take a baseball bat to Miloslav's face. Just to give him a little taste of what I've done to him in the past. Not kill him, of course, but a broken jaw...no solid food for months. Might be the healthy reminder he needs."

"I don't think you going to prison for assault and battery is the solution to our problems," Laurel chided.

"No going to prison," Will added. "Remember?"

"Fine, fine. No prison. But seriously. He has a lot of blood now." Sage threw her head toward Rosemary. "And already tried with you but Asher thwarted him. He isn't backing down. He's using magic in public."

"He talked to Gavin this morning," Rosemary added.

"What!" Lavender shouted. The room around her swirled. Miloslav had been near Gavin? "Is he okay?"

"Yes. I found him as Miloslav was walking away. They...recognized each other."

"Who's Gavin?" Sage, Verbena, and Laurel said in unison.

"Um." Lavender looked at Rosemary, who nodded. "Gavin is my soulmate."

"Wait, you met your soulmate? When?" Verbena sat up in her bed.

"You moved out like two minutes ago and you already have a soulmate? Impressive," Sage said dryly.

"I..." Lavender exhaled.

This was it. After over a dozen years of keeping it all to herself, Miloslav Stoch was here and transparency between all the Bays was needed. She always wanted her sisters to be truthful with her. She should start leading by example.

"When I was in college, I met Gavin. I told him we were soulmates, he knew we were witches, all that. He recently came back into my life."

"Whoa, whoa, whoa." Now Verbena sat up and pushed her legs to the side of the bed. "You've known your soulmate for thirteen years? Have you been doing long-distance? Or ignoring each other's existence? How? Did you do a spell or something? More powerful than the one I used?"

"We broke up. Badly. That was enough to make it bearable. Didn't need a spell."

"Oh, Lavender." Laurel took a step toward her and draped her arm over her shoulders. "How awful. I can't imagine what it was like."

"It's okay," Lavender said quickly, her voice a little too high to be truthful.

"It's not okay," Verbena said quietly. "It's terrible. Was it…was it because of us?"

"No! No." Lavender couldn't stop her eyes filling with tears.

"When did you break up?" Laurel asked.

Lavender managed a small smile. "Two weeks before Mom and Dad."

"It is because of us, then. There's no way the two of you wouldn't have worked it out faster without us in tow," Verbena said, her voice shaky. "Oh, Lav. That's too much. You gave up too much."

"No. Being your guardian, all three of you. And Rosemary to a lesser extent." She sniffed a laugh. "That was what I was supposed to do with my life. You four. You were—are—the most important people. We are a team. We are a family. And yes, we invite more people, every month it seems, to be a part of this team, this family. But there was no way we were splitting up. I made the decision, and it was the right one."

"It wasn't fair to you though," Sage said finally, her arms tight across her chest. "You gave up your soulmate for us? Shit, Lavender. That's terrible."

"I promise it wasn't. If I went back one hundred times, I would make the same choice every single time." Lavender drew all her sisters to Verbena's bedside and flung her arms around all of them. "Being your guardian was the best thing I did with my life. And"—she smiled— "I'm going to get multitudes of lifetimes with Gavin. As far as I can tell, this is the only one where I have all of you."

"Damn, that's really sweet," Verbena said, then hiccuped.

"Everything okay in here?" The sisters released each other and turned to face the doctor, who had a tray of stitching instruments at her side.

"Oh, I'm going to be sick. I can't watch." Laurel rushed out of the room.

"I'll go after her," Lavender said. "Good luck, Verbena. I know you'll do great."

"Yeah, I'm not a baby. I can get my stitches without all of you watching, thank you. Everyone out except Luke."

Lavender ducked out before the rest, who were saying long goodbyes, and rushed down the hallway to find Laurel. After a few turns, she found an exit to a courtyard, where Laurel was sitting on a bench under a light with her head between her knees.

"You okay?" Lavender slid next to her on the bench and rubbed her back.

"Yes. I hate needles. And did you see the thread? Gross." Laurel had the bad luck of absolutely despising all things medical while also being a hedge witch, a discipline with a hefty dose of healing involved.

"Take some deep breaths and stop thinking about it." Lavender sat back and looked at the half-moon hanging in the sky.

"Thirteen years." Laurel slid to sitting. "That's a long time to wait to smooth things over."

"I was a little busy," Lavender began, then stopped herself. "I was afraid."

"It's really scary. All that stuff you said to me, about soulmates breaking each other's hearts? Hurting each other beyond reason?"

"Personal experience," she admitted. "It was a really bad time."

"You didn't tell any of us. I get him not wanting to drop out of college and come play father figure, but why didn't you two stay together? Do long distance, figure things out five years ago when we were all legally adults?"

"Oh. He didn't...I didn't give him a chance to come. We were in a bad place. It wasn't a normal breakup. I thought cutting it off completely would be better than...dealing with all of it. I knew what I could handle, and I picked."

Laurel nodded. “For what it’s worth, I think we all would have done the same thing. I love Owen, with every fiber of my being, but back then? We’d just lost Mom and Dad. And we’re sisters. We stay together, no matter what.”

Lavender put her arm around Laurel and pulled her close.

“No matter what.”

Chapter Eleven

Gavin sat in the plush pink chair beside Rosemary and Asher's front window. Lavender was okay—Rosemary had texted—but Verbena was not. And Gavin was even more confused now. The Bay sisters were in danger; Charles or Miloslav Stoch, was on Star Island and making weird threats.

What was going on?

He pulled his phone out and opened a message to his dad. He hadn't talked to him in over a week. Usually, he didn't let more than two days go by without a conversation. But with Lavender being a sore subject between his father and him, his dad firmly on team "move on," this whole business was set to get much more complicated. Gavin couldn't explain what he'd seen... what he knew. Not unless he wanted his dad to think he was crazy.

Still. He was halfway across the country from where he was supposed to be. He should tell him.

GAVIN: Hey Dad! Hope you are doing well. Decided to take a last-minute vacation for a couple weeks to Star Island. It's by Nantucket. Finally, a vacation after two years without one. Reception here is spotty, but I'll check in when I can. Talk soon.

. . .

A car pulled into the driveway and Gavin shoved his phone in his pocket and scrambled to his feet. He hadn't wanted to badger Rosemary and Asher while they were at the hospital, nor did he want to pry into business that wasn't his own, but he was struggling here.

The door slammed shut, and footsteps ran up the path. Gavin squinted to see if Rosemary looked upset, but it was too dark to see.

"Gavin?" Lavender called as the door flew open.

"Here," he answered. He immediately relaxed once his eyes were on her face. She was okay. The world might be going to shit around them, but Lavender was unharmed and at the moment, that was enough.

"Oh, goddess." She took two large steps, like she was going to fall into his arms, then stopped herself. She pushed her hair behind her ears, then bobbed her head a bit. "Are you all right?"

"Me? Of course. I've been here."

"No, Rosemary said you talked to Miloslav. Charles? That he came up to you this morning after you left the bakery? Alone?" She pulled off her scarf and coat, tossing them on the couch, then yanked off her boots.

"Yeah. Still the monster he was at 15 General. But he said some weird things."

"What? What did he say?" Her eyes were almost wild, a sharp crease between her brows.

"Will you sit down? With me?" He reached his hand out to her, hoping she would take it.

"I...yeah, I'll sit," she answered, but didn't take his hand.

Rosemary and Asher's living room was cozy, if not quite lived in. There were framed paintings and photo prints leaning against the walls they would eventually be hung on, and the built-in shelves were still seventy-five percent empty. Asher mentioned they had moved in less than a month earlier, and with everything going on, Gavin doubted hanging pictures was high on the to-do list.

Lavender slid onto the couch, and he joined her on the other end. She didn't want to take his hand, and he could give her space. As much as he wanted the space part of their relationship to be over.

"You have to stay away from Miloslav, Charles. He's the one who attacked Verbena. He already attacked Laurel and Sage. He kidnapped and beat Sage's boyfriend. Badly. He's not a good guy. He's worse than Charles."

"Why on earth is he attacking your sisters? Are you in danger?"

Lavender hesitated. "It's witch stuff. You don't need to get involved."

"Moonbeam. I am involved. Charles or whatever the hell his new name is knows I'm here. I'm part of it now. Will you please just..."

"Just what?"

"Let me in. Let me help. You don't have to be alone in all of this."

"I'm not alone. My sisters are a part of it too."

"I'm not some green human when it comes to being with a witch. I know those four men are their soulmates. I know their soulmates, human or otherwise, are helping. They aren't going at it alone. Don't push me away again, Moonbeam. I'm not a kid anymore. I can handle it."

She snorted. "I can barely handle it."

"Then let me help. Please. Even if it's only as someone you can talk to."

She twisted her hands on her lap and her eyes fell to the ground. "I don't want you to get hurt."

"I don't want to get hurt. But I think I'm in much more danger of being heartbroken, again, then Charles doing anything."

Lavender shook her head. "He's really dangerous. I don't..." She huffed. "Look, I love you. You know that. It's not some big secret. As much as I tried to make it not true for years. No matter how much time we spent apart, I still love you." She hesitated. "But I don't think this is the one."

"The one?"

"You know, the chance for us. We're going to have a lot of lifetimes, we've had a lot of lifetimes."

"More than just this one and France?"

She nodded. "I haven't wanted to look at anymore, because as you know, it's pretty shitty to see all of it. Statistically, there have been some happy ones, and we will have some happy ones in the future. But I don't think this is one."

"Why?"

"If it was meant to be happy, if we were meant to have a nice quiet life, it would have worked out before. Something would have been different. You would have stayed or my parents wouldn't have died. Or you would have answered your phone, or I would have left a forwarding address. We did so many things to stay apart. Choices stacked onto more choices. And I know a lot of those are my fault. I'm not blaming you. It wasn't one thing. And I can't let you back in to watch me die. Or for me to watch you die."

"Die? What the fuck is Charles doing?" Gavin got to his feet.

"I don't want you to be a part of it."

"Too late. If you think Charles might actually kill you, we need to call the police. Get a restraining order on him. Get him thrown off Star Island."

"It wouldn't work. He...he can mess with people's heads, with their perception of reality."

"Then you need to call a magical cop. There have to be some of those, right?"

"I wish. But at the moment, no."

"Why is he doing this? You didn't do anything to him in France, other than, you know, being loyal to your country. He can't be that petty. It's not even like we figured it out and got him executed for treason. Was he expecting you to sleep with him or something? That's ridiculous."

"You'd be surprised how poorly he has taken that exact situation. Mostly with Sage, but other women too."

"He tried to sleep with Sage?"

"Not this time around. But he's connected to Sage too. And Will."

"Yeah, he said he was always a part of our story. Never far behind."

Lavender rubbed her hand over her face. "I can't convince you to leave?"

"Nope. I'm here. Leaving before was the worst decision of my life. And I am so sorry. I wasn't there. God, Moonbeam, I wasn't there." He still felt so guilty over it. He was off wallowing in the pain of the distant past, and she was alone through it all. "I couldn't...I didn't know how to handle it, any of it."

"We were basically children. It's hard, I know. The way we died, it was awful. Having to relive it was terrible. I was awake for most of it. But I couldn't get to you. All I wanted was to lie in your arms while we faded away. It broke my heart."

Gavin looked down. Fuck, she didn't know. How could she? He never told her. It wasn't like her powers extended into telepathy. "It wasn't that. Oh, Moonbeam."

"What?"

"I didn't die. Not then."

"What?" Her voice dropped low. "No, I saw you, you were under the cabinet. I was awake for four hours, and you never woke up. You couldn't have survived that. It's not possible."

"Crushed pelvis, two broken legs, and a concussion. PTSD for the rest of that life. But I lived. Visited your grave every year. Went back to England once I was deemed well enough. Didn't see any more battle. I died in nineteen-seventy-two." It was a crazy thing to say, especially since he was born again less than twenty years later.

"No. No, I don't believe it. I spent the last four hours of my life mourning you. You were dead. You didn't move. Your chest had no rise and fall. You were not alive, Gavin."

"I was," he said quietly.

"Damn it! Well, and then what? You went back to England? What the hell?! You were alive in nineteen-seventy-two? My parents were alive in nineteen-seventy-two."

"So were mine. Lavender, I went home and I lived the second half of my life without you. A lot of life happened without you."

"Oh, my goddess." She collapsed onto the couch. "Did you marry someone? Did you have a family?"

"Yes," he admitted. "But it wasn't, it wasn't love. It was a sense of duty."

"You married someone else out of duty? Oh shit, did you get someone pregnant?"

"No. No, it wasn't that kind of marriage. We were friends. She was my brother's—you remember Phillip—she'd been Phillip's girl. When he was on leave...he got her pregnant, right before he died. I knew I'd never get over you. And it was a different time. She couldn't fake a dead husband without leaving Suffolk. And her mom was older, needed her help. It made sense."

"Wait. You had a child, or niece or nephew, born in the forties."

"I did. Judith." Gavin still felt a pang when he mentioned her name. Still felt that fatherly loss.

"Is she still alive?"

Chapter Twelve

Thirteen years earlier

Gavin rolled off the bed and hit the floor.

"What the fuck!" he shouted as he scrambled to his feet. God, his head was killing him. He was starving too. There was a bag of tortilla chips on the desk. He grabbed them, tore it open, and jammed a handful in his mouth.

What the hell was that?

"Moonbeam." He crawled back to the bed and shook Lavender. "Wake up, babe. We've been asleep for ages."

She whimpered in her sleep, then thrust her hand out and grabbed him. "Arthur?" she whispered.

Arthur.

Arthur.

It all came rushing back to him like a flood...

A life, a different one. When he was a different man. A child in England, a soldier in France. A heartbroken man, the love of his life killed by Charles...a person he had called brother.

Discharge. His mum and da. Phillip was gone.

Cynthia.

Judith.

"Oh no." Gavin stood up and crashed against the bed. He looked down at Lavender, who was finally blinking her eyes open. "Was that real?"

"It was terrible," she moaned.

"Lavender, listen to me. Was that real? Were we really Arthur and Ruby? Or was that a dream we shared?"

"It was real." Her voice was shaky. "I can't believe it worked. I thought it might work..." She slowly pushed herself up to sit and reached for him. "Don't worry, we're together again."

Gavin looked at her, the woman he had loved before, and felt...

Terrified.

"I have to leave." He grabbed his wallet and phone off the desk and shoved them into his pocket.

"Leave? You need to sit down. We should talk about what happened."

Judith. Judith. Judith. And Cynthia. Oh, hell.

Lavender had her hands outstretched to him. "Come back, come sit with me. You shouldn't be walking."

"I'm sorry," he stuttered. "I'm so sorry."

Gavin stumbled through campus, barely able to keep on his feet. Memories came back like shots on the battlefield. Waking up in the field hospital, every single person he knew dead around him.

Ruby. Losing her had been the worst thing he could have imagined. The rescue team didn't even try to save her at that point. Said she was cold. And Dunk and Timmy and Bobby and Dorothy...

Coming home to a dead brother with a pregnant girlfriend.

His mum sobbing when she saw him as he was after. A shell of the man he'd been before. A quick wedding for everyone's sake. Judith needed a father. He needed a caregiver for years.

He picked up speed and ran to his dorm. He needed to find Judith. That was the only thing he could think of.

He needed to find his baby girl.

GAVIN: I'm sorry I'm doing this over text, but I need a break. I have some stuff to sort through and I need to do it alone. I'm not breaking up with you. There are some things I can't talk about right now. It's too fresh. But I'll come back at some point. But...I don't think we should be in contact for a month or so. I'll find you when I'm ready.

LAVENDER: You're leaving? School? Are you going home to Wisconsin?

LAVENDER: I'm sorry I did the spell. Please, just come talk to me.

LAVENDER: Gavin? Please talk to me.

LAVENDER: I love you.

Chapter Thirteen

"Gavin, is Judith still alive?" Lavender asked again. She sat on the edge of the couch, her hands twisting as she spoke.

"She was. I...that's where I was when I left. I went to find Judith."

Lavender let it wash over her. Gavin wasn't Judith's father, but he'd been as good as one. She could imagine the tie to her would be...intense.

"When I went to look for her, she was still alive. Still in Suffolk. Living only a few blocks away from where we had. Our house was still there. The roses I planted when Judith was seven were blooming, though much more impressive than when I was in charge." He sat beside her and leaned back, gazing at the ceiling. "I saw her, once. It was...tricky. I didn't, you know, tell her who I was. She probably would have called the police if a kid was at her door insisting he was her father."

"What did you do?"

"I pretended I was getting signatures to stop England's involvement in the Iraq War." Gavin smiled a little. "She was very confused why an American student was going door to door in Framlingham instead of focusing on their own country."

"How did you know she wouldn't slam the door on your face?"

"Because I know her. I knew her. My little girl. She was a big protester in the late sixties and early seventies. Always looking to make the world a better place. I got her signature, her email, and a conversation out of it. We talked for nearly an hour on her front step until her husband came home and I had to act uninterested in him. She didn't meet him until after Arthur had died. I was curious."

Lavender sat very still as the silence in the room became heavy. It was a lot. Hell, Ruby died in 1942. She never had kids or nieces and nephews she knew who could possibly be alive today. That world had ended for her thirty years before Arthur's.

"I still can't believe you survived. We were all dead. I thought I was the last one."

Gavin shook his head slowly. "No. When the Americans got there a day or so later, they were mostly looking for supplies. Couldn't believe I'd survived it. Didn't think I would make it more than a few days. Doctor thought I had to have destroyed all my organs. I was also a sorry mess, begging to be left behind. I...I didn't want to go on without you." He wound his hand through hers. "But in the end, I didn't have much of a choice. They dropped me at another field hospital, that's when..."

Lavender was sure she looked like the picture of shock. She still couldn't believe Arthur had survived the bombing. She was a nurse, for goddess's sake. She should have been able to tell whether he was alive or dead by looking at him. Especially since she spent nearly all of her last four hours praying he would twitch.

"My mother wrote. Told me that Phillip had died in Belgium, that Cynthia was pregnant. Suddenly, I had something to live for. Everyone in the village knew that Phillip had been the one to get her pregnant, hadn't done the right thing and married her before he went off and died. I wasn't going to let the love of my brother's life be shamed, his child teased for not having a father."

"That was noble."

Gavin shrugged. "It felt like survival. She needed a partner. So did I. I wasn't going to...I wasn't going to have a normal life. Neither was she. We cobbled together a life for Judith."

Lavender nodded. "You and Cynthia."

"I'm going to be honest with you. I slept with her three times. In our thirties. It's part of the reason I couldn't talk to you about it when we did the spell. I felt like I'd betrayed you by being with her." Lavender let the information wash over her. He'd been with someone else. "But I'd like to continue by saying that in the past thirteen years, I have not been with anyone else. I haven't gone on a date, I haven't had a one-night stand, I haven't kissed anyone at midnight at a New Year's Eve party. I, Gavin Murphy, have been completely faithful to you, Lavender Bay. I knew you were out there, knew that someday I would find you, and I never lost hope. No matter how awful I felt, no matter how many dark empty nights weighed on me, I never, ever thought of being with anyone but you. You are my soulmate and the love of my life, Moonbeam."

Lavender inhaled sharply. Yes, it was all true. Gavin was the love of her life. And Arthur had been the love of her life. But she couldn't fault Gavin for something Arthur had done. She couldn't even fault Arthur. To be alone...to survive such a terrible ordeal, whatever small comforts he needed were forgiven.

Gavin lay his hand open toward her. "I don't want to take any more steps back. I only want to be with you. Please. Let me be with you. I don't care if the world is falling apart around us. I don't care that Charles, or Miloslav, is here and making life dangerous again. I only want you. To hell with that shadow. You and I are all that matters."

She stared at his open hand. She wanted to slip her hand in his, crash her body against him, and forget that anything else existed.

Forget that a blood curse still lay on her family. Forget that Miloslav's soul was intertwined with hers, and his relations were intertwined with her sisters.

But trying to forget was like ignoring the sword above her neck. No matter how much she wanted to fall into a dreamland with Gavin, the world hadn't changed. The danger wasn't only still there, it was creeping ever closer. Miloslav had the blood of three Bays now. He'd be coming after the rest of them, and soon.

She slid her hand in his but responded with hesitancy. "Gav, I want that. So badly. I really do."

"You sound like you are about to say but," he answered.

"But there is a lot happening. And I'm worried I can't protect you."

"You don't have to."

"I do. I have to protect you. And Rosemary. And I've done a shitty job at protecting the rest of my sisters recently."

"A madman attacking your sisters is not your fault."

"I understand that logically. But they aren't just my sisters anymore. They haven't been for a long time. I was their guardian. And while it's not a capital G guardian, it comes with the same job description. I am meant to shield them from harm. That is my role in their lives. And I love you, Gav, I really, really do. I never stopped. My heart hurts with loving you. But I cannot focus on keeping my sisters safe while you are so vulnerable to Miloslav."

"I can take care of myself," he interrupted.

"You really can't. I can barely take care of myself around Miloslav, and I'm a witch. He's a chaos warlock. It's scary what he can do. He changes the way you perceive the world. He rendered a powerful storm witch immobile. He's blessed by Erebus—he's a chaos god, the personification of darkness. The fact that Miloslav has him as a patron." She inhaled sharply. "His power is...I don't know. Warlocks aren't usually this powerful."

"I'm not leaving you." Gavin set his jaw.

"Please—" Rosemary and Asher's car pulled into the driveway, shining lights into the living room. Lavender scrambled to her feet and scrubbed her face a few times. She didn't want Rosemary to worry. There was enough to worry about right now, and Lavender's messy heart was at the bottom of the list.

"You can dig your heels in all you want, I'm not leaving you," Gavin mumbled. "Fuck Charles, fuck Miloslav, fuck the curse over your bloodline. You are my soulmate and I will not abandon you, not again. You are stuck with me, Moonbeam. Until the day I die."

Lavender turned a sharp gaze on him.

"Do not say that," she hissed. "You are inviting ill will on yourself."

"Ill will be damned, you are my fate. I do not intend on losing you early." He met her gaze with a fire of his own.

Lavender could see in the set of his jaw that he wasn't backing down. No matter how many times she told him this was a bad idea, Gavin had made his mind up over her.

He wasn't leaving this time. Even if things turned awful.

"Lavender? Gavin?" Rosemary called as she opened the front door. "Everyone decent?"

"We're in the living room. And yes. Of course, we are decent."

Asher followed close behind Rosemary, his hand wound through hers.

"How is Verbena?"

"Doing great. Her stitches are finished, and she's been released. Everyone else went home together. Laurel and Owen are going to stay at the cottage tonight. Safety in numbers and all."

"Oh. Should we all head to the cottage?" Lavender quickly tried to figure out where everyone would sleep. Luke and Verbena and Laurel and Owen would be fine in their old rooms, but Rosemary and Sage's old room had two twin beds. And Asher was the size of a tree.

"Uh, no," Asher finally spoke.

"Here's the thing. I had a really good idea in the car ride home for a spell to keep Miloslav at arm's reach, at least for a couple days. I don't know if it will work, but it's worth a try, right?"

"Oh. What kind of spell?"

"I think I might be able to sort of...soothe his soul. Like, you know, make him a little high. Enjoy life for a bit. That sort of thing. Might take a bit of the bloodlust out of his brain."

"Huh." Lavender hadn't thought of that. But leave it to Rosemary to think someone who is literally trying to murder them and steal their power might only need to change his mindset.

"Is it a tea? How are you going to get him to drink it?"

"Not a tea. It's a sex spell. So yeah. Would you be able to take Gavin off our hands for at least seven hours?"

"Seven hours?" Gavin interjected. "Jesus Christ."

Lavender couldn't help bursting into laughter. "Seven hours, Rosemary? Seriously? That cannot be good for either of you."

"No, we won't be going at it the entire seven hours. There's a lot of prep work involved! But I think it would be best if no one else's energy was in the house while we are prepping."

"What are you, putting towels down? Covering the couch in plastic?" Gavin smirked.

"Gav!" Now, Lavender burst into a fit of giggles. It was all ridiculous. So ridiculous! Lavender was a witch, sure, but her sister was going to try to bang her soulmate into making their arch nemesis too happy to come after them.

"Towels aren't a bad idea," Asher mused. "Wouldn't want to damage the hardwood."

Now, everyone laughed. Asher wrapped his arms around Rosemary and pulled her tight. Lavender risked a glance at Gavin. She loved his smile. His beard hid the deep dimple he had on his left cheek now, but she could still see a shadow of its presence.

"Seeing as it's already late and Asher and I have a very long spell session to commence, I say this with the kindest heart possible. Lavender, take Gavin to your apartment and get out of my house so I can take off Ash's clothes."

"Please wait until we have pulled out of the driveway," Lavender said as she walked into the front hall and pulled on her boots. "You can see everything through the window in the living room."

"No promises!" Rosemary sang. "You better hurry!" Lavender looked back into the living room just long enough to see Rosemary throw her arms around Asher's neck.

"She isn't kidding, we better move it," Lavender said to Gavin, who was also wrestling a boot on.

"Yes, ma'am. Plus, I'm looking forward to you taking me home."

Chapter Fourteen

Gavin climbed into the passenger seat of Lavender's car and kept his eyes firmly off the front window of Rosemary and Asher's house. Even when purposefully averting his gaze, he swore he saw something hit the glass.

"Does Rosemary really think she can alter the world by sleeping with Asher? That seems...unlikely."

"Well." Lavender huffed a laugh. "When Miloslav's brother, Ivan, came to Star Island to terrorize Rosemary and Asher, he destroyed our street. Like, pulled up the plumbing pipes and cracked the asphalt. It was a disaster. Looked like a tornado had torn up the entire block. I was more than a little convinced we'd have to come clean about our magic finally and basically change the landscape of the world with that. But Rosemary and Asher did a spell and fucked in the front yard, and it fixed the street completely. So yeah. She kind of can."

"Whoa. Seven hours...kind of makes me think of when Cal went out of town that one weekend." Gavin looked over to Lavender, whose cheeks were now bright red. "That was a good weekend."

"It was," she answered quietly.

"I still think about that weekend a lot."

"You do?"

"Hell, yeah. That image of you...on my bed in a tangled mess of sheets and blankets, your arms above your head, skin all rosy. Best image I've ever seen. Beats out Starry Night, Venus de Milo, the Sistine Chapel."

"Oh, my goddess, stop."

"Why? You don't want me thinking about you naked? Sorry, I do it a lot."

"How? After being apart for thirteen years, how do you still even remember what I look like naked?"

"Moonbeam. It's been a while, and I know I don't look the exact same. But if I were a talented artist, which I am not, I could paint every inch of your body still. I could shade the dip above your hip perfectly. Color match your nipples. I could sketch the exact face you make when I sink into you. That beautiful mix of lust and relief. I've never forgotten. I never will. You are seared into my memory."

Lavender was quiet for a moment, concentrating on the road ahead of her. She made a series of turns through the wooded landscape until they finally made it back into town and civilization.

"I thought about you too." She looked at him for a second, then back at the road. "Obviously. I'm not a nun. Far from it with my pagan soul. So, it was always you I thought about. But..."

"Yeah?"

"Sometimes it was too sad. To think about you. My heart would ache when I was simply trying to find a moment of bliss. But I did think about you. And I do remember. Probably to as much detail as you, but I'm not going to wax poetically about your, like, balls."

Gavin laughed heartily. "I wouldn't expect you to do that. My balls have nothing on your nipples."

"Damn it, Gavin, stop talking about my nipples." She giggled.

"It's hard to stop talking about them when I think about them constantly."

"Gav!" God, he loved when she called him Gav. Especially when she used that tone. That mock shock. Like she had to put on a show when he was talking dirty to her. Pretend to be scandalized. But he knew her. He knew she liked it. Loved it.

"Perfectly rosy points. So sensitive. Loved being in my mouth. Especially when you were riding me."

"Damn it. You are...hell, you are talking like nothing changed." She huffed. "You haven't talked like that in ages."

"Been waiting to find you so I could bring my dirty talk back out for you." He leaned in until his mouth hovered just in front of her ear. "Do you still love it?"

Lavender pulled into a parking spot, threw the car in park, and turned to him. "What do you think?"

"I think we should go upstairs and then you can tell me."

Once in Lavender's apartment, the mood shifted. Erie met them at the door, mewling for dinner, which she quickly got for him. Then she headed to the kitchen and started cleaning up the supplies she had out from before getting a call from the hospital. Gavin stood against the countertop watching her quietly. In the car, she had been a former version of herself—a college girl with no responsibilities. But that spell broke the moment they stepped in here and returned to the real world.

"Do you need help?" he asked.

"No, no. You can sit down. Um. Hungry? Or are you tired? I can take the couch tonight." All the hope Gavin held deflated. He'd wanted to fall into bed with Lavender, find his way back to her, trace the lines he'd left on her skin so many years ago.

"I will take the couch," he said quickly. "And I will make dinner. Will you sit down? You've had a shock. I shouldn't have..." He exhaled. "Sit here." He pulled out one of the chairs at her small table. "And relax."

Surprisingly, she listened, dried her hands off on a dishcloth, and sat.

Gavin took her place in the kitchen and opened her fridge.

What had he been thinking? Lavender's sister was attacked. She had the weight of the world on her shoulders. He shouldn't have come in so hard at her. That wasn't what she needed from him right now.

"So. What are you making?" she asked.

"I think I am making some sort of soup and grilled cheese." He pulled out two blocks of cheese—cheddar and parmesan—milk, butter, and a paper bag of carrots.

"The cabinet to the left is my makeshift pantry," she said as she leaned forward on her elbows.

"Perfect," Gavin mumbled as he added two sweet potatoes, an onion, a head of garlic, and a can of chicken broth.

"Oooh. Carrots and sweet potatoes? Sounds delicious."

"It is. Simple, but very good." He pulled open her spice drawer and added paprika, chili powder, and cinnamon to his growing pile of supplies.

"You have stuff like this on the menu where you work?"

He chuckled. "Not really. It's a little fancier. But I did do a version of this soup for a little while a couple years ago."

"Customers didn't like it?"

"Nah, management likes things changing. If the menu stays the same, why would people keep coming?"

Lavender snorted.

"How do you come up with your menu? Owner, head baker, cashier… you do it all over there."

"That I do. Well, my menus are mostly seasonal, but I have a couple year-round items. I don't change up the breads other than one loaf that's seasonal."

"And you've got the whole coffee thing too."

"That's Hazel's territory. Before I hired her, it was straight coffee or tea, add whatever you want at the serve-yourself bar. But Hazel turned it into something else. She came up with all the drinks that aren't staples and then taught Cece and I how to make them."

"It's a pretty amazing business you've built. I've seen the lines." Gavin finished chopping the rest of the veggies and threw them in the pot with the onions and garlic. "I'm really proud of you." He opened the chicken broth and added it, then brought it to a boil. "You ever use anything you learned at DePaul running a business?"

"I mean, I didn't finish my business degree there. Never went to culinary school. Obviously."

"How'd you end up owning the place?" Gavin opened the bread and threw a quick glance her way. Her shoulders were relaxing now, the frantic energy around her dissipating. Good. They could talk until she was calm again. As long as it took. Gavin had waited years to hear her voice. He would rejoice in it now.

"I worked there first. For six and a half years. Then the owner wanted to retire, she didn't have kids, offered to sell it to me. Which I, of course, couldn't afford. But I got a loan. For the first two years, I didn't have anyone else working there. Occasionally one of my sisters would pull a shift if I got sick or had a mental breakdown. That happened twice. But then I started actually making money, and I hired Hazel. Another year passed and I hired Cece. In the summer, I also have three high school or college-age kids helping out. On crowded days, it's too busy for me to work the front and the back. It's worked out."

"Like magic almost."

"Yeah. Probably a little bit of that. My house—my old house—was bequeathed to us by our great-aunt June. She was a hearth witch of some sort. No kids. She still hangs out in the cottage, basically watching over us. I like to think she had something to do with it as well. Making sure nothing really terrible happened. I've owned the place for over five years. Still never had to replace a major appliance. Never had a fire. No electrical problems. I think Aunt June might have something going on. Like she knows all the things already happening were enough, you know?"

"Like a fairy godmother. Except she's actually a ghost."

"My ghostly godmother."

Gavin got out her frying pan and started making the sandwiches. There was nothing like making a grilled cheese. The way the butter spattered and the bread got all toasty, watching the cheese melt. It was a simple pleasure in life. Gavin liked watching food cook. Watching it change into something new. Ingredients mixing together to create something magical.

He shredded the cheese over the frying bread, enjoying the few stray pieces that fell off and were about to turn into the crispiest mouthful of salty goodness in the world.

"It smells amazing," Lavender said. "You sure you don't want me to help?"

"No. You do so much for everyone. Why don't you go put on your comfiest pajamas or a hoodie and sweats, and your plate will be ready when you come out, all right?"

"All right," she answered with a small smile. "I want you to know while this is lovely it's a little hard for me to give up control of my kitchen completely. Cooking together is one thing. Me sitting around is another."

"You're not sitting around," he called as she disappeared into the bedroom. "For once in your life you are resting. Let me take care of you, Moonbeam. Let me remind you what that feels like."

Gavin got to work, pureeing the soup, plating the sandwich, and sprinkling a bit of parsley he found in the fridge on top. He added a giant spoon and napkin to her spot, then went to look for a drink.

"Looks amazing," Lavender said softly.

He looked up from the fridge as she sat down. She had her hair pulled back in a high ponytail. Her sweatshirt had one of those wide necks and was falling off her shoulder, exposing a thin bra strap. His gaze settled on that bare shoulder for a moment before he shook himself out of it and grabbed a glass to fill with water. As much as he wanted to run his hand over her shoulder and pour her a deep glass of wine, he wasn't going to. She needed rest, and he was going to give it to her.

He had time. There was no rush. Taking things slow was the mature choice in this situation, and Gavin would strive to be mature.

"Holy shit, Gavin. This soup is amazing! And the cheeses mixed perfectly!" She dipped her sandwich into her soup and took a huge bite. "Good work."

"Thanks, Moonbeam." He went back to the frying pan and made another sandwich, then got himself a bowl of soup and sat across from her. "You look relaxed. A bit undone. Finally."

She giggled. "I guess I should let other people cook for me once in a while. Take a load off."

"I'm here. Whenever you need that. I am here."

Chapter Fifteen

Goddess, watching Gavin cook was unraveling her soul. His hands on her knives, on her counter. Watching the muscles of his forearms as he chopped. When he told her to go get changed... everything this man was doing was like a balm over her bone-tired body.

Then watching him eat. How he tore into his perfect sandwich, gulped down the soup he had made from scratch.

She'd never felt so animalistic in her life. She wasn't sure if Gavin was the predator and she was the prey, or the other way around, but it felt like someone was about to be devoured.

"Do you want to go to bed?" Gavin asked, pushing back his chair from the table. He grabbed both their plates and bowls, balancing the dishes on his forearm with ease. "You had a stressful day."

Lavender shook herself out of her daze. She needed to get a hold of herself. Yes, it was all well and good to lust over Gavin. Her brain was hardwired to want him, and there was nothing she could do to stop it. But she had to be reasonable. Realistic. Now was not the time to be jumping into anything with Gavin, especially her bed. Their emotions were heightened, and life was dangerous.

"Yes. I should go to sleep." She stood from the table as Gavin started washing the dishes. "You can leave those for the morning. I'm not the kind of person who needs a clean kitchen before I go to sleep. Dirty dishes don't haunt my dreams."

Gavin hummed a laugh. "I'm glad to hear your dishes don't haunt you, but I don't mind washing up the mess I made."

"Okay. I'll...put a blanket and pillow on the couch for you. And I always have a few extra toothbrushes so I'll put one by the sink for you when I'm done in the bathroom."

"Thank you. In my rush to not see your sister screwing Asher, I did leave all of my stuff at her house."

"Oh. Do you want something to sleep in? I might have a pair of flannels big enough for you."

"Nah, I'm good. I can sleep in my T-shirt and boxers."

Lavender nodded furiously, trying to keep her mind on bed. Not bed. Sleep. She needed sleep. She was overtired and her adrenaline was crashing. Gavin in her living room in his boxers was a non-issue. Right? She'd gone thirteen years without being around Gavin in his boxers. She would be fine.

She disappeared into the bathroom and decided her longest bedtime routine was probably a good idea. It would give her time to get her body, heart, and brain on the same page. She flossed, brushed, mouthwash-ed, then flossed again for good measure. Then she washed her face and moisturized. Brushed her hair out (something she never, ever did before bed, but there was no time like the present to add a step). Should she clip her nails? Pluck her eyebrows? Neither needed work and, at this point, she was hogging the bathroom. The ambient sounds of cleaning a kitchen had finished, and Gavin was probably waiting for his turn. She pulled out the extra toothbrush—green against her purple—and walked out.

"I'll grab you a pillow and blanket. You can use the bathroom," she said quickly, then ducked into her bedroom before he could see her. Lavender waited until she heard the click of the bathroom door, then rushed out with the bedding and deposited it on the couch before hurrying back to her room. She wasn't sure if she could face him right now without kissing him, so she wouldn't see him. Gavin wouldn't barge into her room with the door shut. He'd leave her alone. She was in control of herself, for goddess's sake. If she didn't want to climb all over her soulmate, she wouldn't.

She pulled her covers back and dove under her blankets. Sleep. She should sleep. Everything would be calmer in the morning. By then, Verbena would be feeling better. And her sisters were fine. Rosemary and Asher were doing goddess knew what to soothe Miloslav's soul to give them a bit of a reprieve. Everyone was safe. Fine. All Lavender had to do was close her eyes and let exhaustion take over.

A chaos warlock is loose on Star Island. His allies are an unhinged hedge witch and a metal warlock. He subdued a powerful storm witch. He's backed by a god. He messed with my perception of reality in public. He's Charles. And Charles killed me. Almost killed Arthur. I didn't figure it out in time, didn't get help in time. He killed all my friends. He's Jonas Fortworth. He killed the other Bay witches. Burned them alive, cut out Eliza's tongue. He's Lysander. He tried to rape Callistrate. He attacked Laurel. He attacked Sage and Will. He attacked Verbena. He tried to attack Rosemary. He isn't afraid of being seen in public because he can distort reality.

He's unbeatable.

We will fail.

There is no way I can protect my family.

I can't win this battle.

I give up.

I want Gavin.

I need Gavin.

No, Gavin is in danger. Gavin needs to leave Star Island. If he's out of Miloslav's focus, he could forget about Gavin. Even if he kills all of us. Even if he becomes the most powerful warlock ever to live, he could forget about Gavin.

Will the superpower bleed into other lives? Will I be powerless forever, if I fail? What if I can't even separate our souls? Am I doomed to repeat this over and over...Miloslav or Charles or Jonas or Lysander always connected to Sage and me. Will and Gavin. Will Ivan always follow Rosemary and Asher? Will he kill or try to kill Asher over and over? Break Rosemary's heart over and over? Will Morana stick to Laurel and Owen? Out Laurel as a witch and watch her burned alive? Will Boris torture Luke again and again? Damn Verbena to a terrible death?

Are we stuck here?

No. I can unwind us at least. I should be able to break the Fortworth curse too. I need to try harder. I need to put my mind to it better. I am the protector. It is my role. I need to push everything else to the side. I should be working on an unbinding spell right now. No, I need to sleep. My brain isn't working well enough to do good magic. I forgot to put the laundry in the dryer. Damn it. I should go to the bakery tomorrow and make a few extra loaves of bread. I should write down all my recipes so when I'm gone Hazel and Cece can still run the Immortal Cupcake. I need to update my will. Who should I bequeath the Bay cottage to if we all die? The Guardians? The Davies water witches? Maybe Luke's brother, Danny. He could use a break. But it should stay in the Bay line. Maybe one of my uncle's kids will manage to have a magical kid. But what if the Bay line well and truly ends? What if we are all gone at the hand of a chaos warlock? What if after three hundred years, Jonas Fortworth finally gets his revenge? A family line of witches snuffed out because a Bay wouldn't be his wife and do his bidding?

What if?

"Shut up," Lavender mumbled. Her brain could not turn off. Which, duh. Her life was in absolute shambles at the moment.

She kicked her blankets off and flipped onto her stomach. Maybe she needed to get really cold and then get cozy. Trick her brain into thinking she finally had some refuge when there was none to be had. She rolled onto her back and pulled her flannel pants off, then stared at the ceiling.

What a mess. What an absolute terrible disaster. Was this it? Really it? Had the point of her and her sisters' lives been to fall to Miloslav Stoch? He wasn't even a witch. A warlock backed by a god and pissed off by both her ancestors and the soul of her little sister. Even if Sage hadn't murdered his soul at least three times, he was still a dick. A power-hungry dick.

Water. A glass of water would sort out her spinning head. And a cup of Don't Let the Bedbugs Bite! Why hadn't she thought of that before? There was nothing like a mild, magical sedative to calm a racing mind.

Lavender pushed off her bed and tiptoed to the door, then slowly opened it as silently as possible. She padded down the short hall, turned the corner to walk through the living room area to the kitchen and—Gavin was sitting on the couch, awake, on his phone.

"Can't sleep?" he asked.

Chapter Sixteen

He hadn't meant to scare her, but Lavender jumped a mile when he spoke.

"Sorry. You okay?" He dropped his phone, kicked the blanket off his legs, and got to his feet. His eyes took a moment to adjust before he realized...Lavender wasn't wearing any pants.

She'd been wearing pants when she went to bed, but thirty-ish minutes later, she was standing in front of him. Pantless.

"I'm fine. Was going to make some tea. Got a case of the racing thoughts." She pushed past him into the kitchen. "Would you like a cup? It's called Don't Let the Bedbugs Bite. It's a magical sedative. Not too strong though. Gives you a dreamless sleep."

"Uh, no thanks. You want to talk? Before sedating yourself?"

"It's perfectly safe. I have trouble turning my brain off sometimes. Not a big deal. This will turn me off like a switch." Lavender paused with her hand outstretched to grab a mug for a second.

"Like a switch," he echoed. She used to tease him that she could turn him on like a switch. And she could. Still did. He'd be lying if he said his eyes weren't glued to the swell of her ass at that exact moment. The light blue line of her panties against her skin in the darkened kitchen—he could see just well enough to know he wanted to see more. So much more.

"Gavin, I don't think we should." She set the mug on the counter and turned to face him. "I should drink my tea and pass out. And in the morning, I'll wake up early and try out some new spells before I go to work. And that should be it."

He should agree with her. He should lie back on the couch and pull the blanket over him, roll so his back was facing her while she made her tea.

But, God, his heart ached with the thought of all of that. He wanted Lavender—he needed her. And he was pretty sure she felt the same way.

"I want you to tell me how you are feeling, and I want you to do it without using the word should. Because I don't care what we should be doing. I only care what you want. Forget about all the walls and constructs and whatever else you've built in your mind. Forget about punishing yourself for years because some really shitty things happened close together. Forget about all of it. What do you, Lavender Bay, want? Not as someone's sister or someone's protector, or as a soulmate, or as a witch. Just you. What do you want?" The words poured out of him like a tidal wave he couldn't stop. He couldn't believe staying apart was the answer. And he needed to hear from her what she actually felt, not what she thought she *should* feel.

"I can't."

"Why?"

"Because I can't! I don't think you understand how much I have to control, all the time."

"Moonbeam." Gavin took a tentative step toward her. "It's you and me here tonight. No one else. I know you. I know you deep in my soul. You deserve happiness. You deserve reprieve. You deserve to be wanted and adored. I want you. And I fucking adore you." He outstretched his hand. "Let the weight fall off of you. Even if it's only for a day, a night, or an hour."

"I..." Her voice faltered. "I should—" She bit off her own words and shook her head, squeezing her eyes shut.

"No shoulds," he reminded.

"I want"—her eyes popped open and stared at him, a delicate crease between her brows—"you."

"Come 'ere," he breathed. Lavender slid her hand into his.

"There's a million reasons why—"

"I don't want you to list them. Let's pretend, for the rest of the night, that nothing else exists. Or matters. It's just you and me, Moonbeam."

She nodded and turned her face up to his. "Just us tonight."

Gavin wrapped his arms around her waist and enveloped her slowly. He wanted everything about tonight to be slow. They only had one night in which they could be selfish? Only one night until she constructed that wall of control around her heart again? Fine. Gavin was going to enjoy every damn moment of that night.

"I missed you every minute we were apart," he murmured against her ear. He buried his nose in her hair and inhaled. God, that scent, cinnamon and home.

Lavender burrowed against his chest, and he felt her entire body let go as he cradled her against him. The tension in her shoulders relaxed, the pinch of her brows released, and she hummed.

"This feels so good."

"I aim to make you feel a lot better than this," he teased.

She smiled against him. He moved his hand to her face, running his thumb over her jaw, across her lips. He traced her nose and her eyebrows. He couldn't get enough of her.

"Gavin?"

"Mm-hmm?" He moved his hands over her back, one to her neck, the other belting around her low back, skimming the edge of her shirt.

"I haven't...you know, done this in a long time."

"Me neither." He fisted the hem of her shirt.

"I probably look a little different. Than I did then."

"So do I."

"Yeah. You look more distinguished. And I've been working at a bakery. Sampling lots and lots of food. All the time."

"Lavender Bay." He pulled on her ponytail until she dipped her head back and met his gaze. "I am dying to relearn every single one of my favorite places on your body. Let me." He pulled her shirt up achingly slow. She lifted her arms and let him slide it off her perfect body.

"Oh, hell." His eyes roamed wildly. Her bare shoulders, the slope of her breasts, the tips of her nipples, the roundness of her belly, the width of her hips. Her panties blocked him from roaming further, but this was enough to undo him.

"Stop staring and kiss me," she demanded, pressing her body against his and obscuring his view.

He'd get it back. He'd have her naked, flushed, and in full view for him tonight.

He kissed her hungrily, throwing his promises of slow and gentle out the window. She met him furiously, as wild as he felt. Like water slipping over rock. God, her lips were so soft, so wet, so perfect. He felt like he was a kid again, drunk over kissing the first and only girl he'd ever love.

But he wasn't a kid anymore. He was a man, she was a woman, and they were still perfect together. No matter what life threw at them—horrible and heartbreaking things—they found their way back to one another. And now that he had her, Gavin would never let go.

"Let's go to your bedroom," he breathed. He ran his hand up her body, squeezed her breast, then scraped his teeth against her neck.

"I mean..." she gasped. "I live alone. We could stay in the kitchen." She pressed into his hand, her back arching in response.

"We could. But I haven't been with you in thirteen years. I don't want to bang you on the counter for two minutes. I want to take my time with you. As long as I can last." He chuckled. "Which might not be long. It might be short. But I will try my best."

She giggled. "Okay. Bedroom." She turned to leave, but Gavin grabbed her around the waist, hooked his thumbs into her panties, knelt, and pulled them to the floor for her to step out. He kissed her hipbone and followed with a deep groan.

"Now, walk to the bedroom." He squeezed her ass quickly. Gavin kept his eyes on her as she led him out of the kitchen. It was taking all his control not to grab her around the waist and take her to the ground right there. He'd waited so long—so achingly long—to be with Lavender again. He could wait the twenty seconds it took to get to her bedroom.

She flicked the light on as they crossed the threshold, then cast a glance over her shoulder. "Lights on, right?"

He grinned. "Yes. I like a clear view of you at all times."

Lavender walked to the side of her bed and pulled back the white comforter, then sat on the edge. Gavin took in the moment. Her white bedspread and sheets, her three pillows, her stark white walls, showing how recently she'd moved into this space. An empty mug next to a lamp and a very old-looking book on her bedside table. A sweatshirt in the corner on the floor. Small hints that she lived here.

He walked to stand in front of her, then fell to his knees. He skimmed over her thighs, her skin soft beneath his thumbs. God, he missed this. The simple feel of her was enough to drive him mad. He pressed a kiss against one knee, then the other.

"I haven't...mmm...ever had a man in this bed."

"I should hope not. Random men sleeping over sounds like a bad idea." Gavin kept his hands on her thighs, kneading the flesh, worried he might lose control at any moment. He wanted to kiss every inch of her body. Would she taste the same as he remembered? Sound the same? His memories were clear but fuzzy around the edges. They were both changed too. They weren't college students hopelessly in love. They were weathered. They knew what it meant to lose. Everything was heightened now. Gavin knew what life was like without Lavender, and he wouldn't let that happen again.

"I remember what you like, but tell me what you want," he said slowly, dancing his hands from her thighs to her hips.

"I want...everything."

Chapter Seventeen

Want.

What did Lavender want?

She wanted this. She wanted Gavin, on his knees in front of her. In her bed, in her house, sleeping next to her. She wanted to eat dinner with him every night. She wanted him to surprise her at the bakery on slow winter mornings and to steal a kiss from him in the back on busy summer days.

She wanted Miloslav gone, her sisters safe, and some semblance of a normal life for the first time ever.

Most of those things were not attainable. So instead, Lavender would let herself want Gavin, for tonight, and as a balm to the odds of her losing everything else, she would take anything he could offer for now.

Tomorrow she would let her mind grow crowded with every reason this was a bad idea, but tonight she would simply want Gavin and let herself have him.

He slid between her knees, his hips slowly widening her until their chests were flush. She leaned into him, seeking his mouth with her own. Goddess, she could kiss him all day, all night, all life. They'd lost none of their rhythm, none of their familiarity with each other. Kissing Gavin felt like coming home after being lost for so long. The way his mouth moved over hers like a promise, the way he cradled her head against him. It was all so wonderfully comforting.

"You still have all your clothes on," Lavender breathed as his mouth moved down her neck to her collarbone.

"Yes," he mumbled against her skin. "Protection."

Lavender laughed. "I've been on the pill since college. Don't need my period ruining my life."

"Not that kind of protection, but good to hear." He gripped her waist and manipulated her onto her back, hovering over the cradle of her hips. His mouth dipped to hers again, devouring her until Lavender wrapped her legs around his waist. She wanted to hold on to him—with her arms, her legs, her heart. She didn't want to let go ever again. She never should have done that spell when they were kids. She was the reason they were lost to each other for years. And then she was so scared for so long. She couldn't bear to see him and—

"Moonbeam."

"Yeah?"

"You look like your brain won't turn off."

"Sorry. I...I can't believe I screwed us up for so long. How much time we lost. I didn't...I didn't know." She shrugged helplessly.

"No apologies tonight. No overthinking. No thinking at all." Gavin rolled off her, grabbed her three pillows, and arranged them behind her back so she sat at a reclined angle.

"What are you doing?"

"You need you brain turned off. So"—he slid off the bed and knelt in front of her—"you are going to watch me go down on you."

"I am?"

"Yes. You are. I never made a big deal about it before, but I always saw you looking in the closet mirror in your dorm when I did. Watching me work you over. Mesmerized by every move. You always came pretty quickly that way."

Lavender felt her cheeks redden.

"I'm right?"

"Yeah," she answered softly. It did turn her brain off. Watching something happening to her. Seeing Gavin with her. The combination of touch and sight—it was her favorite. "It's been a long time though. I don't know if the same things will work. Or if I'll even be able to finish at all. My mind is a mess and—"

"What if..." He slowly ran his hands up her legs and arranged them on each of his shoulders. "We simply enjoy the process? I'm certainly not in a rush to finish."

Lavender nodded. She shouldn't rush anything about tonight, especially since there was a good chance this would be their only opportunity to be together.

"Hey, Moonbeam?" Gavin whispered, his lips against her thigh.

"Yeah, Gav?"

"I love you." He didn't let her respond. He nestled between her legs, used his mouth against her—teasingly slow. Gentler than her memory could conjure. In a way that made her pant immediately, legs shaking, hands roaming wildly until he offered one of his own to hold on to. Which she did, with both of hers.

It was like an assault on all her senses, crowding out any thoughts that might threaten to pull her away. She couldn't think about anything when he had his mouth on her. Not Miloslav. Not the curse on her line. Not all the mistakes she made in the past.

Not that he had said I love you for the first time in thirteen years.

Her mind was crowded with the sight of Gavin working her over, the sounds she made as he did. The way her entire body felt like it was on fire. As if he was everywhere all at once. All the noise of her life went silent, and she enjoyed Gavin.

She squirmed beneath him—the gentle, languid licks were wonderful but also threatening to drive her mad. She wanted to come, she was ready to come.

"Gavin. Will you...you know...like in college? With your hand too?"

He hummed against her, shifting her further down as he snaked his hand between her legs...pushed two fingers inside her...found the tingling bundle of nerves...his mouth still on her...then took her over the edge.

She cried out, in pleasure, in anguish. Every bit of pain and aching devastation of the past wove with her unending ecstasy and with it, she felt alive.

"Keep your hands on me," she managed to choke out as she drew his body up hers. "Wait. Take your clothes off. You can take your hands off me only to get those pants off. Shirt too. Everything. I want to see you."

He slid off her to stand between her legs, his hands dragging down her thighs as he did, and immediately pulled his shirt off and tossed it to the side. Then he made quick work of his boxers and stood in all his naked glory.

There he was.

He wasn't the exact same. The years had changed both of their bodies. Hell, as a twenty-two-year-old, Gavin had only had the barest hint of a happy trail and no chest hair at all. Now, a fine dusting of black hair sprinkled over his chest, dissipating, and then forming a thick line below his navel.

Below that, it was everything Lavender remembered.

She didn't have a lot of experience. Before meeting Gavin, Lavender had made out with a few boys in high school, but nothing that lent itself to a peek below the belt. So, when she remembered a hard cock, there was nothing in her memory to confuse with Gavin.

"You're staring," Gavin teased.

"I am." She tore her eyes away from his cock and looked up at his face. "You know I've missed you a lot, but him,"—she gestured between his legs—"he's been thoroughly missed as well."

He chuckled and pulled her to stand, then flipped them around so he was sitting on the bed and she was straddling his legs.

"I can in turn say that I missed you with my whole damn heart, and my dick missed you just as much." He pulled on her hips until she climbed onto his lap, hovering just above him. "You gave me a whole 'I might not come' speech. I'm going to give you a 'this might be over in thirty seconds' speech."

It was Lavender's turn to giggle. "Gavin. It's okay if it's over fast."

"If I'd have known we would be in bed together tonight, I would have checked into a hotel last night and jerked off. As it is..."

"You've been staying at Rosemary's house."

"I have." He ran his hands down her sides, up her thighs, over her breasts. He cupped her face and kissed her lightly. "And I also have my beautiful soulmate in my lap. A woman I have dreamed of every night for thirteen years."

Lavender's heart panged. They could talk. They could talk themselves to death through all the hurt and pain and grief they'd caused each other.

But she didn't want to talk anymore. She wanted nothing but him.

She shifted her hips and sank down until his entire length filled her to the brim.

"Oh, Moonbeam," Gavin groaned. "You feel..." He buried his face against her chest. He wrapped his arms around her waist tightly, keeping her from moving an inch for a moment. "Let me...just stay like this a minute." He craned his face up toward her and captured her mouth with his. His kiss started tender, so gentle she could have cried. But then it changed. It became deeper, wilder. Their lips parted, their tongues met. Gavin's hands moved over her frantically. He squeezed her breasts, cupped her face, ran his fingers over her thighs. She wanted to move—she needed to move. She needed more.

Gavin released her and fell to his back, then grabbed her hips.

"Ride me," he growled.

Lavender moaned an enthusiastic, "yes," then dragged her body over his, over and over again. She planted her hands on either side of his face and moved with purpose, enjoying every moment, every inch, every jolt that ran down her spine.

"God, you are so perfect." Gavin moved his hand to the apex of her thighs, just where they joined. "I want to make you come again." His thumb found her and strummed in time as she raced over him. She was so close again. They both moaned and moved, chasing that beautiful moment of release. He bucked wildly under her while working his fingers over her. She threw her head back and let go.

"Gav!" she sobbed through her release. He followed almost instantaneously after and pulled her against him.

"I've got you," he whispered against her hair, still slowly moving in her, drawing up every last drip of ecstasy for both of them. "I've got you, Moonbeam."

She believed him. Even after everything that happened in the past, she believed him.

Gavin Murphy had her.

Chapter Eighteen

"Should I go back out to the couch?" Gavin teased. He stood in the doorway, without a stitch of clothing.

Goddess, Lavender looked amazing. All flushed and well-sated. For the first time since he came to Star Island, she looked relaxed. He wasn't sure how long it would last, but he was going to bask in it while it did.

"Oh, shut up and get in bed with me." Lavender laughed. She pulled the covers back, giving him a glimpse of her beautiful naked body, and patted the empty side of the bed. "It's nice and warm in here. And you won't have to listen to Erie pushing his food bowl around in the morning."

"I'd much rather share a bed with you than listen to your cat." He slid back beside her and immediately arranged her against his chest. They settled against each other like they had so many times before. They'd had sex—unbelievable sex—each used the bathroom and then snuggled into the middle of the bed. It was perfect. This was what Gavin wanted. Yes, being with Lavender, feeling her body beneath his, above his, was something he had missed so much. But lying with her afterward? Getting to sit in her glow? That was the true intimacy he craved. When they were both sated and sleepy and together. Sticky and soft in each other's arms.

"Tell me about your restaurant," Lavender said over a yawn. "What's your favorite thing on the menu?"

"The lamb."

"Really? How do you prepare it?"

"Very simply." He nuzzled against her hair and let his eyes close. He brushed his fingertips over her back as he talked. "It's braised and then slow cooked all morning. I start it around ten and it can't be ordered before six-thirty. Red wine, carrots, my own tomato sauce I make a huge batch of once a week. Lots of thyme."

"Sounds delicious. How long will it be on the menu?"

"Not long. It's heavy, so no one would order it in summer. I fight to keep it from September to March. If it were up to the owner, it would be November to February, but it deserves a longer run."

"Is it your best seller?"

"Nope. Steak is. It appeases the masses."

Lavender giggled. "I don't offer a chocolate chip cookie."

"You don't?"

"Nah. I did. For the first three years. And it was good, but it was boring. It's not my best cookie, but people would always order it because it's safe. So, I experimented with taking it off the menu for one month—December. Told customers I didn't have room on the menu with all the specialty cookies I was making. And it was fine. Once January hit, no one asked where it was anymore. I like forcing people out of their comfort zone when it comes to cookies."

"You, rebel."

Lavender tipped her head up and kissed him quickly. "Do you mind if I sleep on your chest tonight?"

His heart soared. It was back. He'd gotten it all back. Lavender was in his arms and she wasn't going anywhere.

"I'd love that." She flicked the light off, then settled back against him.

"Good night," she whispered and pressed a kiss against his skin.

"Night, Moonbeam."

The room was dark and cold. Lavender was beside him, and he pulled her close, afraid of what was waiting for them.

Three women appeared...their hair made of fire, the skin of their hands and feet burned black.

All three raised a hand and pointed.

"What do you want?" Lavender asked, her hand snaked around Gavin's arm.

"The last time was a gift. Your past still has answers to your questions."

"A gift? That spell ruined us. We're not doing it again."

One of the sisters stepped forward, spoke without opening her mouth.

"You never could have survived seeing the life you are meant to then." She nodded toward Gavin. "It was a gift to him to see his past. A gift to you that you did not see the one you need to."

"No, no, no..."

Gavin pulled Lavender against him as the three women disappeared into nothingness.

She was calling out to him in the emptiness. He needed to get to her.

"Ah!"

Gavin jumped awake and threw his arms around Lavender.

She was shaking.

"Moonbeam? Lavender?" He shook her a bit. Her face was all screwed up like she was having a nightmare. "Wake up, babe. Wake up."

"Gavin!" she shouted. Her eyes flew open, searched wildly, then landed on him.

"I'm right here. I've got you."

She exhaled and sagged against the bed.

"The ghosts are back," she whimpered.

"Were those the three women on fire I saw in my dream?" It all came rushing back to him that moment. It wasn't a dream.

Was it a warning?

"They are the ones who told us to look in the past. That it would help with the curse. It's how Laurel found out how she was connected to Morana, same with Rosemary and Ivan, and Verbena and Boris. And it's how Sage found out Miloslav was Jonas. I thought because we'd already seen ours, and Miloslav was there, it didn't matter anymore."

Gavin sat up and wove his hands through hers. "Tell me everything about the curse. Tell me everything that has happened." Rosemary, Asher, even Lavender, they'd all been talking around the curse. Gavin was sick of being in the dark.

"It's scary."

"I can take it."

Lavender nodded and rolled onto her back. "A witch and a warlock cursed the Bay line in the 1700s. Those Bay witches, the ghosts, were the first ones cursed. Murdered too. Miloslav Stoch, Charles, he was also a warlock called Jonas Fortworth. He wanted Eliza for a bride. When she refused him, he and his sister cursed the Bay line and killed those witches."

"What does the curse say exactly?"

"Any warlock or witch who collects the blood of all living Bay witches will basically steal their powers. We don't know if it will also kill us. But… even if we survive, it will take the part of us that is the most important, most integral to our lives. I don't know who I would be without my magic."

Gavin felt the blood drain from his face. "How many living Bay witches are there right now?"

"Five."

"What? You don't have any cousins? Far-flung?" This couldn't be happening. Miloslav was on Star Island, he knew where Lavender was.

Lavender shook her head. "And he already has Laurel's, Sage's, and Verbena's."

"No." He shook his head. "No."

"I'm so sorry. I didn't want you to know about this. I thought if I could figure this out, then I could find you after. I don't want you to lose me as much as I don't want to lose you." She scrubbed her eyes.

"Hey. I'm not losing you." He slid back beside her and wrapped his arms around her. "I'm not. The witches said we needed to do the spell again. So, we do it again."

"It was awful! It separated us for thirteen years!" She sobbed.

"It won't again. We're older. I know I'm never leaving you. You aren't disappearing again. We can do this. If we need to see the past to fight Miloslav, we do it."

"I'm so scared." Lavender palmed her forehead. "I'm sick with being scared."

"I won't leave you, I promise."

"Promises made in the dark," Lavender whispered.

"Are the easiest to breathe and the easiest to break," he finished. "I remember. But this is a promise I've made to myself in the sunlight. Day in and day out. That if I ever found you, I would never leave you again. And I do not intend to. Someone would have to—"

"Don't say it. Don't tempt fate when we have this hanging over us."

"Then I won't. But you know in your heart I mean every word of what I hold back." He rolled until she was beneath him, her legs wrapped around his waist. He kissed her forehead, her cheeks, the tip of her nose, and her mouth. "I love you, Moonbeam."

"I love you too." She paused, then kissed him hard. "Will you..."

"Go back to sleep?" He paused and kissed her quickly. "Go back to the couch?"

"Don't joke about going back to the couch."

"Tell me what you want."

"I want to be with you again. Right now. And then again tomorrow when I get home from work. If this all falls apart, if everything changes, I want to spend as much time as I can with you." She trailed off. He moved against her, kissing her and caressing her until she moaned and arched up beneath him.

"I want to be with you again and again," he echoed, sliding into her slowly. "And again," he withdrew inch by inch as Lavender shuddered. "And again."

They moved slowly together, drawing out every moment into an infinity of small pleasures. He took his time with her now. He wasn't worried about it going too fast. He kissed her neck, worshipped her breasts, suckled her nipples until she was weeping with need. He pulled out and went down on her until she begged him to fuck her as hard as he could. He gave her what she wanted, hard and beautifully messy until she came over him and he spilled everything he had inside of her and they both collapsed on the bed, sweaty and half-asleep.

Time was never on their side, so he would take everything he could get.

Chapter Nineteen

Lavender was stuck to Gavin in the most intimate way. Her hair was pressed against his chest in strands, her arm fused around his waist. It was the most comfortable she'd felt in years, and she didn't want to move. But the day was beginning.

She slowly peeled herself away, immediately regretting it, but the patrons of the Immortal Cupcake didn't know she'd finally reconnected with her soulmate. They didn't know a curse hung over her like a sword. They still expected coffee and baked goods ready and waiting for them. Which meant Lavender had to get to work.

Even though it was freezing.

Even though the sight of Gavin sleeping naked in her bed had her clenching her thighs again.

Even though all she wanted was to wake him up and have another go. And another and another, until they decided to simply live in bed and ignore all the horrors of the Fortworth curse and the biddings of long dead witches.

She glanced at her phone. Five fifty-two. As it was, she didn't have enough time to make all the cookies she wanted. Or muffins. But that was okay. She needed a shower more than anything right now. She couldn't go to work with "I had three orgasms throughout the night" hair. And that was the look she was currently rocking.

She snuck into the bathroom and switched the water on as hot as it went. More than looking like she had sex all night, she felt it. It had been a long, long time since anything that athletic had happened in Lavender's life, and she was reaping the consequences. Muscles that hadn't been used in years were aching this October morning. Her lower back too. She wasn't twenty anymore. Thirty-four came with a few more aches and pains than she was used to after a night like that.

She grabbed her loofah and worked up a good lather, then ran it over her body in a motion to ease her sore muscles rather than simply clean her body. Though she needed that too. If she walked around smelling like Gavin all day, she would never get any work done. Hell, she would probably close the shop early to come back here and jump him. She definitely wanted to make up for lost time.

She tried to stay focused on Gavin and leave all the business of the Stochs to another day. Yes, the world as she knew it hung in the balance...but right now, right this moment, she would let herself feel something other than panic.

She finished her shower, brushed her teeth, and braided her hair tightly. As much as she wanted to blow it dry, especially with the cold weather waiting for her downstairs, Gavin looked too peaceful wrapped up in her comforter. He'd been through hell too. He deserved a morning of uninterrupted dreaming.

She slipped on a pair of jeans and a sweater and put some food in Erie's dish. Then she grabbed a notebook and ripped out a piece of paper and wrote:

Good Morning. Didn't want to wake you. I'll run home on my break around noon when Hazel comes in. Erie is fed. Make yourself at home. Don't wander around Star Island. I'm sure you've heard there's a chaos warlock on the loose.

Love you.

Moonbeam

. . .

Then she grabbed her coat, hat, scarf, purse, and boots and left her soulmate sleeping away.

It was an eerily quiet morning. Jolene, Ray, and Stephanie didn't come in for coffee, which struck Lavender as very odd. When one of them skipped out, it was normal. People got colds, slept through their alarms. Or Stephanie's husband had a day off and she spent her morning sleeping away. But all three? That hadn't happened in years.

More than that, no one walked by the store. It was like six a.m. was dragging straight on until nine. Sure, it was cold and windy outside, but there were always people going for morning walks before work. Or running to drop something in the mailbox in front of the post office or the library return in the overnight slot.

Lavender walked back into the kitchen and pulled out her latest batch of muffins but held back on making any more. Maybe today was one of those flukes. No one would come in, no one would buy anything. She didn't want to see all that food go to waste, so why make more? She had enough cookies, muffins, cakes, and loaves of bread to serve half of a normal day in October, and for now she would leave it at that.

After arranging everything beautifully in the display case, Lavender checked her phone. Was there a storm coming? No. Just a regular forty-eight-degree October day with normal wind speeds, no rain, and nothing out of the ordinary. She opened the sister group text but the last message was Rosemary at three in the morning and just a series of inappropriate emojis that Lavender interpreted as a sex spell gone well.

Maybe that was why everything was quiet? Had Rosemary's good vibes spell settled over not only Miloslav but the whole island? Was everyone chilling at home having a slow morning and shirking their responsibilities? It wouldn't be the first time Rosemary's meddling caused mass feelings.

Or...this was a warning. The atmosphere was shifting because the tides were shifting.

She hadn't seen Miloslav in days, but he had to be somewhere on the island still. It was too cold to camp. Should she try to find him? Check out the hotel and the motel? Ask some of the rental owners if they'd rented to a particularly menacing-looking man?

Stop it, she chided herself. She could have a quiet morning without a chaos warlock having anything to do with it. She'd had them before and she would have them again.

Lavender left the front counter and stood in front of her large picture window, trying to see if anyone was coming. Was the universe telling her to close up shop and go enjoy Gavin for a while longer? That would be nice. Spend the morning wrapped up in him. Having sex, taking quick naps, eating in bed. Hell, she could even have Gavin cook for her. Or bring back some of these unsold goodies...

As if he heard her thoughts, Gavin turned down the street and walked toward the Immortal Cupcake. She couldn't contain her grin.

He was coming to visit her on a quiet morning.

It was a dream. Everything about the last fifteen hours had been a dream. She pushed open the door and waved.

"What are you doing here?"

Gavin jogged to meet her, looked around, then planted a kiss right on her lips.

"I woke up alone. Those multiple rounds really knocked me out. But then I saw your note. So, I decided to shower and come meet you. Figured if you needed any help in the kitchen I could lend my skills. And if you were slow," he said, gesturing to the store, "maybe we could make out for a while."

Lavender laughed. "Well, I'm definitely slow this morning." She pulled him inside. "I haven't had a single customer. Which is weird as hell." Gavin slipped off his coat and tossed it over a chair at one of the tables.

"Did you get everything made? I can't imagine how hard it was for you to roll out of bed this morning."

"No kidding. I'm super behind, but no customers means it doesn't matter. You want something?"

"Hell yeah. What's good?"

"Everything."

"I'll rephrase. What's your favorite?"

"I'll make you a plate," Lavender said and winked. She ducked behind the counter and piled a plate high—a snickerdoodle cookie, a slice of pumpkin bread, a savory rosemary and cheddar biscuit, and a morning glory muffin. It was more than Gavin could probably eat in a full morning, but she wanted him to try everything she had in the shop.

"Here you go."

"Damn, what should I start with?"

"The biscuit is the only savory thing if you like going that route. Savory then sweet. You want a coffee or a tea?"

"Tea. I'm on vacation. Or at least I feel like it. Probably should start thinking about this place becoming permanent." He took a bite of the biscuit and leaned back in his chair, his eyes fluttering closed. "Moonbeam, that is fucking delicious. I could serve that as an app and make a million dollars."

"I only charge four ninety-nine."

"You should charge more."

"I try to keep the customers happy." She let a beat pass as he took another bite. "You thinking about moving here?"

"Of course."

"Even though you have a restaurant in Chicago?"

"It's not my restaurant. I don't own it. Sure, I like working there. But this place. You own a bakery. That is incredible. Your whole family is here too. Honestly, Moonbeam, the moment Rebecca told me you were living here, I checked out of Chicago. I had a run there. I won't call it a good run because I spent a lot of that time completely miserable, but it was fine. Plus, this is a really nice place to live. Other than my soulmate being here, it's gorgeous."

"Could you handle cooking for tourists every night in the summer?"

"Ha. I basically do that all year in Chicago." He brushed his hands off and stood up, then walked until he had his hands around her waist. "I want you. If you want to live here, we'll live here. If you want to live in Iceland, we'll live in Iceland. My dad is in Florida. I don't want to live in Florida. Nothing is holding me in any other place right now. I go where you go. From now on. Okay?"

"Okay," she answered softly.

"Good." He kissed her forehead, then turned back to his table. "I'm sorry, I have to finish this biscuit. I haven't even tried anything else yet. Oh. Rosemary's across the street."

Lavender followed him to his table. "She works at the florist right there." She peeked out the window just in time to see Asher lay a long kiss on her sister, then get into their car and pull away.

Rosemary stuck her key in the florist door and jiggled it, but the door didn't open. She pulled her keys out, looked at them again, then tried again.

"That's weird," Lavender said slowly. The moment the words left her mouth, a man came running from the alley, sprinting at Rosemary. She heard Asher's brakes squeal.

"Fuck! Miloslav!" Lavender dashed out of the bakery and sprinted toward her sister. She heard Gavin scrambling behind her.

Rosemary was fighting with everything, but in the blink of an eye, Miloslav had her on the ground…his mouth on her arm…Rosemary was screaming now. Her legs thrashed against the concrete while she tried to push him off her.

Lavender felt the world slow down around her. He bit her. He had her blood. Rosemary was pushing him, kicking him, but he was still on her.

Asher appeared and grabbed Miloslav off Rosemary. He punched him in the face, sending him tumbling down the street, then looked at Rosemary.

"I've got her," Lavender choked out as she collapsed next to her sister. "Make sure he doesn't come back." Asher took off after Miloslav.

"You're okay. I've got you." Lavender tried to keep her voice steady. Hell, that bite looked bad. He more than broke the skin, he tore it. Shit, she needed stitches.

"Let's get her inside," Gavin interrupted. He picked up Rosemary and headed back to the store. "Come on," he called back to Lavender.

She searched the street. It was like Miloslav and Asher had disappeared.

"I need to get Asher!" Rosemary yelled. "If I'm not around…it doesn't work if he isn't protecting me!"

Gavin looked at Lavender for an answer. But she didn't know. She had no idea how Guardian magic worked. Only that if Asher was between Rosemary and danger, they were both safe. With Rosemary far behind him…

"There he is!" Gavin exclaimed. Lavender looked up and saw Asher rounding the corner, sprinting toward them.

"Give me her," he said gruffly and took her sister out of Gavin's arms. As a group they raced to the Immortal Cupcake and Lavender locked the door.

"Everyone, get in the back." She switched the lights off, then ran to the kitchen.

"What are you doing?" Gavin asked as she wildly pulled down her jars of herbs.

"Upping the protection of this place."

"Can I help?"

"Yes. Carry these." She handed him the chamomile and sage, then grabbed her dried basil, cumin, and rosemary. She hurried to the front of the store. Her entire storefront was glass. Glass door, glass windows. Something as simple as a brick could destroy it. She lined the entire front with a mix of the herbs, dumping her entire supply, and then arranged them into a thick line between the Immortal Cupcake and the outside world.

"What now?" Gavin asked.

"Rosemary." She dashed back to the kitchen. Her sister sat on the counter while Asher washed out the bite with a wet cloth. Rosemary had her eyes screwed shut and her lips between her teeth.

"Fuck, that looks bad," Gavin breathed.

"It is," Asher answered. "I have to take her to the hospital."

"No," Rosemary began.

"I know. They will call the police. You'll have to give a report. I can talk to Claire beforehand."

"If the town knows someone is going around biting us—"

"They will know something weird is going on," Asher finished for her. "It's too late. He's attacked all of you except Lavender. The police can do something. He has a mug shot. He's been arrested. I don't know how, but it has happened. Same with Morana and Ivan. He can't control everything. You need stitches."

Rosemary looked at Lavender.

"He's right," she agreed. "You need stitches. Asher, why don't you take her to the hospital? I'll...I'll figure out what we are going to do next. Have Claire call me if I need to corroborate anything."

"We will." Asher eased Rosemary off the counter. "I'm going to carry you."

"I can walk."

"I don't want you to walk."

Rosemary nodded and let her soulmate pick her up, then turned to Lavender. "I'm sorry. I should have seen him."

"Not your fault. Good luck at the hospital." She took them to the front door and let them out, then relocked it.

Lavender did not want this to be happening. She turned to Gavin.

"We need to talk."

Chapter Twenty

Gavin pulled Lavender into the kitchen. "First, we need to get out of here," he said quickly. He was sure she wanted to hash out a bunch of shit, including how fucked up it had just been to watch Charles—Miloslav—take a hunk out of Rosemary with his teeth. Like an animal.

"The protection should hold," she started. "But..."

"And that but is why we are leaving." Gavin grabbed her coat and handed it to her. "Is there some sort of invisibility spell you can cast over us until we get to your apartment?"

She shook her head. "If I could do that kind of magic, he'd never be able to find us."

"Then we run." Gavin slipped on his own coat. "It looked like Asher got a few hits. His hands were all banged up. Hopefully, he's still licking his wounds somewhere."

"You think we can outrun him? He can just make us think the world is melting around us."

"We have to try, Moonbeam." He wrapped his hand around hers. "We're not giving up. Right?"

"Yeah," she answered softly. "Wait. Hazel is supposed to come. I think I should be closed today."

"One hundred percent. But you should text her after we get in your apartment."

"Why?"

"Because if we don't make it home, at least Hazel will be heading to work in a few hours and notice some destruction." It was a grim thought, but if Miloslav was going to attack them on the street...Gavin still didn't know what would happen if he managed to get Lavender's blood. Would her magic just disappear in a puff? Would she die? Would he? They were linked together over lifetimes, and he didn't know if the magic is what kept them together. Would they get another chance at happiness if Miloslav succeeded this time?

"That's pretty smart." Lavender shoved her phone in her pocket.

"Wait, wasn't Rosemary and Asher's spell supposed to keep Miloslav at Bay for a few days at least?" Gavin asked.

She exhaled. "It was. It clearly didn't work. At least not on Miloslav. No one has been walking around the streets all day. Maybe it worked on the island, but not on him. He's too powerful."

Gavin could hear the change in the pitch of her voice. She was starting to believe they would fail.

"We need to get out of here," he reiterated. "We can talk about everything else at home." He squeezed her shoulder quickly. As much as he wanted to pull her into his arms and let time stop for a little while, they weren't safe here.

"Okay. I'm ready. Let's run."

He pushed open the door, kept his eyes on the street while Lavender locked it, and then they took off. He held onto her hand for dear life while they ran down the quiet streets of Solaris. It was weird, being so scared in such a beautiful place. Miloslav ruined everything. He truly was a blight following them from life to life, doing everything in his power to destroy their happiness.

They skidded to a stop in front of Lavender's building, dashed inside and up the stairs, and finally burst into her apartment. She immediately locked the door behind them, then ran to the kitchen and grabbed a bunch of herbs.

"Can he get in here?"

"I don't think so. But I'm not risking it. He's been doing a lot of things I didn't think he could do." Lavender spread the herbs in front of the door, then moved to the windows. Erie followed her around the entire time.

"Don't touch this," she chided her cat. "This is protecting us. And you. I can't imagine what a warlock would do to a witch's cat." Her kitten hissed in response and darted under the couch.

Gavin shrugged his jacket off and stared at Lavender. She was hyper focused now, putting away the jars, cleaning up the kitchen counter.

"Moonbeam," he said softly.

"What?"

"Are you okay?"

"Of course. Just tidying a bit. I shouldn't leave things so messy." She kept her eyes off him, her hands shaking as she worked.

"Moonbeam. Come here." He reached his hand out to her.

"If I...I can't."

"Why not?"

"Because if I hug you right now, I am going to cry. Hard. Maybe for an hour. And Rosemary is in the hospital, and I haven't texted Hazel or my other sisters, and there is a goddamn chaos warlock ruining my life. And I don't know what to do."

Gavin nodded. "Give me your phone."

Lavender fished it out of her pocket and walked it over to him.

"Thank you. Now, go sit on the couch." She did as he asked, and he opened her texts.

LAVENDER: Had to close the Immortal Cupcake for a family emergency. Don't come in today. No customers anyway, it's like a ghost town out there.

"How's this as a text to Hazel," Gavin said, then read it out loud.

"That works," she mumbled.

Gavin opened the thread called Sistersssss and saw that everyone was already texting with Rosemary.

"Your sisters already know. Rosemary is texting. I'm going to tell them it's me and that you are safe in your apartment."

"Thanks."

. . .

LAVENDER: It's Gavin. Lavender is okay. She and I are in her apartment, and she added a bunch of protection herbs around the place. She needs a little while to figure things out. Rosemary, I hope you are doing okay. Have Asher call me if you need anything. I'm going to go be with Lavender.

"All done." Gavin sat beside her on the couch. "Can I hold you?"

She nodded slowly and crawled onto his lap, snuggling her head against his neck.

"You can fall apart. I'm not going anywhere."

"It's so hard to...for so long I had to keep it all in. I was in charge. I was the oldest. Even when all I wanted to do was cry my eyes out, I had to put on a brave face. When we first moved here"—Gavin felt the reassurance of a warm tear sliding down his neck—"I was so sad. So heartbroken. But I never let myself cry in front of my sisters. At the funeral yes, and when we left Ohio. But I was determined to show them we would all be okay. No more tears on Star Island. I had made the choice to come here, and I didn't want anyone to think it was a bad one or that I second-guessed myself. So, I became the strong one. I never wanted to be the strong one."

"I wish I could have helped you. But I understand why you did it alone."

"You do?"

"Yeah. It was something you and your sisters were going through. I wasn't a part of it. As much as I wanted to be in your life then, you had a giant upheaval. If I hadn't...if we didn't see the past, maybe things would have been different. But I wasn't in a space to help you. I was a twenty-two-year-old kid who had just met his sixty-something daughter. I was pretty fucked up for a while."

"I'm sorry I did that spell."

"I don't think we should say sorry anymore. We were kids. A lot of bad things happened, and we didn't know how to live with them. But we did our best, and now we're here."

"On the edge of destruction," Lavender interrupted, laughing for a moment through her tears.

"What is it about our souls finding each other in the darkest of times?"

She shrugged and looked up at him. Her cheeks were wet with tears, her nose and eyes red, and Gavin still thought there was no one in the world as beautiful as her.

"I think we're both the light in the darkness. You're my light, and I'm yours. And when the world around us becomes too dark to bear, that's when we find each other."

"That's very beautiful. I only wish it wasn't so depressing on top of it."

She giggled. "What would you prefer?" They snuggled back down to the couch.

"One of these times, I would like to live a simple life with you. A fishing village with a little cottage and a roaring fire. Just us. No world wars or chaos warlocks. A quiet life with our fish and our vegetable garden. Making up recipes together."

"That sounds nice. And if it was seventy years ago, that's sort of what Star Island was. Mostly fisherman and their families eking out a living off the ocean."

Lavender's phone dinged, and Gavin looked at it.

"Hazel says, 'hope everything is okay, let me know if you need anything.' That's nice."

"She's a good employee. And a good friend."

"I think we should get back in bed," Gavin began. Lavender ticked her eyebrow up. "Not like that. We stayed up pretty late. Your sister was attacked in front of you. The bakery is closed. You need to rest."

"I should probably go to the hospital and check on Rosemary. Meet with my sisters and come up with a plan."

"I think right now the most important part of the plan is to keep you safe. I wish I had the same powers as Asher, but if I jump between you and Miloslav, nothing magical will happen. The hospital is probably where Miloslav is waiting for you." Gavin gathered Lavender in his arms and stood from the couch. "You need to rest. I know you want to fix everything as soon as possible, but this isn't going to be something you solve right now."

"I could work on an unbinding spell," she said as he carried her down the hall and into her bedroom.

He set her down, and his hands went to her shirt. "No outside clothes in the bed, right?"

She nodded. He took off her shirt, then her jeans. Gavin pulled the covers back, then guided her into bed.

"There's so much to do," Lavender complained. "And the ghosts..."

"There's always so much to do." Gavin pulled his shirt off and stepped out of his pants, then climbed into bed beside her. "Come here." She snuggled against his chest and he held her close. "Even if you can't fall asleep, you need rest, okay? Just rest."

Lavender nodded against his chest and sighed.

He may not have the ability to get between her and a chaos warlock and keep her safe. He didn't know any spells, and he wasn't even a particularly strong fighter. But he could make sure she slept. That she ate meals. He would take care of Lavender in every way he could.

Gavin pressed a kiss to her forehead and closed his eyes. He was going to keep his Moonbeam safe.

Chapter Twenty-One

Our line is not one to be trifled with. You must look into the past again, find the truth of your soul.

Lavender looked into the eyes of Eliza Bay and cowered.

I command you, witch!

Lavender shuddered awake, the ghost's voice still in her mind. It was dark and quiet outside now. She was pressed against Gavin, his thigh trapped between her legs, his hands spread wide on her body. She pushed her memory of Eliza Bay out of her mind and focused on Gavin.

Goddess. How had she gone so long without him? This was...perfect. Being in his presence was a balm to her broken soul.

"Are you awake?" he whispered.

"Mm-hmm. What time is it?"

"I think around five-thirty. I woke up a little while ago, and the sun was setting."

"Did I sleep for like seven hours? During the day?" Lavender was a little horrified. She never napped. Never got more than her eight exact hours a night. Hell, she should have been trying to figure out how to stop Miloslav. And she needed to call Rosemary and—

"Your mind is racing," Gavin interrupted. "Tell it to be quiet a little longer."

"I'm worried about Rosemary. I need to—"

"Asher texted." Gavin fished his phone off the bedside table. "About three hours ago. Rosemary filed a police report. She needed four stitches. They are home already. There's a warrant for Miloslav Stoch's arrest. Asher wasn't confident the police would catch him, but they might. They have before." Gavin scrolled through his texts. "Verbena, Laurel, and Sage plus Luke, Owen, Will, and Danny are all at the Bay cottage. Will is going through the library looking for something?"

"He's a Zetic warlock. He can consume a book in like two minutes."

"All right. Cool trick."

"We should probably head over there."

"Nope," Gavin insisted. "All your sisters said you should stay here. Miloslav might not know where you live, and we are not going outside. We are staying behind these nice herbs you have set up. We have enough food for a few days at least."

"I can't keep the Immortal Cupcake closed for that long," Lavender interrupted.

"True. But it is closed today. And I think you should keep it closed tomorrow."

Lavender mulled it over. It probably wasn't the worst idea to take tomorrow off. That way she could have more time trying to figure out an unbinding spell.

"Okay. I will. But I need to get out of bed. I need to work on the spell. If I can split the connections between our souls...that would work, right? Miloslav wouldn't be able to find us again. I just need to make sure that we don't continue to be reincarnated on the same timeline. I should also make another loaf of the past-life bread. I have all the ingredients in the kitchen, and those ghosts aren't patient."

"Mm-hmm." Gavin rolled her onto her back and kissed her neck.

"Time is probably of the essence," she continued as he peeled her bra straps down her arms until the entire garment slid down to circle her waist.

"It is," he mumbled before running his tongue around her taut nipple.

"Ah!" she cried out. "And...and if I get to work now"—she moaned as his hand teased her other breast—"I could get a few trials in before dinner."

"You do whatever you need." Gavin's mouth moved over her breasts, down her belly. He pulled her panties off her body, then settled his face between her legs. "I'm going to do something I need to right now. Let me know if it works for you." He split her open with his tongue, and she shuddered.

"It does," she panted.

"Good." He snaked his hand up to her face and brushed his thumb over her lips. "You deserve to feel really good right now."

Lavender stood in the kitchen in Gavin's shirt. It barely covered her bare ass, but she wasn't going to burn her tits trying to banish Miloslav from her life. He'd caused her enough grief already.

"Goddamn." Gavin whistled as he exited the shower. "I've missed that view."

"Me cooking in just a shirt?"

"I don't think I've ever seen you cook in just a shirt, and I do like it. But no, I missed seeing you in my clothes."

"Does something for you?"

"I'm just a caveman underneath all this modern man nonsense. You wearing my shirt is like you agreeing to be mine."

Lavender smiled. "I've always been yours." She set down the bundle of dried herbs she was holding and turned to him. "Always."

"If I hadn't promised to let you work for an hour, I'd be dragging you back to bed right now."

Now she laughed. "I didn't think men in their mid-thirties were supposed to have this sort of turnaround time."

"I'm making up for over a decade of lost time. Give me three minutes and a look at your boobs and I'll be hard in no time."

"Gavin!" Lavender exclaimed. "Not in front of the spells."

"Is it going to mess with your work? Me being horny around you?"

"Maybe. I'm trying to make an unbinding spell. If I start thinking about...binding to you, it won't work."

Gavin nodded. "The last thing we need is you to accidentally really attach Miloslav to us. I don't want that soul as my sibling in any life." He walked to the couch and sat down but kept his eyes on her. “I promise I’ll be good. Tell me what you are working on.”

“Basically, I’m trying to curse us all in a way. Our souls are all stuck together right now, following each other throughout our lives. If we look at another life, I’m pretty certain Miloslav would be in it. He was in four of Sage’s, and she only saw three of them.”

“Is this man being reincarnated over and over again? How is he managing that?”

Lavender shrugged. “I don’t think there are any living witches or warlocks who understand how it all works. Why we are living at certain times, not at others. The first Bay witches Miloslav killed when he was Jonas Fortworth still haven’t been reincarnated. And they were alive over three hundred years ago.”

“Hell. I was barely off the planet.”

“You had an abnormally fast turnaround time.” Lavender tossed a handful of dried white sage into her mortar and began crushing it. “I doubt most souls have so little time at rest.”

“Hm. I wonder what we’re doing when we’re at rest.”

“Well, Aunt June is hanging out in the Bay cottage. Boris Varga was torturing his son. My parents don’t seem to be tied to this realm anymore. So, who really knows? Seems like a plethora of options.”

“I don’t think I’d be up for haunting anyone. Friend or foe.”

“Oh, really?” Lavender pulled down a jar of salt she had dried herself last summer. Taking the time to collect seawater and let it dry in the sunshine until you had salt gave it much more power than regular table salt anyone could buy at the market. She sprinkled a bit on top.

“Nah. It sounds exhausting. Plus, would I really want to haunt anyone? Even Miloslav or Charles or whoever. I don’t want to hang out with him. He sucks. Plus, could you imagine watching him do all his evil warlock shit and just being an incorporeal being floating around watching? I’d lose my mind.”

“Well, you should probably request to come back as a phantom then. They can at least move a lot of shit around. Verbena could explain it more to you. There are all sorts of undead spirits hanging around earth. Some more annoying than others.”

“Either way. I think I’d rather chill in the ether with you.”

"That's sweet. I'd like to chill in the ether with you too." She sighed. As much as she wanted to stop working and climb into Gavin's arms so she could melt the afternoon away talking and touching, she needed to work. And he was a distraction.

"I need you to go in my room. I have to concentrate, and you are distracting me with your sweet words and handsome face."

"Sorry, Moonbeam. Can't control my irresistibility around you," he teased.

"Get out of here." She laughed. "I'll take a break in a little while. I promise."

"I'll hold you to it. Good luck," he called as the door shut behind him.

Lavender looked down at her wares. Salt, white sage, cloves...she needed something more.

She scanned her shelf...maybe oil? Oil and water? They were normal ingredients for a cake, but if she took on the attributes of one...

"Holy shit." She exhaled.

Oil was the key.

She scrambled around the kitchen and grabbed her dried rosemary, lavender, verbena, sage, and bay laurel. She added each to her mortar, crushing them together until they were inseparable. She added more salt from the Atlantic, used a funnel to get every last herb into a glass bottle, and filled the bottle with olive oil.

Now she needed to let it infuse. This oil would contain each of the Bays. And she would make a water for the Stochs.

A layer of oil cake with a layer of water cake and a cream filling neither could pass. It could work. She still had to figure out a way to get Miloslav, Morana, and Ivan to eat it...and that still left Boris somewhere in the ether attached to Luke and Verbena. It wasn't perfect. But it was a start.

Now, it was time to make a loaf of bread.

"Gavin?" she called as she pushed the loaf pan into the oven.

"Coming," he answered, padding down the hall. "Ready for a break?"

"Sort of." She walked to stand in front of him. "In sixty-five minutes and then fifteen minutes of cooling, the past-life bread will be ready. I think we should eat it again. I know it almost destroyed us, but I know how to separate all of us from the Stochs. I came up with a recipe and I know it will work. If we can split our souls from theirs, and if the answer to the Fortworth curse is somehow in our past…"

"We should do it," he interrupted. "I'm not afraid of what I'll see. I already lost you. If this can show me a way to keep you safe, I will do it."

Lavender slid into his arms. "We'll be okay," she whispered. "I know we will."

Chapter Twenty-Two

Kat turned her face to the wind and smiled. The cloying humidity of yesterday was now gone, and a chill laced through the air.

Autumn had arrived.

She hurried down the back steps and into the garden, her woven basket tucked under her arm. She still had an hour or two until her father woke, and it was the perfect time to do the work she wanted, rather than what he bid.

She pulled up the last of the lavender, rooted for a few rose petals still left on their flowers. She added some sprigs of thyme and marjoram, a few oak leaves that littered the ground, then knelt beside the birch tree at the edge of their property. She dug a bit of the soil surrounding the tree and sprinkled it into a handkerchief.

Kat pushed up to her knees and dashed back into the house and to the kitchen, her cloak loosely billowing behind her as she moved.

Old Maggie was in the corner getting breakfast started, but as usual, she ignored Kat. Technically, Kat was the lady of the house, and therefore mistress of the kitchen and all who worked there, but her father was the true master of this space, and Old Maggie was kind to turn a blind eye toward Kat's comings and goings. Plus, the old woman was more than half deaf and starting to lose her eyesight. She could always feign ignorance if asked if she saw anything.

Pulling out a mortar, Kat crushed the soil, lavender, and rose petals with her pestle. She left the rest of her collection in the basket for later use.

Now, she focused on the movement of her wrist as she mixed, whispering over and over again...

"Come to me, come to me, come to me, come to me, come to—"

"What are you doing?" her brother's voice shocked her out of her work, and the pestle clattered against the mortar. Damn, she'd felt so close that time.

"I'm working on something new," she answered quickly.

He sidled up beside her and peered at the mash. "What is it?"

She scooped up a handful and spread it over her arms. "Anti-aging. The women will love it. I don't think it's perfect yet, though."

"Hm." He furrowed his brow. "Shouldn't you add mulberry?"

"I thought of that, but it would dye the skin. You know how our customers are. No one would use it if it made them look like a berry."

"True." He glanced at her. "You look like a farmer. Go take a bath. I'll tell Nelly to bring the water up."

"I can tell her," Kat interrupted.

He laughed. "No, I have something I would speak to her about as well. And before you go up, Lady Edgeworth is coming this afternoon. She'll want more of the tonic. Gather anything else that you may need." He walked out of the kitchen, calling to poor Nelly as he did.

Kat set her jaw. She needed to figure out how to make a potion to keep him from the servants. But between her work for her father and trying to make something that could get her out of this forsaken household, she was stretched too thin.

The least she could do was shorten the time Nelly had to deal with her brother. Kat rushed back outside and clipped some more lavender, plus rosemary and mugwort. Lady Edgeworth was plagued with terrible dreams of the deaths of her children. While Kat knew this tonic only gave her a dreamless sleep and would not banish the dreams forever, it was the least she could do.

With a full basket, she hurried back into the kitchen, left the basket, then went to find Nelly.

"Lady Edgeworth, welcome to our house." Kat's father's voice dripped with venomous honey. "Please, sit for a moment." He led her to the parlor where Kat waited, her hands twisting as she sat perfectly still in her work clothes. She didn't mind Lady Edgeworth, but these noble customers...they often wanted more than she could give.

"Thank you, Mr. Fortworth. Your last tonic did wonders, but I need more. I ran out three days ago and the dreams...they are getting worse. Last night I saw poor Samuel. He was in such pain." She lifted her handkerchief to her eyes. "I cannot bear it."

"Of course, my lady. I've already made another bottle for you." He slipped the tonic Kat had prepared this morning into her hand.

"There's something else," Lady Edgeworth said, her voice lowering. "I think it might be worth us speaking alone," she added, throwing a look to Kat.

"Oh, do not worry. My daughter is completely under my control. She works as my assistant and would never breathe a word of anything heard in this room." He patted Lady Edgeworth's hand. "Go ahead."

"It's my husband. He...he wants a son. A son who lives. It is not enough that I have given him three taken so young. He does not want the title to pass to his nephew." She took a deep breath. "I need to provide an heir."

An heir? Kat held her tongue, but Lady Fortworth was at least forty-five. A pregnancy could kill her. Her last birth three years ago nearly did.

"Yes, my lady. It will be expensive. And take time."

"Is that wise?" Kat interrupted. "The lady has two healthy daughters but a history of early labor and—"

"Excuse me," her father cut in. "Katherine, you may leave this meeting. Why don't you go tinker in the *garden*?"

The slight sting over his pronunciation of garden had a familiar terror settling in Kat's gut.

She would pay for that remark.

Kat nodded and fled the parlor, first going to the garden so that if any of the servants saw her, they could tell as much to her father. But once she was outside, she kept walking until she hit the fence at the back of their property.

She hitched her skirts up, climbed over the fence, and ran down the beaten path toward town.

Her father would come after her, but if she was going to face him, she would have the beginnings of a potion for Lady Edgeworth to ingest.

It was a lovely day to lay bricks.

Richard Mason took a moment from his work and turned his face toward the sun. Soon, the warmth would be a memory of brighter days, when the heavy rain and dark clouds came, but today Richard would allow himself to be happy.

His belly was full, his work plentiful, and by the feel of the wind on his cheek, he could tell it would be a good day.

He settled in to his pattern: apply mortar, place brick, apply mortar, place brick—over and over again until the movement became a sort of dance he did, the din of the city as his music. He relaxed while he worked, letting his mind wander as he did. There was a pair of songbirds in the tree just above him, singing the day away in joy.

Richard rocked back on his heels to give his back a break when a woman caught his eye.

She hurried down the street toward him, her brows pinched in worry. Her white bonnet couldn't hold back the brown curls that escaped out the sides, and she fisted a handful of her dark green dress to make walking more quickly possible. It looked as if she muttered to herself as she wove through the crowd, something important on her mind.

"Ah!" the woman cried out as her foot caught an uneven spot and sent her tumbling forward, her knees smacking against the ground in an unpleasant thump.

"Miss," Richard said as he sprang to his feet and ran to her side, leaving his work unfinished. "Are you all right?" He offered her his hand, which she took. As he got her to her feet, her leg gave out again, proving she was injured.

"Here," Richard began. "Sit and take a moment." He led her to a flattened tree stump, not far from where he was working, then retrieved her basket from the street and returned it to her.

"Thank you," she said softly, her eyes never leaving his face. "You are very kind."

"I don't know if I am very kind. I should hope most would stop to help a beautiful young woman after she's taken a tumble in the street." The moment the words left his mouth, Richard felt his cheeks warm. Why had he said that? Yes, she was lovely, lovelier than he'd ever seen before with her golden-brown eyes, but she was an unknown woman. He wouldn't have blamed her if she slapped him right then.

But she didn't slap him. Instead, she smiled and set her hand upon his forearm for a moment. "What is your name?"

"Richard," he answered, then quickly amended. "Mister Mason."

"Well, Mister Mason, I am Miss Katherine Fortworth. But those dear to me call me Kat. I think very soon I shall count you as one of my closest friends."

"Oh," Richard mumbled. "If that's the case, would you allow me to escort you home? If you are feeling well enough, that is."

Katherine's smile fell, and she worried her lip a moment. "I believe I will sit here a little longer before I return. You do not have to wait with me if you have something to attend to," she added.

Richard motioned to the half-finished wall. "My only work is here. I can work while you rest." He turned back to the wall, lining up the bricks that would be placed soon.

"You are a bricklayer?"

"I am."

"And do you like your work?"

"I do." He smiled and turned back to look at her. "I would ask what your work is, but you have the distinct look of a lady."

"Do I?" she mused.

"Yes." Richard picked up a brick and placed it.

"And what about my face and dress makes me look like a lady? Look here, I've dirt smudged on my skirt. And my shoes are hardly impeccable."

"Hm," he began, spreading a layer of mortar before throwing her a grin. "You have no freckles. And your skirt looks freshly dirty. It isn't stained. I would guess...you are a lady who has a garden."

"A garden?"

He nodded. "I bet you grow the most beautiful roses in all of Mayfair—all of London!"

She laughed then, covering her mouth with her hand as she did.

"And there! So proper even when you are laughing. You must be a lady."

"Well," she said, lowering her voice and leaning toward him. "I'll tell you a secret. I am a lady, but I am a lady with an occupation."

Richard ticked his eyebrow in response. He'd never heard of a lady with an occupation. The only women he knew were working class, and work they did. They were seamstresses or laundresses or did the books for their husbands blacksmithing or brewing. But a lady working and making money? She had to be jesting.

"I'm an herbalist."

Richard searched his brain for the meaning of the word.

"A healer? I've studied all sorts of plants and how they can help people."

"Ah. So, you are a gardener."

She giggled in response, this time keeping her hand away from her mouth.

"I suppose I am a gardener of sorts. Though, my garden wouldn't win the praises of the ladies of Mayfair. And, for the record, I'm not Lady anything nor do I live in Mayfair."

"Where do you live then? Since I'll be walking you home soon."

"Covent Garden? Not far from here."

He knew the place. It may not have been as desired as the new builds in Mayfair, but Covent Garden still sat as a neighborhood above his own station. He chuckled. "Another garden for my gardener. Now, in this garden in Covent Garden, do you grow roses?"

"I do."

"And are they as beautiful as you?" Richard let the compliment fly before he could stop himself. This woman was clearly so far out of his league he thought nothing of bestowing her with flowery language that in any other setting would land him with a sweetheart, maybe even a betrothed.

But she didn't go cold or blush, only looked at him with her kind eyes.

"You'll have to be the judge when you walk me home," she answered quietly.

Kat had had half a mind to run away and never come back. The wrath of her father was never easy to endure, and if Jonas joined him in his efforts? Kat had scars down the left side of her back to prove her father's anger and no older brother to defend her if it became bad again.

But then…he appeared.

Her soulmate.

The man she had begged for only this morning.

Was it a sign to stay in London? That escape was close at hand? Kat had to think so. And while she had fallen and bruised her knee, she could have gone home immediately with no problem.

But she had wanted…more.

She could tell Richard was human-born. No magic coursed through his veins other than the magic that knitted them together. He would find her fascinating because of this connection, but nothing more. She couldn't very well beg him to take her away this instant, run away with her to the continent, without risking him thinking she was mad.

So, she feigned worse injury than she had and enjoyed a full hour talking quietly with him as he laid bricks under the lovely October sun. Only when the sun began to dip close to the horizon and darkness was on its way, did Kat concede to being unhurt and an escort home from the bricklayer.

It truly was a fine autumn evening, the air crisp and crackling with the building power of Samhain. Kat's mother had stayed long enough to teach her the important things about being a witch.

Keep the sabbats even when the men do not.

Give offerings to the gods of the land, even when that land is London.

And never, ever tell anyone that she was a witch.

She hadn't told Richard, not really. Admitting that she understood herbs…well, there was a woman on every block of the city who could do that. The human healers did well with their work, delivering babies into the world and easing suffering souls out of it. Plus, no one knew that Kat muttered her charms and spells over the herbs she worked with. No one knew that the dreamless sleep potion she gave Lady Edgeworth would have nothing for her if Jonas or Kat's father prepared it.

But when she looked at Richard, her heart told her she could trust him with anything—her love, her body, her secret. She knew they'd lived lives together before and would again. That this was one in a long line of lifetimes she would spend with this man.

Oh, it would have been easier if he was a warlock or at least an aristocrat. Not that Kat needed anything other than a garden to tinker in. But her father would never willingly allow her to marry a common human.

"You look lost in thought," Richard commented. "Is something troubling you?"

"No, of course not. Only wool gathering," she answered quietly. Here she was, silently planning their future while Richard only knew that he walked a woman home.

But he had to feel it too, right? Even if he wasn't magic, he must feel this pull. It was like a string tying the two of them together. Kat couldn't help but believe he was being tugged toward her as well.

"Do you often walk the streets of Soho?" Richard asked, his hand tightening over hers where she held his arm.

"Not often, but I go to the markets there when I can."

"Will you be visiting those markets again in the next five days?"

Kat smiled. "Do you have five days left of work on that wall?"

"I have four, but I could stretch it into a fifth," he admitted.

"What if"—Kat paused their walking and turned to face him—"you gave me your address. And the next time I am out walking, I come to call at your house."

"That doesn't seem proper, a lady coming to call on a man."

"True, but if you came to call on me, my father would turn you away."

"Right." Richard dropped her arm. "I shouldn't have...it was improper for me to suggest—"

"Oh, no!" Kat shook her head. "My father would turn away any man he hadn't invited himself. And I don't care much for the opinion of my father, sin it may be to say. But I, Katherine Fortworth, would like very much to see you again. And I do not mind a walk. In fact, I quite enjoy them."

With that, Richard smiled a terribly warm smile, and in a flash, Kat could see a future with him.

A quiet house, away from the city, perhaps on the coast. Brick, laid by himself. A baby or two between them. She could have her garden, make remedies and tinctures for the nearby villagers. He could build and repair houses. It could be a lovely life between them.

"I'm right near the White Chapel, in the green building. I'll wait outside all Sunday if it would please you."

"I think it would."

Sunday could not come soon enough.

When Richard had said goodbye to Katherine a full block from her house, his heart had panged with letting her go.

It was ridiculous, really. She was a beautiful woman with a townhouse in Covent Garden. He was a bricklayer with a small apartment in East London. It was too big of a dream to come true.

But he would live, for a while, in this dream with her. They could walk and talk, and Richard would allow himself to daydream about what life with a woman like Katherine could be, even if it never would be.

He walked outside Sunday morning just as the sun came over the horizon. The streets were already bustling, as they always were in his neighborhood. He once quipped to his father that only between the hour of two and three in the morning was his street empty. That the church bells rang at two to tell everyone to get the hell out of the gaze of the White Chapel and then again at three to let them all know it was safe to return.

He said hello to his neighbors, waved and nodded at passersby. Once the sun was well and truly risen, he grinned at the children running and playing in the streets, clearly kicked out of their homes by parents already dreading the winter when they'd all be huddled around the hearth for warmth.

Just as the church bells were ringing for noontime, she came.

Her dress and bonnet were blue—as blue as the summer sky. Her hands were bare, like they had been before, and gave away that she'd been in the garden before coming. She held a basket, with a white cloth tucked over something.

Richard strode to her, stilling himself just enough to keep from running. What would his neighbors say if he was seen running to a woman they didn't know? The rumors would be out of control.

"Miss Fortworth," he said formally, bowing slightly in her direction. "I am glad to see you."

"Oh!" She mimicked his bow. "Mr. Mason. I am glad to see you as well." She lowered her voice. "But you really must at least call me Katherine. I am so rarely called Miss Fortworth that it does not feel as though the name belongs to me."

"Katherine, then," he answered quietly, a bloom of warmth opening in his chest. "Please call me Richard from now on."

"Richard," she said, his name curling wonderfully against her tongue.

He cleared his throat before he thought too long of his name in her mouth and offered his arm. "I thought we might walk to the park and have a meal there. I know the best carts for a noon luncheon."

"How wonderful!" Katherine exclaimed. "Oh, it's been years since I've had a meal in the park. And what a beautiful morning for it. I simply love autumn in London. I can't imagine anywhere in the world as perfect."

Richard must have pulled a face because Katherine immediately began laughing.

"What? You do not enjoy London in autumn?"

"Well, I do not mind the sunny days, few as they are. But the rain and chill and the damp? I could do without them. I much prefer a June day if I'm being honest."

"Always be honest," she said sincerely and somewhat seriously before lightening her tone again. "I don't mind the rain and the cold. I love a night next to the fire or working in the garden to find the last sprouts still clinging for life. Perhaps I like this time of year because soon I will have a break from the garden. All will be harvested, and there is nothing to do but wait for spring. Do you do much bricklaying in the winter?"

"Only repairs. We try not to do any new builds in the rainier months."

"Does the water stop the mortar from hardening?"

"Rarely, but it makes the bricklayer much grumpier."

"Ah, well. I could see that. But sometimes...I do love being out in the elements. I love my kitchen and turning—taking my herbs and crushing them for those who need the remedies." She was talking quickly now, so quickly Richard was afraid he might not follow. "It gives me a purpose in life. So many women of my station, they do nothing but wait for something to happen. Wait for a suitor, wait for a proposal, wait for a wedding, wait for a baby. I love doing rather than waiting." She stopped abruptly. "Sorry. I am talking too much."

"Don't stop. I like the sound of your voice." Richard brushed his shoulder against hers for a moment.

"Oh. Well. That is very kind of you to say." She blushed a little, the pinkish tone climbing up her neck to settle on her cheeks. She cleared her throat, then settled her gaze ahead of them. "Have you always lived in London?"

"Always."

"And was bricklaying your father's profession?"

"It was."

Katherine chuckled a little. "You're not being very responsive in your answers."

"I suppose you are right. I have lived within a mile of where we stand at this moment my entire life. I've never left London, not even to visit the seaside. My father was a bricklayer, as was his father and so on. I don't have any siblings, I've never had a sweetheart, and this is the first walk I've taken with a woman in a very long time."

"Not first ever?"

"No, I used to walk with my neighbor Abigail when we were children," he teased. "The last time I stepped out with her, we were both thirteen. She's married. Four children."

"You're teasing me," Katherine laughed. "I've never walked out with a gentleman before," she admitted.

"Nothing gentle about this man," he quipped.

"No, don't say that. Because while you may not have the last name or the house in the country to match the one in town, I am very good at reading people."

"Are you?"

"Yes. Excellent. And when I look at you, I see a gentle man. A kind man. A good man. A man I would be lucky to spend more time with."

"You can tell all that from looking at me? Sounds like magic." The moment the word left his mouth, it settled over them like a blanket.

"Magic," he whispered again as he looked at Katherine. It was like a shimmer was surrounding her...a million tiny raindrops catching the sun and glistening over her. As soon as it arrived, it disappeared, leaving Richard simply staring at Katherine.

"Are you all right?" Katherine asked quietly.

"Yes. Of course." Richard closed his eyes and shook his head a bit, trying to knock out whatever had possessed him that moment. "Only a little dizziness," he lied. "Should we make our way to the park?"

He walked with purpose now, hoping it might clear his head.

As Katherine sat beside Richard, aching to weave her fingers through his, she made her mind up.

She would leave her father, and she would leave with Richard.

It couldn't happen today, or even this month. She needed him to fall in love with her first, to understand. She would ease him into her life, her powers, and explain the prison she currently found herself in.

But none of that could happen yet. So, she would enjoy this October day with her soulmate and dream of the future they would build together in the years to come.

"Are you taking on clients behind Father's back?" Jonas accused on a particularly freezing February morning.

"Why would I do that?" Katherine stopped grinding the oregano for a moment and blew into her hands, trying to warm them up. Even in the kitchen the air was frigid today.

"Money. You were always a little miser."

"A miser? Me? I haven't enough money to squirrel any away, you know that. And furthermore, you should be careful what you say to me." She was in a foul mood this morning. She was supposed to sneak out to see Richard tonight, but with this blasted cold her father would never let her out for a walk.

"Why would I be careful around you?" Jonas scoffed.

Katherine lifted her pestle and pointed it at him. "Because. I am a witch, and you are a warlock. And while I am stuck in this house as long as our father wants, he will not live forever. And I doubt very much that you will want to live in a house without a working witch."

"And where would you go? The streets?"

"I wouldn't have to go to the streets. Half the aristocracy uses my potions. You think you would keep position among them without me?" She huffed. "Doubtful."

"That is not true. Soon I will have a bride as powerful as you."

Katherine set her tools down and turned to her brother now, his chin raised in the air.

"You have a betrothed? Who?"

"Well, she is not my betrothed yet, but soon she will be." He paused. "Eliza Bay, of course."

"Eliza?" Katherine had known her since they were children. Witches were not open about their powers now, nor would they be ever again after the trials that swept through England, the continent, and the colonies alike. But their mothers had been friends and confidants for years. Long before Kat's mother married her father. Long before she left.

"You still speak to Eliza?" Kat had seen her...three years ago? She hadn't even known Eliza was still in London.

"I pay her calls frequently. She will be a perfect wife for me. Powerful witch, good family line. Her mother had five children, so I can expect the same out of her."

"How romantic," Kat muttered, turning back to her work.

"Either way, you will be the one needing me in the future. I will have the powerful wife, I will have the long line of children. You will die an old, childless maid lucky to be allowed to live and work in this house."

Kat sighed. "Please leave me to my work, Jonas." She said it quickly and as if she had been defeated. She needed him out of the kitchen before her cheeks went red and betrayed her secret.

For while she was still a maid, she did not feel like one. There had been many stolen hours in Richard's apartment, when they used each other's flesh for love and lust and the greatest pleasure Kat could have ever imagined. She'd tasted his lips and his skin and he had done the same to her.

She'd known a man, if not completely, and he had known her, from the freckles on her nose, to the dimples in her thighs.

He knew all of her secrets now...her lineage, that they were destined to be together, how her mother had left her when she'd needed her most, and how her father and brother treated her ill at any chance. And she knew his secrets. That he'd been terribly lonely for years and never understood why finding a wife to work beside more than to love was never something he could do.

They had a plan: in April, when the sea was fair, they would go to Dublin. Neither had any family there, but a bricklayer and a healer could find work in any city. No one would think to look for them either. Kat's mother was rumored to be in Scotland, so when she turned up missing, her father was sure to look there first. He hated the Irish. It would take him years to debase himself to travel to the green island.

It was a perfect plan. All they had to do was wait.

Richard hated these cold months.

He wished he could damn the weather and take Kat away this very morning. But the ships running to Ireland were few, crowded, and likely to go to the bottom of the sea. He needed to wait.

Even if waiting was killing him.

Yes, he wanted her fiercely. He wanted to make her his wife, legally and binding. But more than that, he wanted to get her out of that house.

When she'd taken her dress off the first time—all the way off and left in a puddle on the floor—then shimmied out of her corset and shift until there was nothing but air between the two of them, he'd seen the scars. The bruises. The marks of a man evil of heart.

He'd begged to leave that day.

But Kat was smart and a good planner. She'd insisted they only wait a little longer. That she could stand it all a little longer.

Richard had gotten down on his knees and promised never to raise a hand to her or any children they would make, he swore on the fate of his soul.

He slid another log into the fire, cursing the wind and snow. He wanted Kat here, safe, well-loved, and taken care of. Every moment they were separated he worried.

He worried her father was hurting her. He couldn't bear the thought of Kat befalling any ill when he could stop it.

Two more moons. A boat to Dublin. They'd have the ship captain marry them before they disembarked so they could begin their new lives as Mr. and Mrs. Mason.

If Richard could jump to April, he would.

She made a mistake. A small one, but a mistake nonetheless.

After two weeks of miserable cold and wet weather, March third was a timid spring morning. It wasn't warm, no, but it was dry. The wind was strong, but favorable. The dim light of late winter finally seemed to be relinquishing itself to a brighter spring.

Kat couldn't wait any longer.

She gave some stupid reason for leaving early to Old Maggie. Something about a market in Mayfair, before she dashed out of the house.

She forgot her basket.

Kat hurried to Richard's and found him before he left for work that morning. They dashed inside, and like any couple who hadn't known the sweetness of each other for weeks, within moments, Kat was beneath him in his bed, their limbs and lips a tangle of want and lust, a race to finally quench the need that had been building.

"You came," Richard whispered against the bare skin of her shoulder once they were quiet again.

Kat smiled. "I've hated the winter this year. Before I met you, I used to sit in every season, see it for its strengths and its faults. But this winter I've seen nothing but endless cold and being separated from you."

Richard rolled onto his back and arranged her to lie against his chest. "In Dublin, you'll love winter again. Think of how lovely it will be next year. You and I on quiet mornings, when there's no brick to be laid, no family needing a tincture. We'll take our time getting out of bed, sit beside the fire, drink our tea, and eat our breakfast. Only you and me. Nothing hanging over our heads any longer."

She smiled softly and snuggled against him. "So soon."

It was only an hour later, when Richard needed to leave for work, that she dressed and walked out of the apartment she'd come to view as a sanctuary, her hand tucked beneath Richard's arm, that she came face-to-face with Jonas.

He stood outside the door, staring the two of them down, until finally he spoke.

"You whore." His mouth screwed up into the wickedest snarl she'd ever seen.

Richard pushed Kat behind him and took two large steps toward the man spewing hate at the woman he loved.

"What did you say?" Richard challenged. This man was all fancy clothes and soft skin. He looked like he'd never done a hard day's work in his life. And if this toff thought he could come into his neighborhood and call the woman he loved such a foul name for no reason—

"Richard, stop," Kat called, rushing beside him. She tugged on his arm until he looked down at her. "This is my brother."

Shit. Richard relaxed his body against every instinct he had.

He wanted to punch this man in the face for not protecting his sister. For allowing their father to treat her so terribly year after year.

But he could not assault him in the middle of the street.

Instead, Richard dipped his head in the man's direction. "Mr. Fortworth. Pleasure to make your acquaintance, I am Mr. Mason."

"A Mister Mason, Kat? Really?" Her brother looked him over with disgust. "If you were going to whore yourself out, you should have chosen someone high born. At least then you would know any bastards would be taken care of."

The blood whooshed in Richard's ears.

"What do you want, Jonas?" Kat interjected, her hand immediately going to his and squeezing. He needed to remain calm. Jonas held all the cards at this moment.

"I have need of my dear sister, of course. Of her particular skills. Come, Kat, you cannot leave a customer waiting."

Kat looked up at Richard and nodded.

"You cannot go with him," he mumbled quietly and tightened his grip on her hand.

"I must." Kat pulled him back to the doorway and turned her back to her brother. "I know my brother. I need to go."

"Please don't. Stay here. We can leave today. There are a million places we can hide before our ship." He risked stroking the soft skin of her cheek. "What if he tells your father?"

"There's nowhere in England we could go where he wouldn't find us." Kat smiled softly. "I will handle Jonas. He is always able to be bought."

"What will you give him?"

"Whatever he wants."

Kat wanted to kiss Richard goodbye, but even without her brother staring at them, she would have been scandalized to do so openly on the street. Instead, she lingered in her hold on his hand, until finally releasing him and following Jonas into a hackney cab.

She settled into her seat while Jonas stared, a smile like the devil on his lips.

"So. You've ruined yourself."

"I'm a witch. I was never going to make an advantageous marriage. Plus —" She held her tongue, but Jonas was already piecing it together.

"Oh, my word. Did you meet your elusive soulmate? I thought those were just stories for children. But did you look at that man and know that no other would scratch that itch for you?"

"Don't be crude."

"Crude? Me? You're an unmarried woman carrying on an affair in the slums."

"It's not an affair when it's with your soulmate."

"Tell that to society." He paused, then snarled. "Tell that to father."

"Fine, Jonas. I am a whore. What do you want to keep it to yourself?"

"I don't know what you could have that I could ever want."

Kat ran her tongue over her teeth. She knew what he wanted. He wanted her abilities.

Warlocks were not, by nature, powerful creatures. She'd heard, of histories past, of a time when warlocks could hold as much power as witches. But during the trials, women were not the only ones who burned. And witches were far better than warlocks at hiding their powers. Yes, many innocent women, witch and human, were lost over the hundreds of years of violence, but Kat had never heard of a human man going to the stake or the noose or the lake to be drowned. They were all hubris men, convinced their powers would see them through the trials. Convinced they could survive when so many before them had not. Now the only warlocks who lived were those too weak to cause their own demise.

She knew Jonas would ask. She hoped that what he wanted wasn't beyond her abilities.

Or her morals.

They reached home more quickly than Kat could have anticipated, but as they pulled up to the curb and before the driver banged on the carriage to let them know they'd arrived, Jonas spoke.

"I will keep your secret, but you will pay me for it. And soon. So do not think to disappear in the night. I will have one hundred men out searching for you. I will tell a million tales of how Mr. Mason of White Chapel kidnapped my sister, raped her, used her ill, and is forcing her to marry him. There are dozens of young men in London looking to make a name for themselves as a hero. Hell, the King might even grant a knighthood for such a heroic act. Saving a lady from a hoodlum. It is the dream."

Kat bit back a thousand curses and nodded.

She was his now, whether she liked it or not.

Kat hadn't come in ten days.

Richard secured passage for them on a ship called William II. He found a coachman who would take them to Liverpool three days earlier. He packed his life into one small case, sold the rest of his possessions. He hid the money in a pocket he'd sewn in the interior of the leg of his pants. He sent a letter to the bricklaying guild in Dublin introducing himself.

On the eleventh morning, he'd nearly lost his mind and walked to her house. He stood outside, until he saw the outline of her figure against the candlelight.

She was alive.

He left a piece of paper, crumpled in her garden, with only "APRIL 3, 5 O'CLOCK. R" written, hopeful that Kat would find it and know to meet him then.

Now, he could do nothing but wait.

Life had changed considerably.

Kat never left the house. Even the garden was off-limits. Jonas was ever watchful. The only time he left her side was in the evenings when he would call on Eliza Bay as Kat and her father had dinner.

"Your brother is going to marry a powerful witch," her father said on one such night while Kat sat by the fire mending the hem of one of her spring dresses. She had planned to wear it once they arrived in Dublin. It was a lovely pale blue.

Kat didn't answer, only nodded in response.

"They will live here, of course. You can play nursemaid to whatever offspring come our way. Hopefully a break in the warlock...predicament." Her father took a handful of chestnuts for himself. "I think it would be wise for you not to marry."

"You do not wish me to carry on the family...power?" Kat raised an eyebrow as she carefully spoke.

"Hm. I've thought long on it. And there is a warlock...Cassius. His family is slightly flamboyant. They live in Wales where one can be less discreet. He has written to me. I knew his older brother at school. But I fear he would gain too much control over you. And his last two wives died childless, which does not bode well for offspring. But, if you were to marry him and he somehow got you with a child, our line would inherit his wealth."

"How... What is his age if he's lost two wives already?"

"Cassius? He must fifty-five, at least? He was only a year or two behind Tiberius and me. But, for now, I think it is better that we focus on Jonas and the Bay girl. No need to send you to Wales when you can be of use to us here."

Kat looked back to her mending. Life seemed hopeless at this moment. She would never be rid of Jonas. Never be rid of her father unless he married her off to an elderly warlock in Wales.

Gods, how she wanted her mother.

"I have thought of a way for you to pay me."

Kat looked up from her work in the kitchen. She was bleary-eyed and had already mistaken thyme for oregano twice. She needed to be outside, but still...Jonas did not allow it.

"How?" she asked. At least now...maybe she could have some relief.

"Eliza Bay refused me. Said she would never marry me."

Kat was shocked. Oh, how she wished she had the courage of Eliza Bay to stand up to her family.

"I...I am sorry, brother. But there is no spell to make someone fall in love with you, nor to bend to your will. I cannot force Eliza to marry you."

"That is not what I want any longer." Kat watched any semblance of humanity leave her brother's face. "She laughed at me. Said terrible things. About me. About our family. I don't want to marry her any longer."

"Do...do you want me to find someone who will marry you?"

"No, Kat. I will find my own bride in my own time. I want you to make me the most powerful warlock in the world."

Kat almost laughed as it was such a strange request. But she held her tongue and only asked, "How?"

"I've been reading the Fortworth history. There was a family, four hundred years ago, called Allwright. Their daughter, a girl named Edith, cursed a family. An entire line. She declared that any living witch or warlock who collected the blood of an entire line and ingested it would become imbued with their powers." He stepped toward Kat. "I want you to put such a curse on the Bay line. I want to take Eliza's power. I want to bury her line, to end the Bay witches."

Kat froze in her horror. Lay a curse on the Bay line? She could not do that. It was...impossible.

"I cannot...it would destroy me. My soul. For a witch to curse another... it would be begging evil to rain upon me."

Jonas shrugged. "Think on it for a day. By tomorrow night, you may choose to pay me with this curse, or I will tell Father of your Mr. Mason. And you know how poorly he will react. I would hate to think of Father... taking a personal offense to the man who deflowered his only daughter. He will be quite inconsolable."

Kat tried to swallow, but it was as if her throat was filled with wool. "Why are you like this?" she hissed.

Jonas exhaled slowly. "We all play our parts. I am a man with designs above my station. You are a woman with designs below yours."

"Why do you bring him into it? He is innocent. He is good and kind, and he doesn't deserve whatever Father would do to him." She shook her head and let her gaze fall to her brother's feet.

They'd been happy as children, hadn't they? The years seemed so far away now. It had all changed when their mother had left. When Father's cruelty had landed on both of them instead of her. Jonas had learned to be his ally, turn it all on Kat. He'd abandoned her.

"Punish me instead," she begged. "Don't hurt Richard. Don't hurt the Bays. Rain all your ill will down on me. I won't mind. I've known that this life is not a happy one. Make up another lie, I won't tell Father the truth. Find another witch, I'll help you woo her. Just leave Richard alone."

"Tomorrow," Jonas answered. "By noon. You'll need to go to the markets to collect your supplies."

That night, Kat sat awake in her room, searching for any spell that could get her out of this house. Their grimoire was a tattered thing, and only thirty pages long. Her mother had once spoken, almost as if it were a myth, of magical families having full libraries of books on the craft written by witches before the trials and hunts began. She should have tomes upon tomes to draw upon, but instead she held flimsy paper, barely bound, with nothing of use. She needed a spell to cloud her father's vision, to put him and Jonas to sleep. She needed a potion that would give her more time. A tincture that would warn Eliza Bay of her brother's obsession with punishing her.

She had none of those things.

She had her instincts. She could brew lust and sleep and beauty. She could weave good will over those she loved.

Kat sat up in her bed and walked to the window.

A curse of that kind was not beyond her abilities.

When she spoke a spell, she knew before it left her lips whether or not it would work.

It was how she knew that she could curse the Bays. And that she could never outrun her father and brother.

She knew in her soul that magic she was capable of.

Now she simply had to decide whether or not saving Richard was worth it.

And, of course, he was.

Richard felt like a man without a heart. He ached for Kat every moment of every day. He was sloppy at work, left the mortar to harden if he thought he caught a glimpse of her. Had she changed her mind?

What was her father doing to her?

He was a warlock, a man with unnatural power. Kat had been clear that Richard would never have been able to do anything against him. It wasn't a matter of fighting with fists, but on a plane completely different from the one they lived on.

She had begged him never to come.

But how could he abandon her to such a man? A man who never deserved to have her as a child.

No.

Richard could not leave her to the whims of a villain.

Cursing a line was not easy spell work.

There were black thorn branches and stinging nettle. Foxglove and giant hogweed. Her skin split and bled and swelled with pain. Blisters and cuts covered her from fingertip to shoulder. All the sleeves of her dresses were torn.

This was no spell that could be done indoors in the kitchen. Kat lived in the garden, barely sleeping, barely eating. Everything she was, she poured into the spell.

It became an effigy beneath her oak tree.

It was as tall as she, a woman built of wicked plants soaked with her blood.

She muttered under her breath at all times, even when she slept fitfully. She wound the power of the Bay witches' line with her own. As she felt the curse on them growing, her own powers depleted. Kat didn't think she could make a tincture now. She couldn't give Lady Edgeworth a dreamless night or a healthy son. She couldn't soothe a baby's cough or a broken bone. All that she was became this curse.

On the third day, she realized she wouldn't survive it. It was evil work, terrible craft. Death was an appropriate sentence for her failings as a witch.

But if it saved Richard from an awful death, it would be worth it.

Finally, on the fifth morning of spell craft, her father came.

He didn't speak for some time, only watched as his daughter shaped branches, blood running down her arms, only listened to the babbling words that escaped her mouth. She was turning into a wild animal before his eyes, but there was nothing he would do to stop it.

The effigy now looked like a witch…there were dead leaves woven through the branches as hair, dried flowers running down its arms. A creature made of things once living. A perfect base for a blood curse.

"This is…impressive," her father finally spoke, jolting Kat out of her trance.

A compliment? That man did not compliment her. He did nothing but reprimand her and take credit for her work. He'd used her powers since she was a child, made a name for himself in the world on her talents. He was rotten, rotten to the core.

Kat should have left him years ago.

She turned to him and bared her teeth as she spoke. "I am impressive. I am a witch of the Fortworth line. I am made of ancient power and stand in the company of the most magical women in the world. And you...you and Jonas and every other warlock in this world are *nothing* without us."

She turned back to the effigy.

What a waste.

The most powerful work of her life, the work that would end her life, and it was a curse on witches.

She was too far gone now to turn back. To abandon it. The curse was flowing through her veins, pounding in her heart.

Tonight, it would be cast.

She threw a look back at her father, one that didn't feel entirely human, and for the first time in her life, she saw a flash of fear cross his face.

Good. He should be afraid.

On the morning of April second, Richard awoke with an awful feeling. He'd long realized that he and Kat were not going to Dublin. There would be no escape to the seashore, no boat to a new life. He wouldn't lay bricks for the people of Ireland; she wouldn't heal their woes. They were trapped in London. And she was trapped with her father and brother.

He tried to think of a way to save her. Rush in and kidnap her? Pay a man to kill her father and brother? She'd told him no human could stand against her father. And he did not have time to find any other magical beings in London. That could take years.

He couldn't wait anymore. He didn't care what would happen. Nothing could be worse than abandoning Kat to whatever fate she currently lived in that house.

Richard looked over his apartment, the little quiet life he'd been content with until Kat walked into his world six months earlier. It had been so empty without her. There was nothing left here for him. So, he took all his food and gave it to the nice widow who lived upstairs with her four children. He gave her his blankets as well. Then, he collected his clothes and gave them to a beggar who frequented his corner. The man could either wear them and hope to gain employment or sell them and use the proceeds for a meal.

Richard knew in his heart something would happen today. Either they would escape, or he wouldn't survive facing Kat's father, or some unknown third option, but no matter what, his former life no longer mattered. He carried all his money, in case they were able to escape. They could set up a new life somewhere. Anywhere.

He left the rooms, locking the door behind him. He didn't know what the day would bring him, but he didn't want to wait any longer. Kat was his. His love, half his soul. His only regret was on that first day in autumn, that he did not simply take her away right then. It would have been so much easier when no one knew they had even met. They could have disappeared then.

He walked down the front steps and turned toward Covent Garden.

She collected the kindling.

The last moment of the spell would come as soon as the sun set. This sort of evil had to be done in darkness. Even the light of the sun was too good. It wouldn't be long now.

Kat felt closer to death than life now. Her body was wrapped up in the curse as much as her soul. How much had she bargained away for this? She was stretched so thin. Her mind was clouded. It was spring. The world was coming alive again, but not Kat.

She didn't know what was worth anything anymore, only that she would do anything to save Richard from a life like this. From a father like hers, or a brother like Jonas. How lovely it would have been to have been born powerless. To have been allowed to live a simple life with the man she loved.

But that wasn't possible, so instead she would trade whatever she had to give him a chance at a quiet life. Her body, her life, her very soul. They all hung in the balance.

The sun set.

She lit the effigy.

And she watched as her work cursed one of the oldest and most powerful lines of witches in the world.

The fire crackled and popped and jumped. The pieces of dried flowers and leaves were the first to crumble into ash. Then the giant hogweed...it released a smell like death as it burned. The foxgloves puffed gray smoke into the air, and finally, the black thorn branches burned.

She could hear...

She could hear a line of women crying out in anguish. She could feel their pain in her bones, spreading like a fever over her body. She cried out at what she had done.

Kat fell to her knees, pressed her face against the earth, dug her fingers into the dirt. How could she ever be absolved of this?

She could not.

She was a witch who had cursed witches.

There was no salvation for her. Not in this life, not in any other.

Moments, minutes, hours passed until at some point, Jonas stood over her, surveyed the damage, and left.

He found her outside.

She looked dead.

Richard rushed to Kat where she lay in a heap. It was freezing out. The sun was gone from the sky; a chill had settled in the air.

He yelled out when he saw her—not her name or for help, but a cry of loss so deep in his soul.

When he reached her side, he fell to the ground and gathered her against his body. She mumbled a response.

"Oh, thank God," he prayed loudly. She lived. He shrugged off his coat and wrapped it around her, then stood with her in his arms. "We're leaving. I'll take you to a healer. I'll find us an inn. You won't stay here another moment." It all rushed out. He'd found her. All hope was not lost. They could still be together.

He walked to the side of the house, Kat barely stirring in his arms, but as they came closer to the property line, she began to thrash against him.

"It's Richard," he said, trying to soothe her. "We're going to get help."

"No!" She finally spoke. "Take me back...to the ashes. I...can't leave. I'm bound."

"You need to see a healer. Or to get out of the cold." He eyed her father's house. Would he dare bring her inside?

"No." Her eyes were wide and alert now. "Take me back where I was. I cannot leave this place. Oh, Richard...you do not know what I have done this day." She gritted her teeth and squeezed her eyes shut. "I am damned."

"No," he said firmly. "You are not. You are good and kind and—"

"I have committed an unforgivable spell." Suddenly, a dawning washed over her face. "No, you can't be here. Why are you here?"

"I hadn't seen you in weeks, I was worried—"

"Put me back and leave. If they...if they find you, it was all for naught. I need you to leave."

"Kat, no. I will not leave you," he said firmly, but walked back to where he had found her. As they came closer to the spot, he felt her relax in his arms.

"I can't leave the...ashes."

Richard knelt, then sat, keeping her in his arms the entire time. He cradled her delicately now. She looked...

She looked a breath away from death.

Richard remembered when typhoid swept through his neighborhood. Took his parents, his aunt, boys he'd grown up with. Right before they went, there was a look in the eyes...a surrender.

Kat had surrendered.

God, she grasped his collar, turned her face up to his, and smiled. "Thank you for all you gave me these months. Now, I beg you. Leave before my father or brother find you and make everything I've done worthless."

In that moment, Richard felt his own surrender. He believed Kat, deep in his heart, that if he was found out, with her in his arms, he would not survive. Her family was magical. He was not a particularly good fighter. It would come to pass.

But he also knew that death was the only thing that could ever pull him from her side.

Richard arranged Kat to lie on the earth, then slid beside her, wrapping his arms over her body.

"You need to go," she whimpered.

"I can't. As you can't. So, we will lie here together until the worst happens."

Kat's face trembled now, tears streaming through the dirt on her face. She placed her chilled hand against his face, and he pressed a kiss to her palm.

"I wish I could have taken you away from here," he whispered against her skin. "We could have made a lovely life in Dublin."

"A home of our own," she added.

"With a cup of tea for any who visited."

"Dried herbs over the hearth. A quilt on our bed."

"God, I'm so sorry I didn't give you that life, Kat." Richard kissed her forehead softly.

"We'll have another chance," she mumbled. "We aren't once born. We will...get the chance to be happy. I know it." She tensed up again, gripping his arm. "He's back," she hissed.

"Didn't work!" Jonas shouted as he pounded toward them. "Do you know how hard that was? Killing all of them? And it didn't work, you hack."

Richard sat quickly, pulling Kat into his lap as he did.

"It worked," Kat spat. "Exactly how I spoke it."

"What?" Jonas seethed.

"All. Magical. Bays. Not one line a mile away from you in London. All of them. Their entire line, wherever they may be. You want to be the most powerful warlock in the world? Fight for it. You thought I would make this easy for you? You're a murderer. You want the Bay power? Find it."

"You bitch," Jonas muttered, his eyes going dark. "Father!" he yelled now.

"This is it," Kat said, squeezing Richard. "I want you to run."

"I won't."

"Then, let me say, I love you with everything I have."

"I love you, Kat Fortworth." Richard kissed her softly, then pulled her into an embrace.

"Who is this?" a sharp voice asked in the darkness.

"My soulmate," Kat replied as Richard said, "Mister Richard Mason."

He looked over Kat's father. Thinning gray hair, a slight build. His skin hung loose on his face; his eyes were cold.

"You, stupid girl," her father accused. "Soulmates are for the weak."

"I've had more happiness with him than I have all the days I've spent in this damned house."

Her father moved slowly, but Richard was frozen in his space. Her father knelt beside them, stroked Kat's cheek once, then turned to Richard.

"I hope she was worth it," he said, then grabbed his face.

She was screaming.

She didn't think there was anything left in her, yet she screamed while she watched.

Kat had seen her father snuff out the life of a being before. Birds, small mammals, the family dog nearly a decade earlier. The young man who'd tried to burgle them.

But nothing could have prepared her to watch her father kill Richard.

It was over quickly, a flash. One moment, he held her in his arms, the next he was prone on the earth.

She wailed and howled as she grabbed his shoulders.

It was all for nothing.

"You," she spat, pointing first at Jonas. "You will never find peace. You will never..." Her voice faltered, but she thought it.

You will fail.

Jonas scoffed at her words, but Kat watched as the ashes of the effigy glowed behind them in the darkness. Her power was still here.

"Father. I..." She closed her eyes and concentrated. Fratricide was a terrible crime against one's soul.

She didn't care.

She grabbed her father's hands, pulled every bit of witchcraft that sat in the earth, lingered in the air, and stirred in her soul, and poured it into her spell. She fashioned a curse, as strong as the one she'd just made.

"I curse you, Bartholomew Jacob Fortworth, second of his name, patriarch of the Fortworth line. Your magical line ends here. You will be human born from this day forward. And you will die before the turning of the moon." She gasped the last part, her breath already leaving her body, her heart slowing.

Her hands were cold, and her feet. She slunk to the ground, trying to draw breath. She cast one last glance at the ashes, which pulsed with light.

She'd done it.

"Idiotic girl," her father mumbled. "You really think you can curse me?"

She smiled and let her final breath leave her body.

She needed to find Richard.

Chapter Twenty-Three

“Kat,” Gavin mumbled.

No, Kat was gone. As was Richard.

He reached to his side and found Lavender, his darling Lavender Lily Bay, still groggy but slowly shifting out of the stupor.

He pawed around his head for a moment. It had been a flash, dying that time. A terrible headache and then darkness.

“Moonbeam, wake up,” he said, pulling her toward him. “Come here,” he said. He needed to hold her. Hold her until she was completely awake. He wasn’t leaving her this time, wasn’t leaving her ever again.

“Oh no,” she whispered, her face pressed against his chest. “No.”

“It’s okay,” he began, his hand going to the back of her head. “It’s going to be fine.” The memories of that life were sharp and stinging—oh, the pain of watching her suffer. His stomach twisted with every new image rushing into him.

“It was me,” she cried. “Oh, Gavin. I cursed us! And he still killed you. I did exactly what Jonas wanted and I still lost—” She broke off, sobbing. God, it broke his heart to listen to her cry.

“Lavender, listen to me. You are Lavender. You were Kat. A very long time ago. And you were dealt a very hard life. Without many choices.” Gavin held her face a few inches from his. “They were terrible to you.

Your father, Jonas. You did what you could to give us a chance to get away."

"He killed all those Bays because of me. It's all been my fault. I am the curse maker. Not Jonas, not some shadowy witch from the eighteenth century. Me. It was all me. Everything. In this life too. It's all because of what I did back then. Morana and Ivan and Boris and Miloslav. If I'd just refused him...we would have ended the same."

"Jonas was a monster. So was Charles. And Miloslav. And whatever names he's gone by when Sage has known him before. You were tied to a monster."

Lavender nodded. "He was a monster." She scrubbed her tears off her face. "He is a monster." She looked up at him. "Oh, poor Richard."

"It's okay. The last thing I remember you were in bad shape..."

"I died very soon after you. I..." She took a deep breath. "Before I died, I cursed them both. I barely had anything left, but I remember feeling like they had worked."

"What were the curses?"

"That my father never be magical again in all his reincarnations. I cut his line." She shook her head. "If only I'd done the same to Jonas."

"What did you do to him?"

She hesitated. "It worked," she began quietly. "I cursed him to fail. And Jonas did. But...I don't think that curse extended past that life." Her face crumpled.

Gavin ran his thumb across her cheek. "Hey, no one is going to separate us this time. I promise. Maybe we need to leave. Run before Miloslav has a chance to show us if he's as bad as Jonas."

"We can't leave my sisters."

"Then we all go. We split up for a few years. He can't chase all of you."

"He doesn't need to chase all of us. He only needs to chase me. I'm the only missing piece of a curse of my own making." Lavender pressed a kiss against Gavin's jaw. "I'm sorry I couldn't save Richard."

"I'm sorry I couldn't get you away from there." Gavin wrapped his arms around her and buried his face in her hair. "Fuck, I forgot just how shitty it feels to do that. Like physically. I'll never forget how my heart felt when I woke up."

"And how is that?"

"Like it's been ripped open so I could see everything. Like I couldn't save you from your family and give you a better life. Don't like that feeling one bit. All I want is to make your life better." Gavin pulled back so he could look at her face. "I really hope there was a quiet life at some point where we were just together. And normal things bothered us like our roof leaked. Or the vegetable patch was overrun with beetles one year."

"That would have been pretty detrimental to our survival depending on where and when we were," Lavender pointed out.

"True. But it's a problem we would face together without Jonas or Charles or Miloslav waiting in the wings." Gavin groaned. "Ugh, I never thought I would hate the brother of the woman I love, but damn. I really hated him when he was your brother."

"I hated him too. That was so strange. I love my sisters with every fiber of being; I gave up my twenties for them. I had nothing like that with Jonas. My entire family was terrible."

"I didn't care for your father, either," Gavin added. "How on earth did you have such a terrible family then and such a wonderful one now?"

"I don't know. Rosemary had an awful father when she was a Viking. And Sage's mother abandoned her at a temple in Ancient Greece. We really won the lottery in this lifetime when it comes to familial relationships."

"Agreed."

Lavender untangled herself from Gavin and fluffed her pillow, then sat against the headboard. "I remember the spell. So perfectly. Hell, I was powerful."

"More powerful than now?"

"Yes. Which is odd for the time period."

"How so?" Gavin pushed himself to sit as well.

"The witch trials were a very real thing, in both Europe and America. We mostly think of the Salem Witch Trials, but they only lasted a little over a year. In Europe, women were hung, burned, drowned, for hundreds of years. Most of them were not witches, but some of them, like Laurel when she was Amée, were. People didn't really practice magic in the seventeen hundreds. We still had it, deep in our souls, but it was left as something to simply be passed down until the time was safer."

"But your father, I mean Kat's father, he was openly running an apothecary. How on earth did he escape persecution?"

"Well, for starters, we were rich. And he was serving those even richer. Plus, it worked. I was really a witch. I could make potions, and they didn't fail. I would think a lot more women who were simple herbalists at the time would be dragged before courts or mobs if what they were selling did what it was intended to." Lavender paused. "I did a lot of cool stuff."

"Like what?"

"Like I made a coagulant. I didn't survive long enough to see Lady Edgeworth deliver...but she probably did. And I still remember it so clearly. I bet I could make it again."

"Will you?"

"No, that is highly unethical," she said while swatting his arm playfully. "I'm not in the business of playing God. Not anymore," she added. "I can't believe I'm Katherine Fortworth."

"But you're not. You were her, yes. A long time ago. You share a soul with her. But you, Lavender Bay, are not her. You are surrounded by a loving family. You had a wonderful set of parents. You use your magic for good."

"That is true," she said quietly. "Hell, I cannot believe I was a Fortworth and now I'm a Bay. And then the prophecy telling us it would all be over by Samhain. Maybe..." She quickly chewed on her thumb. "Maybe there's a reason for that."

"What do you mean?"

"Well, Miloslav is here, he knows about the curse, he forced me to cast it. But I'm the last Bay whose blood he needs. And I am the true curse maker. If...if anyone could unweave a curse as strong as this one...it should be the witch who laid it down, right?"

Gavin felt a sense of unease creeping up his chest. "Does this mean we are staying here? Not running from Miloslav?"

"I can't run from him. As much as I would love to disappear to some small town on a different coast and fix a leaky roof with you and try to keep a vegetable garden alive, I have to face him. It has to end now. There will not be another life with him."

Chapter Twenty-Four

Lavender stared at the ceiling.

She was Katherine Fortworth.

How? How was this possible? She was the matriarch of the Bay family. She'd met Eliza Bay! And the ghost had said nothing about her being the one who'd cursed them. Not a peep!

She rolled to her side and looked at Gavin. He was snoring softly, his hand loosely wrapped around her wrist.

She thought of Richard...and Arthur...and college. She'd lost him so many times. Given him up once. Lavender snuggled a little closer to Gavin.

She wasn't losing him again.

Kat built the curse.

It had killed her, but she'd created it. With no spell books or help or any semblance of a mentor. She'd constructed an effigy and had woven a curse into existence.

Lavender remembered all of it. The pain and suffering she'd endured, the weakening of her body. The overwhelming shame that had come with hurting witches in the name of a warlock.

But...Laurel had broken a curse of her soul's making. When Laurel had been Amée and Morana had been Flavie, she'd cursed the woman who sent her to the pyre. And Laurel had unwoven the curse a few months ago. Before that, Laurel had been a pretty normal hedge witch.

Maybe...maybe Lavender wasn't actually a normal kitchen witch.

Maybe she was a kitchen witch who could break a curse.

"I feel like I'm going to throw up," Lavender moaned as she slid lower on the couch.

"Moonbeam, it's going to be fine." Gavin sat beside her and wrapped his arm around her. "They are your sisters and they love you." He looked at his phone quickly. "Rosemary is here."

That was good. Lavender could tell Rosemary anything. She was the most judgment-free soul in the history of the world.

Gavin gave her a squeeze, then got up and let Rosemary into the apartment.

"Hey," she said softly. "Everything okay?"

Lavender looked at her sister, who moved as if she was approaching an injured wild animal.

Lavender felt a bit like an injured wild animal.

"I did something really bad," she burst out. "It's all my fault."

Rosemary rushed to her side and sat beside her, grabbing both of her hands immediately.

"It was me. I was Katherine Fortworth. I made the curse. I...I did it because I thought it was the only way to save Richard—Gavin. All those poor Bays died because of me. And Miloslav took your blood. And Sage's and Verbena's and Laurel's. Everyone is in danger because of me. It's all because of me."

Rosemary was quiet for a moment, her eyes round with worry, her grip strong on Lavender.

"Oh, Lav," she soothed. "It's not your fault. But what a terrible thing for you to carry." Rosemary pulled her into a tight hug, smoothing her hair as she did.

Lavender was the oldest sister. The protector. The one who made all the decisions. But she'd be lying if she said she could have done any of it without

Rosemary's unending support. She was the fun adult when Lavender had to be strict. The one who'd kept them all from wallowing in their despair those first few years. Rosemary was the one who had gotten Lavender through it all. She was the heart of the family.

"Was it awful? That life?" Rosemary asked.

"Yeah. Pretty much the whole thing."

"You and...Richard didn't get any time to be happy?"

Lavender sighed. She and Gavin hadn't been lucky in the past. A few months together as Ruby and Arthur. Less than half a year as Kat and Richard. Hell, they'd been together in college for almost two years before it all came crashing down. She'd already gotten so much time with him this life. And she's squandered most of it.

"Stolen moments. No more than that."

Rosemary shook her head. "I am truly sorry for that. Gundrun and Skáldi had so many happy years. Hard, but happy."

"I can remember the curse," Lavender said slowly.

"Details?"

She shrugged. "Yeah. I could redo it if I wanted. But casting it killed Kat. Katherine. Me."

"Please don't do it," Rosemary said quickly. "We can figure something else out. Don't need you cursing the Stochs."

"No, I would never do it again. But...what if I could do a similar spell to undo the curse?"

Gavin walked over from the kitchen the moment she said it.

"No," he said emphatically.

"You just said it killed Katherine," Rosemary pointed out. "The counter would probably kill you."

"We don't know that," Lavender said slowly.

"Do you even know how to counter a curse like that? Did Katherine's memories come with that kind of information?"

"No." Lavender slouched back defeated. Even if she thought she could awaken the power to counter the curse, she would have no idea how to actually do it.

"Then we figure it out some other way," Rosemary answered. "We can do this."

The door buzzed and Gavin looked at his phone. "Verbena, Laurel, and Sage are here."

Lavender turned back to Rosemary. "Okay. Time to tell everyone."

There were more tears involved in telling everyone else. When the initial fear of admitting what she'd done wore off, Lavender let herself mourn her actions. Her entire life had been wrapped up in protecting her sisters, and this curse had been the last huge hurdle she needed to clear in order to get them out of danger. Knowing that she had created the single most dangerous thing any of them would face would take a long time to process.

"I love you so much." Laurel sobbed, her arms thrown around Lavender. "And I always will. And I don't care that you cast this curse. Not you, Katherine. Katherine cast the curse. I did the same thing. And I did it because I was pissed I was dying. You did it to save the man you loved. You are a nobler curse maker than me."

Lavender laughed softly as she patted Laurel's back. "We both made choices we've had to deal with."

"Why are *you* crying?" Sage snapped at Laurel. "Cool it. Okay, let's think. This is probably a good thing, in terms of intel."

"I don't know if it's a good thing," Verbena said slowly.

"It is. The curse exists. We knew it did. Now we know who made the curse. And exactly how it was made. With wood and shit. We also know that when Miloslav was Jonas, he wasn't powerful at all. I knew he wasn't anything special, but this proves he really needed a witch. Yeah, he's got the whole chaos magic thing going on. But! You all have an earth witch on your side. Me. We've got one sister who has broken a curse, one who has called a goddess to her aid, one who killed a ghoul, one who isn't affected by his magic, and the actual curse caster. If you're trying to build a team to take down a chaos warlock, we're not in short supply of players. We can beat this asshole. No problem."

"I don't know if I would say, no problem, but we definitely have a fighting chance," Rosemary piped in. "So. Should we make a plan?"

Sadly, the plan the Bay sisters came up with that night was a simple, don't die for now. Lavender would try to figure out a way to break the curse without dying in the process, but other than that, they were still adrift when it came to fighting the Stochs.

"Did Laurel seem okay to you?" Lavender asked Gavin as they cleared the glasses left behind now that they were alone.

"I think so? I don't know her very well. Not yet."

"She's been a bit...I don't know. It's almost as if she's expecting the worst to happen. I don't like it."

"There are a lot of hard things happening. It's probably pretty normal to be scared when there is a curse of that nature on your line. And she's had her blood taken twice. That can't be fun."

Lavender shook her head. "That isn't why I'm nervous. Laurel can see the future sometimes. What if—"

"No what-ifs tonight," Gavin interrupted. "Unless you are going to finish that sentence with what if we get into bed and you let me rub your back until you fall asleep."

"I can't promise I won't worry, but I will surrender to having my back rubbed while I try to sleep."

Gavin grinned. "That's all I can ask from you."

Chapter Twenty-Five

Lavender had to go back to work.

And as much as Gavin wanted to keep her locked in her apartment, she had a job. Beyond that, she employed two people and owned an establishment the residents of Star Island had come to need. But they took precautions.

He sat at a table in the front corner to keep an eye out for Miloslav the entire time. The rest of the family worked in shifts of two, so there were always three members of the Bay family in the bakery at all times. One in the back and one joining Gavin in the front. It wasn't perfect, but it was something.

Lavender was oddly calm today. She seemed almost resigned to whatever would happen between now and Halloween. The prophecy had said something about Samhain being the end of the soulmate-meeting-crazy-dangerous-times for the Bay witches, so for Gavin, it couldn't come soon enough. Hopefully, they just had to wait out Miloslav and when the sun rose the day after Samhain, he would disappear like Cinderella's pumpkin carriage at midnight and never bother them again.

But that was unlikely.

For now, Gavin was content to watch Lavender all day in the bakery. He tried everything she made, and he'd yet to find something that wasn't perfection. Though...his chef brain couldn't turn off. If she offered a few more savory things on the menu, hired a few more people, she could stay open for dinner, more in a grab-and-go capacity, at least in the summer months and on the weekends when she still had loads of customers. It would increase her sales exponentially, and with a bigger staff, wouldn't add too much to her plate.

He took to bringing a notebook with him and taking notes on some ideas that might work with her current menu. Definitely his carrot soup she loved. They needed a bunch of soups for weekends in the fall and winter. And they should offer them frozen as well. Sweet potato bowls with spiced chickpeas and pomegranate seeds, roasted vegetables and fat hunks of feta. Grilled cheese on Lavender's sourdough with turkey, sliced apple, and cherry jelly. Hearty pastas with chucky tomato sauces and homemade meatballs. They could make a family-style meal out of them all, adding a loaf of bread and box of cookies to finish it off. The year-rounders on Star Island would have their weekend dinners sorted from now on. His chef musings definitely helped keep him from spiraling over what might happen to Lavender.

Laurel and Owen walked into the shop, giving him a quick wave. Owen ducked into the back after saying hello, and Laurel got herself a slice of pumpkin bread and a hot drink.

"Any sign of anything untoward?" she asked, sliding across from Gavin.

"Not yet."

"Yeah. I don't know what their plan is. Will they all attack in broad daylight? Maybe." Laurel rifled through her bag and pulled out a deck of tarot cards, then started nervously shuffling. "I saw Morana about an hour ago."

"Where?" Gavin looked around the bakery wildly, as if the Stochs might all be hidden in plainclothes.

"On the street. I was in Owen's truck with him."

"Did she see you?"

"Yup. We locked eyes. She gave me a big ole smirk. I assume to say that she wasn't with the Guardians anymore and that I could rightly fuck off."

"You worried she's going to come after you?"

"Not really. She already has my blood, and her brother is three Bays ahead of her. She's probably just here for moral support. Or to dance over my dead body if it comes to that."

"Shit, Laurel."

"I don't think it's going to come to that. Plus, if Morana comes near me, I can always throw her in the Hedge World again. It worked perfectly well as a prison for a month." She set her tarot cards down and took a bite of her bread. Gavin didn't know what the Hedge World was, but he knew the woman sitting across from him looked the entire part of scary witch. Maybe that was the key to bringing down the Stochs: that the Bay witches were scary in their own ways.

Gavin leaned in and lowered his voice. "What can you actually do?"

Laurel grinned. "I'm a hedge witch. I can go to the Hedge World. I can also read minds, but I hate doing it. And I can see stuff."

"What kind of stuff?"

She shrugged. "Future stuff. Not like lottery numbers, but I get some pretty good glimpses as to what's going to happen."

"So, what's coming?"

"The Tower." Laurel sighed. She picked up her deck and rifled through it until she slid one card out and in front of him. It was a building about to collapse and on fire with several people jumping out of the windows.

"Fuck."

"Don't take it at face value. It's the upheaval card. It means everything is going to change and it's going to be batshit crazy as it does."

"And you got this card about the future?"

"I've gotten this card seventeen times in the last six months asking about the future. There's no escaping it." She tucked it back into the deck and shuffled. "You want a reading?"

"I'm afraid of what you'll see."

"I think of it more as a heads up than anything. What's going to happen will happen. Me looking at the cards won't change it. But they can give you advice."

"I don't know."

Laurel nodded and tucked her cards back into her bag. "If you change your mind, just text. I'm always up for a reading."

Gavin nodded but he didn't think he'd change his mind. If that tower card was any indication, the future wasn't looking bright. With the past being what it was, Gavin felt like the only time he had with Lavender was the present. He'd enjoy what he could.

"Hm," Laurel mumbled. "Is that..."

Gavin popped his head up in time to see a blur of blonde hair disappearing down the street. He jumped to his feet and ran to the door, swinging it open to get another look.

"What's wrong?" Lavender was at his side in a moment, ignoring the customer who she'd been serving.

"I thought...I think I saw him." He looked down at Lavender and wrapped his arm around her waist. "He didn't stop. It could have been someone else who looked like him."

"But," Lavender began.

"Probably was him."

Lavender nodded and squeezed his hand. "Only two more hours until close."

"I'll keep my eyes on the street." He snuck a quick kiss on the top of her head, then returned to his seat by the window. He and Laurel turned their chairs toward the glass and sat in silence, watching and waiting, until they all went home.

Days passed, each one shorter. Now when Lavender locked the door at five-fifteen in the evening, the sun already kissed the horizon. There'd been a few times Gavin thought he saw Miloslav, a blur in the distance. But he hadn't contacted them. He stayed in the shadows. They traveled in groups still, Asher and Rosemary taking the last shift for safety reasons. Rosemary wrapped her arms around Lavender while Asher walked ahead and Gavin behind.

Once Lavender and Gavin were in the apartment, it was always a fury of tearing each other's clothes off, searching for skin to worship, then tumbling into bed while they drew out whatever pleasure they could. Then Gavin would cook and Lavender would work on her spells, and he would grasp her all through the night wishing Samhain would arrive faster, and they had already survived and this could all be over. That they could have time, quiet time, lovely time.

It was so damn unfair. If Gavin had been a religious man, he might have complained to whichever deity cursed them to these lives over and over again. He wanted his chance with Lavender.

He wanted more time. They were never given enough time.

"Gavin, Gavin?" He jumped awake, Will shaking his shoulder.

"Oh, sorry." He had fallen asleep in his chair in the corner of the Immortal Cupcake. He hadn't been sleeping well. He had taken to watching Lavender most of the night, afraid that the next day would be the one when they were ripped apart again.

"Look, you should come with us," Sage started. "You need to sleep."

"But Lavender still has...four hours of work."

"I know. But Luke and Verbena are here. Asher and Rosemary will come to walk her home."

Lavender stepped out from behind the counter. It was quieter today. No steady stream of customers, just a couple here and there. Gavin watched the solitary customer push through the door and leave. "Go sleep. I know you are staying up to watch me."

"How do you know if you are sleeping?" he teased.

"I'm a witch. I'm magic, remember?" She gripped his hand. "I'll be okay. Luke and Verbena won't leave me."

Gavin looked at her and relented. "Okay. But I'll come back to walk you home with Asher and Rosemary."

"I'll be waiting." Lavender raised to her tiptoes and kissed him quickly.

"Gross," Sage announced loudly. "Ready?"

Gavin nodded and eyed the pair. Sage with her beat overalls, baggy fleece zip-up, and worn beanie and Will in houndstooth pants, a brown sweater with a collared shirt underneath it, and a darker brown wool trench coat.

They made an odd pair.

He followed them out of the bakery and waited a few minutes before asking, "So how is it going for the two of you?"

Sage pulled a face. "What do you mean?"

"You know. You're pretty young still. Both of you. Living with someone you just met and all."

Sage grumbled. "It's going fine. We're in our mid-twenties, not like we're eighteen. And we didn't just meet, not really. Same as you and Lavender. We've been together a bunch of times before."

"That is true." Will squeezed her hand, then let it drop. "We're doing better than most. Hell, my friends are seriously jealous that, in their minds, I fell into a relationship with a woman with a house."

"Who provides almost all your food! I'm a goldmine." She winked at Will, who blushed.

"I'm glad it's been easy for you two."

"It hasn't been easy. Fuck, Miloslav kidnapped Will. Beat the hell out of him and attacked his mom. Then, he bit me on my fucking shoulder. It's our lot in life. It's not going to be easy. But Miloslav has never beaten me before. I don't intend for this life to be the first time."

Gavin felt a bit of relief hearing Sage talk like that. Lavender had a former brother and chaos warlock after her. But she also had a sister who didn't take shit from anyone and had been the one to kill Jonas Fortworth.

He didn't want Sage to have to kill anyone in this life...but it was comforting to know she'd done it before.

Chapter Twenty-Six

Lavender was glad Gavin went home. She knew he wasn't sleeping. Anytime in the past week when she woke up to go to the bathroom, or her alarm went off, he was up. Basically staring at her.

It'd be creepy if she wasn't completely in love with him.

It was so strange how feelings just trampled their way back into your heart so immediately. Sure, Lavender had never stopped loving Gavin, but there were days, weeks even, when it became like background noise. It was something she got used to, to the point that it didn't dictate her every thought.

Now, it was like she was twenty again and falling off a cliff with how much she cared about him. At this moment, her heart ached a little that he wasn't in the bakery. Which was ridiculous. He was literally in her apartment. She was going to see him in a couple hours.

Lavender ducked in the back and said hello to Luke, then grabbed a tray of cookies to bring to the front. She'd scaled back on her wares for the day, but she ran out of double chocolate chunk cookies before school got out. She popped in a solitary batch so her usual suspects who walked to the bakery before going home could have their choice of cookies.

Her heart panged for a moment. What if Miloslav came during the after-school rush? Would he have any scruples if kids were around? Or would he be as awful as he always was?

Lavender shook her head and looked back at the cookies. She wished the world would stop from now until the day after Samhain. But it wouldn't. She had a business to run, money to make, a community to serve. But that didn't stop a low level of terror from coursing through her veins all day long.

She arranged the cookies in the display case, enjoying the rich scent as she did. She should bring one of them home for Gavin. He liked chocolate. And he'd been on edge even more than she had. Even if they had completely reestablished their sex life as if they hadn't missed a beat since college.

Lavender hadn't expected that. They were both older. Plus, there was the whole bakery and chaos warlock horning in on their time. But that didn't seem to affect anything. When she got home from work, she'd ride Gavin like a newly deflowered nineteen-year-old learning every inch of how to make her partner—and herself—feel amazing.

And it did.

Everything with Gavin was fire. The way he moved over her—in her—she blushed just thinking about it.

"Earth to Lavender, you've been holding that tray of cookies about to display them for over two minutes." Verbena looked up from her laptop.

"Sorry." She quickly added the cookies, then set the tray on the back counter.

"No worries. We're all pretty distracted right now."

Lavender looked around the seating area—one customer with headphones on who was just starting their coffee and muffin and another deep into work on a laptop. She took the opportunity to slink into a chair across from Verbena for a minute.

"How you doing?" Verbena asked, closing her laptop and giving her sister her full attention.

"Stressed."

Verbena smiled. "Yeah, me too. You know us. We don't like it when we aren't in control."

"So obviously, our foe is going to be a chaos warlock."

"Seems appropriate." Verbena reached her hand across the table and squeezed Lavender's wrist. "We're going to be okay. I'm working on some stuff. Boundary spells. I don't know if it's going to work. But I have some ideas. I'll try it on me and Luke first."

"What would it do?"

"Basically, it will set a boundary around our souls. Because Luke is a Stoch technically, I can't block all of them. I'm going to try to just block Boris. His soul. Make a boundary that he can't cross no matter what lifetime we're in."

"That's brilliant."

"Yeah, it would work a little better if my soulmate wasn't on their line." She smiled. "But I'll make do."

Verbena's phone rang and she looked at the screen. "Shit, I should take this."

"Go ahead." Lavender stood and walked back behind the counter.

She grabbed a few dirty espresso cups and headed into the back to get a jump on dishes.

"There we are," Miloslav said the moment she pushed into the kitchen.

"Shit." Lavender dropped the cups and looked at Luke, who was frozen near the back door. He didn't look hurt. More like...stuck. His eyes were trained on Miloslav and his limbs moved slightly, almost like someone was holding him back.

"Lucky Luke was back here. Anyone else...whew. He's really the only one I have qualms about murdering. Blood relative and all that. Those sorts of stains don't leave you."

"Didn't seem to stop you before," she said through gritted teeth.

Miloslav's eyes flashed as he stared at her. "Before? Oh...is Katherine finally with us?"

"Fuck you," she spat. "You broke a promise to a witch. Dangerous territory."

"A little more bite than before? Technically, Jonas broke a promise to a witch. And another technicality, Father did it. A warlock who you cursed."

"You're a monster."

"Right back at you, sis." Miloslav shrugged and picked up a muffin sitting on the counter, then took a bite. "This is burned."

"That's why I didn't bring it out."

Miloslav tossed the muffin back to the counter, then brushed his hands off. "Here's what we're going to do. I don't love getting thrown down the street by Asher. I also don't love your pain in the ass little sister killing me in every lifetime."

"She didn't kill you in France."

"Blech, I know. Firing squad and all that. Hell if I know where she was during World War II." Miloslav leaned against the counter and locked eyes with her. "I want your blood. And I want to get it without a lot of fanfare, you know? I attack you here, you and your sisters all drop dead wherever you are, it'll be a big thing. Especially since Rosemary and Verbena both went to the hospital. I'm sure you've given them a full report on all of it."

"You don't know if it will kill us. Katherine didn't put that in the curse."

"True. I'd say your chances are fifty-fifty when it comes to surviving. But...magic is entrenched in our souls. Wrapped up within us. Who knows what would happen to us if our souls took such a hit? Anyway. I'd much rather you all gather in your house. So, the cops can say there was a carbon monoxide leak or whatever. Easier all around. You don't want to be the reason witches have to step into the light, do you?"

"You expect me to make your attack easier for you?"

"Yes, I do. First of all, you seem like a morally sound person. Do you know what would happen to the world if suddenly everyone knew what magic was? We'd be looking at another two centuries of witch hunts. Also, I have something to offer you." Miloslav stepped toward her as if he was approaching a stray cat. "Tell Richard, Arthur, whatever the hell you call him this time, to leave. I won't go after him if you do exactly as I say."

"As if I would believe you."

"I thought you might say that." He cleared his throat. "I, Miloslav Stoch, solemnly vow that if Lavender Bay gathers her sisters into her cottage on Samhain night to allow me to take her blood, without a fight, I will never hunt down Gavin Murphy. That's his name, right?"

"It is."

"There you are. You have my vow."

"Why would your vow be worth anything?"

"Ask Sage. She has experience with my vows. Come on, curse maker. Here's your chance to end the evil you made." Miloslav smirked, then his expression shadowed. He breathed heavily and grabbed his belly. "Sage has my number. Text me your answer." With a groan, he dashed out of the bakery, door banging behind him.

"What the hell?" Lavender ran to Luke, who crumpled to the ground.

"Did it work?" Verbena shouted as she barged into the back. "Luke! Oh, my goddess!"

Lavender moved aside and let Verbena slide beside her soulmate.

"I'm okay, I'm okay. Fuck, I hate Miloslav."

"What do you mean, did it work?" Lavender asked.

"I tried changing him. Bones...they were stronger than I thought. Couldn't change them into jelly like I originally planned. But...organs. Organs were easier. I changed his pancreas into a muscle."

"What the hell?"

"I know! I can't believe it. I'm sure it's back to normal by now, but if I can figure out how to change his heart into, I don't know, an appendix, he'll die, right?"

"Verbena. You shouldn't kill him." As much as Lavender wanted Miloslav dead...she didn't want her sister to carry his murder for the rest of her life.

"He's going to kill us, Lavender. I could hear what he was saying. I don't think if he steals our power, he'll be walking away from us."

"Okay. Don't kill him unless he's actively killing one of us. Deal?"

Verbena shrugged. "I'll take it into consideration. There's a lot of bad stuff he could do that would warrant me fucking with his organs beside murder. What if he's torturing one of us? Or burning down our house? Or casting some sort of chaos spell on the entire island? I'm going to reserve the ability to fuck around with his insides."

Lavender furrowed her brows. "Maybe stick with things that won't kill him immediately for now."

She didn't call Gavin. She called Rosemary and Asher, texted Sage, Will, Laurel, and Owen. Then, she had Asher and Rosemary come to walk her home, knowing full well that Miloslav wouldn't be back tonight.

Lavender knew there was no guarantee that if she sacrificed herself, Gavin would stay safe. Once Miloslav had the full power of five witches added to his as a chaos warlock, there was no telling what breaking a vow would even do.

But she did know that Gavin needed to leave Star Island.

This was a magical battle. Humans were fragile. Gavin couldn't circle his wrists and protect himself. He couldn't bake food that would mess up the people who ate it. He couldn't get between her and a warlock or turn Miloslav's organs into something else. He was unprotected.

And right now, she needed to put as much space between Miloslav and Gavin as she could. Because she wasn't going to give up, but if Miloslav thought she was...

They might just have a chance.

Chapter Twenty-Seven

The sound of Lavender's keys in the door had a weight the size of an elephant coming off his chest. When Asher had texted and told him to stay put, he'd been worried something terrible had happened. But now she was home.

"I missed you. Is everything—" He stopped talking. Her face was crumpled, and she dropped her purse on the ground.

"Holy shit." Gavin ran to her. "What happened?"

"Miloslav came to the bakery."

"What? Why didn't you call me? I would have come. I would have—"

"Can we sit down?"

Gavin's mind stopped racing at the sound of the question. He needed to stay calm, for her sake. "Of course. Do you want me to make you a cup of tea? Or pour you a glass of wine?"

"I'm fine." She sighed as she pulled off her boots and shrugged off her coat, leaving both in a pile by the door. She collapsed onto the couch beside him.

"I want you to know that I love you. Okay? I really, really love you, and the last few weeks with you have been the best weeks of my life."

"Even with a chaos warlock fucking everything up?"

"Yeah. I'm going to say some things that are going to upset you. But I want you to listen to me. Actually, logically listen to me."

"Fuck, did he get your blood? I'm going to kill him. I don't care what the consequences are."

"No. Not yet. But he might. Right now, I don't know if I still have faith in us beating him. I need you to be safe."

"And I need you to be safe."

"Gavin. He...made me an offer. A vow, actually. That if I went along with it, with him. Did as he asked, and you left Star Island, he vowed he would never, ever come after you."

"Well, that's bullshit. We know him. He's Charles. He lied to us for months."

"It's different when it's a vow. I talked to Sage. She had one over him before. He never broke that vow. And she doesn't think he'll break another."

"So what, he expects me to fuck off and leave you to die?"

"I might not die."

"But you might! Sorry I don't trust the guy that's killed you at least twice before! And hasn't he killed Will? If he manages to steal your powers, all of your powers, and becomes some sort of souped-up chaos warlock, what's to stop him from erasing you five from anyone's memory? He messes with reality." He shook his head. "No. I'm not leaving you."

"I wouldn't ask unless I thought it would work." She inhaled sharply. "I'm not giving up. I promise. The curse...I might be able to figure it out. If you asked me to recreate it again, I could do it. But I'm just not sure I can undo it. But I know I can separate us from him. I have faith in that spell. I can make sure that we never see Miloslav again. In another life. We could still have a chance to be together."

"Your next life? Lavender, you're thirty-four years old. You aren't going anywhere. I won't let it happen. We deserve to have each other in this life. I'm not...you don't know what it was like. When I was Arthur. I lived without you for such a long time. I was so sad, bone-deep sad. It was an ache that never left me, no matter how many years passed. You can't ask me to choose that path."

"You're human!" she shouted. "And vulnerable. And I can't protect you. I'm not Sage. I don't have a vengeance goddess watching over me. I've never killed anyone. And I'm not Verbena. I can't turn Miloslav into mush. Or throw him into the Hedge World. I'm a weak kitchen witch who is trying to take down a chaos warlock, a metal warlock, and a hedge witch with a fucking cake! And I can't watch you die again. I can't. You have no idea." She was hyperventilating now.

"It's okay," he began.

"No! Listen to me. Two times! Watching as you died. Waiting to die. I can't let him kill you again in front of me. I can't watch the minutes pass on the clock again, or stare at the stars. I cannot do it! If Miloslav hurts you—"

"He won't.

"He almost killed Will! This time. Not in Ancient Greece when he actually killed him, but this September! He isn't good. He's rotten. You can't beat him. Please, Gavin, don't make me watch, I can't. I can't."

He grabbed her and pulled her into his arms, holding hard. He may have been hurting her, he didn't know, but he couldn't let go. He wouldn't.

"Please," she whimpered, her hands wild on him. She tugged his shirt over his head, scraped her teeth over his shoulder. "Please."

He pulled her shirt off, matching her intensity. In a fury, she undid his pants, slid her skirt up her waist, pushed her panties away, and seated herself on him. He buckled immediately. Lavender dragged over him at a frantic pace, her hips moving wildly. "Please, please, please," she moaned over and over like an incantation. Like if she begged enough he would leave her.

He flipped her onto the ground, thrusting on top of her. He felt so full… full of love for Lavender, full of anger at Miloslav, full of fear for what might happen. His heart felt like it might burst.

"Aw, Moonbeam," he groaned against her. "Fuck, I love you."

"You need to leave me," she begged.

"I can't. Don't make me. Don't make me leave you again." He buried his hand in her hair and rutted like an animal in heat. Like he'd never get a chance to be with her again. His perfect Moonbeam.

"You'll find me again." She screwed her face up and dug her nails into his shoulder. "Ah! You'll always find me. I won't hide. I promise I'll never hide again." Her legs gripped him like a vise as she spasmed around him. She whimpered through her orgasm, the sound between a moan and a sob.

Gavin leaned back to his knees, dragging her hips with him. He pumped into her until his desire took over and he couldn't hold off anymore, pouring himself into her in one last attempt to bind them together.

He collapsed to his back but didn't let go of her. She draped over him, her breasts pressed against his abdomen, her right hand gripping his shoulder.

"I left you once and it ruined my life, Moonbeam." He tried to catch his breath. "Don't ask me to do it again."

Lavender didn't answer but peeled her body off his and slid to the floor beside him.

"We're a team," he whispered. "Better together."

Chapter Twenty-Eight

It was hard to argue with a man who'd just made you come harder than you thought was possible.

Lavender felt like her body and soul had been separated on her living room floor. Her body was sticking to the hardwood. Her soul was on another plane entirely.

At some point, Gavin rolled far enough away from her to grab her throw blanket off the couch and arrange it over them.

And they lay on the floor and stared at the ceiling until Lavender felt the day slipping into night and her slipping into her favorite spot against Gavin's chest.

Tick, tick, tick. Seconds became minutes, became hours. Drip, drip, drip. Water. Blood. Hope. Magic. Time. It all ran out.

Lavender woke when it was still dark. She slid to her knees and looked at Gavin in the dim light cast from the nightlight she kept in the bathroom.

He looked so peaceful. She hadn't seen him this relaxed since...

Since college. The night before the spell. It was weird, how certain memories stuck with you. She'd been in his dorm room, asleep. There was a crash or something one room over, and she'd woken up with a start. Gavin had slept on.

His face took on that same youthful innocence. She hoped he was having good dreams. Because she hadn't changed her mind. When he woke up, he needed to pack and get the hell off Star Island. At the very least, Miloslav needed to believe she had sent him away and he had listened. If Miloslav thought she was compliant...it would help.

She pressed a kiss against his brow, then rocked back on her heels to stand, and walked to her room. She grabbed a pile of clothes and headed to the bathroom. She needed a shower and some thinking time. Having a chaos warlock to vanquish was no easy feat. Lavender needed a clear head. And a chance to wash off some of the pheromones that were all over her. She couldn't concentrate smelling like Gavin.

"What time is it?" Gavin mumbled.

"Five-thirty. I have to go to the bakery."

"I'll come. Just give me a second to get ready." Gavin got to his knees, then his feet, groaning as he did. "I should have been chivalrous and carried you to bed last night. I can't believe we slept on the floor."

"Might have still hurt your back. Gavin, we need to talk."

"We can talk while we're walking over."

"No, we need to talk before we leave."

"Moonbeam." He stopped walking and turned to her. "I am not leaving. There's nothing to talk about."

"I need you to listen to me and to take me seriously." Lavender took a deep breath. "I'm not throwing you out of my life. I am making a decision based on what I know about Miloslav and beyond that, all of the Stochs. I am compounding a lot of information that you don't have. How Morana and Ivan acted with Laurel and Rosemary. What Sage knows about Miloslav's other past lives. He's been more than just Jonas and Charles. A lot more. We're not simply fighting him, we're fighting a curse I laid down on our line. We're fighting fate, and we're fighting his family. And I need him to think I'm losing my will to fight."

"But you aren't. You can win this, I know it. I won't let you give up."

"Asking you to leave isn't me giving up. It's giving me a chance. Because he needs to think he's winning. I think there's something to do with Samhain—Halloween. I don't think anything is going to happen before that. So, I have five days to figure this out."

"I don't want to leave you."

"You're not leaving me. Not in a permanent way. You just need to get off Star Island for a little while. I'll still call and text and tell you when it's safe. But I...If I am worried about your safety, my concentration is going to be shit. This will help."

"I don't see how us being apart will help anything."

Lavender took his hands in hers, kissed his knuckles, and looked up at him. "I need you to trust me. I'm not disappearing. I'll be in contact with you the whole time."

"And what if he kills you?" Gavin shook his head. "I'm not doing that again. Life without you is dark and awful. If he's taking you out, I'm going with you this time. I don't want to spend another forty years muddling through life without you."

"I can't promise that won't happen. But you won't be alone. Your dad... don't make him go through that. Think about what losing Phillip did to your parents."

Gavin scoffed and looked away, his eyes brimming with tears.

"We've lost people we love. It's horrible and hurts. Miloslav, absolute bane of my existence that he is, he offered me a small grace. You will survive, no matter what. What if I survive and you don't? I'll never forgive myself if I could have kept you safe and didn't."

He cradled her head and drew her to rest against his chest. "I would never blame you."

"But I would destroy myself." She pressed a kiss against his chest. "I'm going to open the bakery late. Let's get you on the ferry."

"I love you, Moonbeam. Always have, always will."

"I love you too. Love of my many lives."

The ferry came at ten in the morning. She'd hung an "opening late" sign on the door of the Immortal Cupcake as they walked by. The weather was appropriately gloomy with a thin mist of rain. Were the goddesses telling her it was a mistake to let him go? Or just matching the weather to her miserable mood?

She didn't want to send him off. She wanted to take him back to her apartment, crawl into her bed with him, and pretend nothing else existed. Pretend that if they stayed in bed, nothing could happen. Miloslav would eventually give up and all would be well again. Better than it had ever been. Because she could have everything now. Her sisters were grown and happy. Her business was thriving. And best of all, Gavin, her soulmate, had returned to her. And she'd had the good sense not to run him off. Or run away. Everything she wanted was within her grasp, but one man stood between all of it.

Miloslav Stoch. Jonas Fortworth. Charles Wright. Ruiner of lives. Murderer of witches.

"I don't have to get on the ferry," Gavin said as he pulled her into a hug. "We can walk to the bakery and open it."

"No, you do." She couldn't lose her nerve now. She had a strong feeling someone was watching her right now. Miloslav or maybe Ivan or Morana.

"Okay. But." He pulled away to look at her face. "I can come back whenever you need me."

"You should really go back to Chicago. Figure things out at work, you know. For when you can come back permanently." She said it like it was a wish. Truthfully, she wanted him as far away from Miloslav as possible. He should be going to Japan.

"Hell no. I am staying in Chatham. That's as far as you'll get me from you. I can figure out work in November." He blew out a breath. "Fuck, I hate saying goodbye to you."

"Me too."

"I'm going to call you the second I'm off the ferry."

She nodded.

"God, I love you. Remember that, okay? I'm only leaving because you wanted me to."

"I don't want you to leave. I need you to." Her voice shook now. She couldn't hold back tears from falling down her cheeks. "I love you so m—" Gavin cut her off, crashing his mouth against hers. They kissed furiously, not caring that they were in public. Not caring that Lavender heard a gasp, and a man yelling "get a room!"

She kissed Gavin like it might be the last time she ever got to in this life, in this body. She kissed him like Lavender Bay was saying goodbye until she was someone else again.

In short, she kissed him goodbye.

It was a flurry after that, Gavin rushing to board in the small crowd. Lavender pulling him in for one last hug, holding his hand until the very last minute. Waving from the pier until the boat became a speck against the water and...

He was gone. And she was alone. Again.

Maybe this was her lot. She had a soulmate, who she loved with all her heart, but it was her fate to be alone. To face the worst of it by herself. If it wasn't their childish stupidity, it was a chaos warlock making certain they stayed apart.

Even Rosemary had said she and Asher had years of happiness in their past life. Lavender and Gavin never got that. Months spent hiding their love in the shadows was all they were ever allowed.

She found a bench and sat and cried. Because it didn't feel like it mattered if anyone saw her or was watching her. In this moment, nothing mattered. She was utterly shattered. The pain in her chest was as sharp and nauseating as the first time they were separated. But somehow, now, everything felt worse. Because thirteen years earlier, Lavender didn't see a future that was anything but blinding pain. Now she could picture it so clearly it was like sweetness dancing on her tongue.

Oh, how she wanted to crawl into her bed and cry. Give up for a few days. Let her soul wallow in its devastating pain.

But she wiped her eyes on her coat sleeve and stood. There was work to be done, there always was. But more than that. She had to perfect her unbinding spell. She had to break her curse.

And talk to her sisters.

She still had them.

It was time for a family meeting.

Chapter Twenty-Nine

Lavender walked into the Bay cottage and exhaled.

It was still home. It was as comforting as a hug.

It felt safe here. Like Miloslav couldn't touch her under the protection of this house. It wasn't true; Morana had attacked Laurel in the parlor less than six months ago. Ivan had destroyed the street, pulled apart the kitchen. Boris had trapped Verbena on the boundary of the property. Nowhere was safe, but for the moment, standing alone in the house that had been hers for thirteen years, Lavender Bay felt settled in her soul.

She was pleasantly surprised by how tidy Sage and Will had kept it, though was instantly disheartened when she saw four take-out containers balancing on the kitchen counter. Had they been eating out every night?

"Not on my watch," she mumbled, then walked into the kitchen. The pantry was still stocked, the freezer too, plus Sage had mountains of fresh produce in the fridge. Lavender would be remiss if she didn't get a few things going while she waited. Plus, it would help keep her mind busy while she waited for her sisters.

Thirty minutes later, a baked ziti was in the oven, pumpkin soup simmering on the stove. Bread dough was rising under a clean white dishcloth, and a batch of cookies was cooling. Lavender sat down at the dining table feeling like she had done well by her baby sister.

She ran her hands over the table that had sat in their house in Ohio. It had been a nonnegotiable. Even though it was huge and Lavender had been trying to fit as many personal things as she could in the moving truck, there was no way she was leaving it.

As a family of witches, a table was so much more than a table. It was the meeting place. Where they came together in joy. In sorrow. In solidarity.

"Who's here so far?" Rosemary called as she pushed through the front door.

"Just me," Lavender answered. She leaned back in her chair to look at her sister.

"How are you doing?" Rosemary set down her bag and hugged Lavender from behind. "Did dropping Gavin off go okay?"

"I cried. In public. For over fifteen minutes."

"Oh, Lav. It's okay. Everyone needs to cry in public sometimes. Did he call or text yet?"

"No. He won't be off the ferry for a while still. And then I told him to find a place to stay before he called. A small part of me is hoping that there won't be any open hotels in Chatham, and he'll change his mind and fly back to Chicago. Get more space between himself and Miloslav."

"Can't see that happening." Rosemary took a seat beside her.

"Why not?"

"Because that would also put more space between the two of you. And Gavin has been wanting to close that gap for a long time. He's not going to give up on you."

"I don't want him to give up. I just want him to survive."

Rosemary ran her fingers against the table. "You know, when I was Gundrun and Asher was Skáldi, losing him was unbearably painful. It's faded now, but I do think when you lose your soulmate, especially early when you are both young, there is a certain grief that is terrifying to think about ever experiencing again. Gundrun, who, you know, is me and isn't me, made a lot of strange choices. But when I think about why she didn't try to escape Fáfnir and instead joined Skáldi in the afterlife…it's weird. I had two beautiful children. Who I loved more than anything. But I felt so resigned to that being the end for me." Rosemary paused. "Gavin lived his last life without you for decades. He lived so much longer without you than with you. So much longer. And the way things went this time, if the worst thing were to happen, he'd have to live through that again. So, I don't fault him for wanting to stay as close as possible. I know that the moment you call for him, he will come back. Because he loves you so fiercely. And you deserve every ounce of his love. Don't push him away because you are scared. He's scared too."

"Shit, Rosemary." Lavender wiped her eyes and her nose with her sleeve. "Now I'm going to sob."

"Sob away! I don't mind. I cried for two hours last night."

"You did?"

"Yeah. I'm scared as hell. I don't want to die, and I also don't want to lose my powers. I love being a garden witch. I can't imagine what my life would be like without it. And Asher is scared too. It's fucking terrifying."

Lavender blew out a breath and looked at her sister. "I don't want any of us to die. And I don't want any of us to lose our powers."

"Me neither."

"We need to get to work."

Within the hour, everyone was there. The Bay sisters stayed in the dining room, Asher stayed at the front door, Luke at the back, and Owen and Will went to the attic. Will had yet to absorb the entire library, but he was working on it. Anything they could use on chaos warlocks or curses that was hidden in there needed to be in his mind to give them a fighting chance.

"We can do this," Lavender began. "Let's go around the table. I think I'm almost done with an unbinding spell. It's in cake form. We'll need Miloslav, Ivan, and Morana all to eat it, which might be tricky. And then the five of us need to eat it as well."

"Do they need to eat it willingly or can we, you know, jump on their backs and shove it down their throats?" Sage asked.

"Honestly, I think either would work. As long as some gets in there, we're probably good. But, that won't work on Boris because he's not currently living."

"It's okay. I'm about seventy percent done with creating a boundary between him, Luke, Danny, and me. I should be able to finish it tonight. I won't know for sure if it holds until...well until we never see him again in another life, I guess. So hopefully I just never see him again."

"Thank you, Verbena. I'm really glad you have that in place." Lavender opened the notebook in front of her and wrote down everything so far. She'd decided to keep track of everything they did. Maybe one day she'd type it up and make it into a book. So, if in one hundred years, a family of witches found themselves cursed and bound to a chaos warlock, they could learn from everything the Bays did.

"Nemesis and I have been talking," Sage mentioned, then took a cookie from the plate on the table.

"Care to elaborate?"

"I don't think she or Erebus are going to intervene. I think this is one of the fights they are going to leave to the mortals. Almost like when they saw that they were on opposite sides of this fight, they didn't care about us anymore."

"I'm sorry, since when can you talk to Nemesis?" Laurel asked.

"I'm not talking to her like that. She's been coming to me in my dreams. Mostly giving me pep talks? But very much coded that I'm on my own but that I can do it." Sage shrugged. "If I had to face down her dad, I don't think she'd be that positive."

"Asher and I have been talking to the Guardians," Rosemary mentioned.

Lavender's ears perked up. "And?"

"Miloslav did break Morana and Ivan out, and it wasn't without casualties on the Collective's part. No one died, but there are some pretty bad injuries."

"Holy shit."

"This did officially mark the Stochs as dangerous supernaturals, which is apparently some sort of category the Guardians use. They've been labeled as wanted for questioning and...basically the Guardians are on our side. Asher has been talking to a few about how they can help keep the Stochs away from us, but it's tricky. Without their charge, a Guardian is basically non-magical. So..."

"The Guardians would have to convince the magical person they watch over to help us," Lavender finished. "And witches rarely get involved in other witches' business."

"Some of them don't even guard witches. Asher's mom was an animan," Rosemary pointed out.

"I'll put the Guardians down as a soft maybe in terms of help." Lavender looked down at her notebook.

So much for her North American Witches' Council coming to their aid. It had been a dream, after all. And one with a very tight timetable if she had hoped to have it put together before things came to a head with the Stochs. But organizing all the witches on an entire continent had been a little more than Lavender could handle. The Bay witches were going to have to face this on their own.

She had scribbled down NEW EFFIGY in the margin.

"I think..." She paused and rethought how she needed to approach this. "We should collect some sticks. And larger pieces of wood."

"No." Laurel answered.

"It might be our only way to stop him," Lavender said slowly.

"I am good with straight up murdering Miloslav again," Sage interjected.

"Also, no," Laurel repeated.

"I'm just throwing it out there as a last resort. If things are getting really bad, I'm cool with taking care of that. I can be the one."

"You're not going to be the one who kills Miloslav," Verbena said. "You're the youngest. I could probably turn all his organs into Jell-O for ten minutes. That would have to kill him, right? And probably pretty undetectable in an autopsy."

"He'll only come back again in another life," Lavender interrupted. "And another. I should be the one to deal with it. Now."

"No!" Laurel reiterated. "It could kill you. I have just as much curse laying experience as you do. If you can tell me what to do, I could do it."

"You also died immediately after laying your curse," Sage pointed out. "Fun fact: I have never immediately died after killing Miloslav. Always survived at least another couple of months. Sometimes over fifty years."

"Stop!" Lavender yelled, and all four of her sisters jumped. She rested her head against her hands. "Just stop," she added quietly.

She couldn't do this, argue with her sisters over who was going to sacrifice themselves to stop him.

If anyone wasn't making it to the winter, it was Lavender.

She was the oldest. She was the guardian. It was her greatest privilege to protect her sisters.

She wouldn't stop now.

"Are we thinking this is all going to come to a head Samhain night?" Laurel asked slowly.

"Probably. It would be on brand for both Miloslav and the universe in general. Such a drama queen," Lavender tried to joke.

"I should move some stuff around. I've got a full schedule of tarot readings on Halloween, and on the chance we all survive and I still have to make a living, that cash will be much needed."

"We are going to survive! Don't cancel those readings, just move them earlier. If I know the Stochs, they are all about the dramatic flair. Nothing is happening before sundown," Rosemary pointed out. "And more than that, we are the Bay witches. Come on! Verbena can turn a pancreas into muscle. Chaos warlocks have nothing on Sage. Laurel can throw Morana into the Hedge World. I made plants attack Ivan. And Lavender—"

"I cast a curse in a past life that put us in the predicament?"

"No. You are a master spell caster. You created the past life spell that has opened all of our eyes throughout this entire mess. You have held us together for thirteen years." Rosemary grasped her hand. "We've got this. I promise."

Lavender looked over her sisters.

She could do it.

She could save them.

Lavender snuck up to the attic alone. Will was downstairs eating and taking a break from absorbing the library, and each of her sisters had slowly coupled off to bring their soulmates up to speed.

She needed a minute.

Gavin had texted her that he had landed and would let her know when he was in a hotel. She would talk to him once she was home and truly alone.

It was quiet in the attic. And drafty. It wasn't an ideal place for books. Cold in the autumn, winter, and spring. A freaking furnace in the summer. But it was always a perfect place to be alone.

Lavender ran her hand over the piles of books on the table, some open, some closed and in tight stacks. This was their legacy. If the Bay witches ceased to exist in five days, this was what they would leave behind.

She should tell Owen to have his cousins come get them. She didn't want a human coming across the collection and thinking it was anything less than precious.

"Lavender Bay," a voice called out, causing her to jump and knock a stack of books off the table. She whipped her head around and came face-to-face with...

Eliza Bay.

"Oh shit," Lavender breathed. "I'm so sorry. I'm so, so sorry. I shouldn't have done it. I should have let him torture me or kill me. Richard didn't even survive, none of it was worth it." She snapped her mouth shut to stop from babbling.

Eliza fluttered closer to her, her mouth staying firmly shut, but somehow speaking.

You did not cast the curse, Katherine Fortworth did.

"Yes, but I was her. We share the same soul. It was me; I have the memories."

No, you are not her. She was a witch stuck in a house with two warlocks who hated her. She was a witch whose mother abandoned her. She was a woman who fell in love with a man she could not. You are none of those things.

Lavender furrowed her brow. This didn't make sense. She *was* Katherine Fortworth.

New lives are always a new chance. Seeing that life was a gift. Now you know what to do. You know how to undo it.

"Laying the curse killed me. Won't undoing do the same?"

Eliza shrugged. *I do not know. But laying a curse is so much worse than lifting one, isn't it? Katherine was the curse maker. What will Lavender Bay be?*

Lavender stood with her mouth open, unsure how to answer the ghost in front of her.

That man is not Jonas. He is only himself.

As quickly as she appeared, Eliza was gone, and Lavender was alone in the attic again.

Miloslav was not Jonas. She was not Katherine.

She was Lavender Bay, daughter of Holly Bay, sister to Rosemary, Laurel, Verbena, and Sage.

Soulmate to Gavin.

Chapter Thirty

Gavin checked into a small hotel in Chatham, Massachusetts, and began the awful, terrible, unending task of waiting.

Waiting for Lavender to text him back. Waiting for Halloween to come and go. Waiting for her to give him the all clear so they could actually begin their lives together.

He didn't want to leave her. It felt like shit doing it. And if it was August instead of October, he may just have jumped off the ferry and swam back to Star Island while it was still feasible.

But Lavender was the witch. She understood magical enemies, something he was still trying to wrap his head around. If she believed Miloslav might cool it if Gavin was gone, he believed her.

That didn't mean it didn't absolutely destroy his heart.

"Room 103, down that hall, past the ice machine, on your right. Would you like any maps of the surrounding area?" The front desk woman cut into Gavin's thoughts.

"I'm fine."

"Well, there is a bus to the railroad museum tomorrow at ten, and one to the beach at noon. Though the beach can get pretty wild this late in the season. Definitely dress warm if you are planning on visiting tomorrow."

"Thanks," Gavin mumbled and took the key card from the desk and followed her directions. While he felt like he had a million things to do while waiting to hear from Lavender, none of them would take him out of the hotel room.

"Radka's."

"Hey, who is this? Eli? It's Gavin."

"Gavin! What the fuck, man? Where are you?"

"Vacation."

"Seriously? You've been gone for almost a month. I've known you for, what, eight years? You've never taken a weekend off, let alone fucked off right before the holidays with basically no warning. You okay?"

"Yeah. Is Austin there?" As much as Gavin liked Eli, he had to get this over with.

"Sure. You taking a longer sabbatical than planned?"

"Something like that." Eli put him on hold and before Gavin could even take a minute to gather his thoughts, Austin was on the line.

"Is this a resignation call?" Austin asked abruptly.

"Wow. Cut right to the chase." Gavin huffed a laugh. "Yeah. Yeah it is."

"Damn. Did you get an offer somewhere else? Want to give me a number and see if I can work with it? I'll have to call the owners but—"

"It's not that." Gavin took a breath. "I met someone. It's for the long run. She lives back East. I'm going to move to be with her." It was the simplest way to frame it. He had met someone thirteen years ago. He's known the moment he talked to her that she would be his forever girl, his Moonbeam. And now she lived in New England. None of those were false.

"Well, shit. I don't think I can compete with that. You coming in anymore? Or is this goodbye forever?"

"I'll swing past to say goodbye when I go home to move my stuff out. Radka was a great place to work. I appreciate all the risks you let me take in the kitchen."

"I can't believe we're losing you permanently. It's been a mess without you the last week."

"That's a lie. I know Maisie is doing just fine without me. Probably better since she's not trying to impress me."

"She's so young, though. Twenty-five? She can't run a kitchen like you do."

"No, but neither could I when I started working there. Give her a chance. Hire a line cook instead. Let her show you what she can do."

Austin chuckled on the other end. "All right, Gavin. Best of luck to you. Be sure to stop in when you're back in Chicago. Hope it all works out for you."

"Yeah, me too." Gavin hung up and tossed the phone on the bed next to him. One uncomfortable call down, a few more to go.

By six in the evening, Gavin had his apartment listed for sublet and movers hired for December first. That gave him some time to figure out how things were going to work with Lavender. He was cool with moving into her apartment, but he hadn't asked. While it felt like the most natural thing in the world for them to suddenly live together, she might feel different. Thankfully, there was a Realtor in the family. If he needed to find housing quickly, Verbena would help him out.

He browsed flights back to Chicago mid-month. He'd need to clean out his apartment and pack, say goodbye to everyone.

There was the one phone call he still hadn't made. He needed to tell his dad. It wasn't like Gavin kept his dad abreast of his non-existent love life, but a move halfway across the country wasn't something he could hide. Plus, his dad usually came up for Thanksgiving. Gavin couldn't spring that on him the week before.

Fuck.

He picked up his phone and called his dad, his stomach in knots.

"Gavin! Long time no talk, how was your vacation?" His dad sounded chipper as could be. Great. He was about to ruin that mood.

"It's good, Dad. Real good. Actually, I was calling to tell you that I'm—I'm planning on staying here. Moving here. I need to work some things out, but I've decided."

"Wait, what? You're moving to an island off the coast of Massachusetts? Why?"

Here goes. "This is where Lavender lives."

"Oh, Gavin." His dad's voice took a low turn. "You can't...Look. I love you. You cannot stalk this woman."

"What?"

"You have to let her go. She broke up with you in college. Made herself impossible to find. You need to let her go. I'll come and get you; it'll be easier that way."

"No, that's not what's going on."

"I don't...I don't need to know the details, but you have to respect her wishes. You might think she's the one for you and all that, but if she doesn't feel that way, she isn't."

"She does. Feel that way. We love each other." Oh, God, that sounded lame when he said it to his dad. Conveyed nothing of the actual feelings he had for Lavender. Damn, this was not going at all how he thought it would. His dad thought he was stalking Lavender? Hell. "I'm not with her right now. But soon, I'll bring her to Florida, okay? Of her own volition. You can sit down with her, without me, make sure you feel okay about it. But I promise. She missed me as much as I missed her. It just took us a long time to forgive each other for some stuff that happened in college."

His dad was silent on the other end, not fighting Gavin on it but also not giving him any affirmation.

"So," his dad finally began after minutes of silence. "What's Star Island like?"

Gavin chuckled. "Like a movie set. It's really beautiful here."

"Hm. I was never one for New England. Sort of pretentious, you know? Not as laid-back as the Midwest."

Gavin grinned. His dad was set in his ways. Hell, he was surprised he'd actually moved to Florida. But Gavin would get him on board with Star Island.

"You know I love a good lake," he replied. "Especially Lake Michigan."

"Sure you do. You're a Great Lakes kid. I wouldn't have been surprised if you told me you were moving to Toronto or Cleveland. Hell, if you moved to Duluth and I had a place to visit in the summer on Lake Superior..."

"Dad. I could not live in Duluth. I'd freeze my balls off."

His dad laughed now, hard and loud. “You probably would.”

They chatted a bit longer, staying away from Lavender as a topic. It felt good to have the weight off his chest. Gavin needed his dad to know what was going on. And as much as he didn’t like talking about it, he didn’t want to keep anymore secrets than he needed to.

After they hung up, Gavin opened his text to Lavender. Damn, he wished he was with her rather than across the water.

GAVIN: I told my dad about us. He is worried I am stalking you and said that I should leave you alone and let you live your life.

MOONBEAM: I’m sorry, what?

GAVIN: Eh, I was pretty vocal about looking for you for a few years. Didn’t tell him about the whole soulmate thing, so he thinks I was a little deranged over you. Wanted me to move on.

MOONBEAM: Please tell your dad you are not stalking me.

GAVIN: I may have promised him to bring you to Florida at some point to meet him so you could tell him in person. Make sure I wasn’t forcing you.

MOONBEAM: Oh, my goddess...yes that is fine. But let’s go in January when the weather here is shit and business is very slow.

GAVIN: I’m in. You doing okay?

MOONBEAM: Yeah. Long day. I’m back at work finishing up some bread dough for tomorrow. Asher and Rosemary are waiting to walk me home.

GAVIN: Good. Damn, I wish I was there. I want to hug you so badly.

MOONBEAM: Me too. We’ll get there.

GAVIN: Finish up and text me when you get home. Or call if you want to talk.

MOONBEAM: I will. Love you.

GAVIN: Love you too. Be safe, Moonbeam.

Chapter Thirty-One

"Damn, it's freezing out there!" Hazel burst in the front door, the wind whipping the door shut behind her. "Are we going to have snow on Halloween? I hate snow on Halloween."

"I hope not," Lavender answered as she finished ringing up a customer. "I don't like snow until December." She stared at the space beyond Hazel, waiting for Miloslav to rush into the bakery. She trusted Verbena's spell work, but so far, Miloslav didn't seem to be affected by boundary magic. He'd entered the bakery twice.

Hazel ducked into the back, then popped back out, hands washed, jacket free, and wearing her apron. "Busy this morning?"

"Normal. Lots of pumpkin spice lattes and pumpkin bread."

"Got to get the pumpkin fix before it disappears from the menu!" Hazel said in mock horror.

"They still have a full month. I won't take any of that off until December first. Autumn goes through November no matter what the forecast decides."

"True, true." Hazel lowered her voice. "Is Laurel giving tarot card readings in the corner?"

"She is." Lavender had decided it was as good a cover as any as to why

Laurel would be hanging out in the bakery all day. Plus, it fit the time of year.

"Ooh. Maybe I'll get one. Some of my friends swear your sister is actually psychic."

Lavender laughed. "She'll be glad to hear it."

"Do you let her read your cards ever?" Hazel picked up a rag and started to wipe down the back counter.

"Very rarely. I'm not really a tarot card person," she answered flippantly.

"Scared of what she might see?"

"More like I don't want my little sister in my business."

Hazel cackled and nodded. "Yeah, I don't think I'd want my sister telling me personal stuff."

The door blew open with the half-day preschoolers and parents crowd, and in a moment, Lavender had a line nearly out the door. Any talk of Laurel being actually psychic faded while she and Hazel handled the customers.

Cookies and muffins and coffees and hot chocolates were ordered, and by the time that crowd was handled, another was on their way in. The rest of the afternoon was a flurry of activity, with barely any time for Lavender to check her phone and talk to Gavin. She kept her eye on the door though. Even as she filled orders and exchanged pleasantries with regulars, Lavender couldn't let her guard down. Miloslav might have enjoyed dramatics, but what was more dramatic than a public showdown?

Lavender missed Gavin deep in her bones. Even though it had been less than forty-eight hours since he left, she missed him. She shouldn't miss him. She'd gone thirteen awful years without him. A couple of days should have been no problem. But instead, here she was, dealing with a pang in her heart anytime the store quieted down enough for her to form a coherent thought.

She wanted to hug him. And kiss him. And wrap her body around his so they could never be separated again. Gah! This was *her* plan. She had decided to make Miloslav think he was winning. To somehow give him peace of mind so she could...force him to eat cake and then attempt to dismantle an effigy and break a curse.

When she really thought about it, it appeared she had a shitty plan.

Maybe she should call Gavin and have him come back. They were better together, right? It had been stupid to—

"Ow!" she screamed. Her hot pad had slipped, and Lavender had set her hand on a baking sheet straight out of the oven. She quickly put the tray on the counter, then rushed to the sink and stuck her hand under freezing cold water. Burns were a hazard of the work environment, but that didn't mean they didn't hurt like hell.

"Are you okay?" Hazel called, and she was quickly followed by Asher and Rosemary who were both waiting in the front scrambling into the back of the bakery.

"I'm fine. Just burned myself. Really. No big deal."

Hazel looked at her, eyebrow ticked up. Then she turned to Rosemary and Asher. "Can I talk to Lavender for a minute? Just us?"

Asher took a step toward them.

"It's fine," Lavender said quickly. She didn't need her brother-in-law acting like Hazel was an undercover Stoch.

"We'll be just in front," he reminded, as he and Rosemary disappeared back through the door.

"Okay, Lav. What the hell?"

"What? I burned myself."

"Yeah. I know. You've also been crazy distracted. Like way more than I've ever seen you. You look like you're waiting for something terrible to happen."

If Hazel only knew...

She took a breath. "Cece and I talked about this last week."

"Please don't tell me you are both quitting." Lavender couldn't handle her business falling apart on top of everything else.

"Oh, my God. No. We are worried about you. You have some serious signs of burnout. You need more help. And we both think you should think about closing the store for a few days. At least. Maybe even a month."

"Closing?"

"Yes. You need a break. A real break. And you need to hire another baker. I'm a whiz with drinks, I know it. And Cece is great at, like, remembering to take things out of the oven. But you need another baker who can actually make stuff. Someone you will trust not to mess up your recipes so you can have serious time off. You need at least two weeks a year. I think you took maybe two days this year? Including your family emergency."

"I took a couple half days for the dentist and doctor appointments."

"That doesn't count! If you are here at three in the morning baking, that counts as a workday." Hazel set her hand on Lavender's shoulder. "Look, if I thought Cece or I could come even close to making your recipes as well as you do, I would offer for us to take over. But we can't. And you've created a flawless reputation. You need to hire someone who is as good as you. Or nearly so. But until then, I think it might be a good idea to close up for a week or two."

"Close the bakery?" Lavender almost shrieked.

"Not permanently. And we're usually a little dead over Halloween with all the candy everywhere. Give yourself a vacation for the first time ever. If you want, Cece and I can still open coffee service for a few hours in the morning, just no baked goods. Come on, Lav, you need some time. I don't want you to have a mental breakdown over this. Especially with the holidays coming up. You can't go into Thanksgiving and Christmas season worn out. It'll be a disaster."

Lavender's head swam with every single reason she shouldn't close. First, she'd lose a ton of money. Her regulars would be pissed.

But...she was a witch who believed in fate. Halloween was in two days. She had a chaos warlock after her. Maybe, the universe was throwing her a raft in the middle of a storm. The Immortal Cupcake wouldn't fall apart if she closed for a week or two. It could survive.

"Let me think about it," she said softly.

"Please do. Like really think about it. Don't just say that and then work yourself to the bone until you fall down one day in the kitchen."

Lavender nodded and went back to closing up. She was nearly done. The cupcakes that she'd just pulled out of the oven were a special order, and Hazel was delivering them tonight.

She was distracted. And who could blame her? It was like every part of her life was reaching a head.

"Hey, Haz?" Lavender called once the cupcakes were cooled and frosted, all the ingredients were put away, and the kitchen was ready for the cleaning crew. "It's a good idea. I'm going to close the bakery for the next week. We don't have any special orders after this one and...you're right. I do need a break. A serious one. I'll still pay you and Cece for the week, of course. But we could all use a little time off."

"I think that's a really good idea." Hazel pulled Lavender into a hug. "Give yourself a break. Both literally and figuratively."

They closed the bakery, and Lavender added a "closed until November 6th" sign to the window. She'd get complaints, and there would be some busybodies who might come to the Bay cottage and demand she open, but hell. If Lavender didn't close the bakery when a chaos warlock was trying to steal her powers and kill her, when would she ever close it?

Lavender stayed up until two in the morning. She made unbinding cakes. She cried as she washed her dishes. She held onto Erie and took deep breaths. She texted Gavin a million times that everything here was fine. She sent him a picture of her boobs to prove it.

And then, when she finally climbed into bed with two cakes cooling in the refrigerator and a design for an effigy on a notebook next to her, she felt a burst of confidence.

Maybe.

Maybe she could do this.

Chapter Thirty-Two

Lavender and Gavin...Ruby and Arthur...Kat and Richard... Charles...Miloslav...Jonas... they stood on the ocean's edge, cold water splashing over their feet. He was between them, always between them, pushing them apart, driving each of their souls into the darkness alone.

No, no, no. She couldn't be alone. She needed him. They were two halves of the same soul. That monster couldn't do this.

Why was he so strong? Warlocks weren't supposed to be this strong.

She reached out to him, but he faded into darkness.

"No!" Gavin shouted, kicking the blankets off his legs. "Lavender!" He shook his head. Where was he? The hotel. In Chatham. Lavender had asked him to leave.

"Damn it." The dream had seemed so real. Jonas—no Miloslav—standing between them. He was separating him from Lavender. Taking her away.

Was that his actual plan? Were they stronger together?

Gavin jumped out of bed and paced the room. It was only four in the morning. Lavender would be up in an hour. He could call her then, make sure she was okay. But it was October thirtieth. Tomorrow was the day Miloslav was supposed to attack. How was he supposed to sit here in Chatham when the love of his life was in danger?

"Nope," he finally said, set in his decision. He didn't care what Miloslav Stoch wanted. He was Lavender's soulmate and he would see her through any hardship. He wasn't going to sit fifty miles away with the ocean between them while that monster wreaked havoc on the woman he loved.

He grabbed his bag and threw everything he'd brought in it. He never should have left her.

The daily ferry left Chatham at eleven, and Gavin was the first person on it, coat pulled tightly around his neck, baseball hat on. He doubted Miloslav had spies on the ferry, but if he did, he wasn't going to make it easy for them to recognize him. The sea was wild today, waves tossing the boat around reminding every passenger that humans are nothing if not at the mercy of the elements at all times. Gavin kept his eyes on the horizon, in the direction of Star Island, and concentrated on Lavender to ward off any seasickness.

Though the rest of the passengers opted to cram together in the interior of the boat, Gavin stayed on the deck. There was something about the cold wind in his face keeping him focused. Reminding him of another life, when he'd needed this type of focus before battle.

Gavin hadn't enjoyed being a soldier. But he had been English and twenty years old in 1939, when the entire world he'd known had completely gone to shit. Those years had been like a nightmare. Nearly every one of his friends had died in the war. His brother, Phillip. His cousins, Robert and Matthew. His father had died six months before it all had ended, knowing one son had beaten him to the afterlife.

And Ruby. A nurse who had signed up to heal, not kill, cut down by someone meant to be an ally.

He didn't relish the idea of another battle.

While facing the Stochs might not be on the same stage as a world war, it felt as imminent and hellish. He'd seen evil on the battlefield, participated in it, and when he looked at Miloslav, he felt that same dread he had a lifetime ago. Miloslav was a man who would burn the world for his vision. He didn't care who he hurt or whose lives were ruined in the wake of his destruction.

When Katherine's father had killed Richard...it was like a light turning off. There was no great pain or even fear—it all happened too quickly for that. But he feared them now. If any of the Stochs could snuff out a life like that man, this battle would be far worse than anything he'd experienced.

Gavin may not be magical, but he could not sit idly by. He believed in Lavender, trusted her completely. But...it was the distance. And this ocean currently crashing around him. If she were on the mainland, he would have had no problem driving an hour or so and waiting for the all clear, but he could not be beholden to a ferry timetable when his soulmate's life was at risk.

And maybe none of that mattered. Maybe if she were sitting in Boston, he'd be on his way there to hide in the shadows.

When they docked, Gavin picked up his bag and kept his head down as he disembarked. He stayed with the crowd for a while, melting in with a group of locals returning home from whatever business they had in Chatham or beyond. Then, he turned quickly away from the harbor and made his way to the hotel. He walked with purpose, like he knew where he was going, what he was doing. He kept his eyes glued to the sidewalk in front of him, then turned into the foyer of the hotel and stomped his feet before going to the front desk.

"I need a room," he said plainly, adjusting his bag on his shoulder.

"For how long?" the woman replied, typing away on her computer.

"Three nights."

The thirtieth, the thirty-first, and the first to be safe. By then, he would be back with Lavender. She would be safe in his arms. They could finally begin their lives together.

But for now, he needed to stay hidden.

MOONBEAM: How's Chatham?

GAVIN: Haven't seen much of it. Mostly hanging out in my hotel room. Told work I was leaving. Told my landlord I'd be subletting the rest of my lease.

MOONBEAM: Whoa. That's a lot.

GAVIN: Are you surprised?

MOONBEAM: No, but you didn't say anything.

GAVIN: Pretty sure I said I love you at least a hundred times this month. I'm not going to be going back and forth between Star Island and Chicago. You have an established business here. I'm obviously moving here.

MOONBEAM: Oh yeah? Where you living? LOL.

GAVIN: There's this real cute witch who likes having me around. Figure she might let me crash with her for now.

MOONBEAM: For now?

GAVIN: Yeah. Her place is kind of small. And I take up a lot of space. We might need to find someplace bigger soon.

MOONBEAM: Interesting. You seem to have it all figured out.

MOONBEAM: Are you sure you don't want to call your boss and landlord back and tell them you might be back? Just in case.

Gavin stared at the last text, his brows pinched in worry and anger. He clicked on Lavender's name and called her.

"Hi," she answered.

"Don't talk like that."

"I know. But there's always a chance—"

"I don't care if there's a chance. I love you. You love me. We get longer. We get to be happy. We get to have that life where we sit by the ocean and just enjoy each other, okay? I'm not playing into any plan that doesn't have both of us coming out of this okay. Got it?"

"Yeah," she answered softly.

"Good. Where are you?"

"My apartment. Erie is helping me finish frosting the unbinding cake."

"How's it going?"

"It'll work. As long as I can get some in every Stochs' mouth and get them to swallow it, it'll work."

"You're brilliant, you know that?"

She scoffed.

"I'm serious. You made a cake to unwind a soul from ours. That's insane."

"It's witchcraft."

"Pretty sure none of your sisters could handle that."

She laughed. "That's probably true. Only kitchen witch in my line."

"Did you write that recipe down? All your special words too?"

"I did. In case there's another witch with a chaos warlock bound to her soul who she needs to cut out of there."

"And..." Gavin took a deep breath. "You're sure it won't separate us?"

"It won't. I promise. You aren't going to eat any. None of the men are. You will stay bound to me, and Miloslav will be gone. You won't be reincarnated without me, and he can't have one with me. It's going to work. I can feel it." She didn't sound nearly as optimistic as he wanted her to.

"But?"

"But he might still win. He might still get my blood, take my power. I don't think it will stop me from finding you again. So, we will still have another chance but..."

"You think you might not be a witch anymore?"

He heard her breath catch over the phone.

"He won't."

"How do you know?"

"I just do. I have a good feeling about this life, Moonbeam. There's no war outside. No reason a lowly bricklayer can't whisk away a young lady. There's one really annoying, fucked-up monster of a man, who has a couple of sidekicks. There's no axis forces he can sell your secrets to, no father to lord over you. And you have four badass witches with you this time."

She laughed and sniffled. "True. I can't imagine what the last time would have been like if Sage was there."

"I think we've established a pattern. She would have murdered him. God, the one time I met Sage before, she was like twelve years old. Who knew that middle schooler was going to grow up to be an angel of vengeance?"

"Ha, we all did. Honestly, knowing that she is blessed by Nemesis, it makes so much sense."

"Really?"

"Oh yeah. Sage has always been like...a dark deliverer of justice." She sighed. "I wish you were here."

"I can be there as soon as possible—"

"No. Stay in Chatham. But goddess, I miss you."

"I miss you too, Moonbeam."

"I should finish the cake."

"Good luck." He paused, feeling a twinge of guilt that he could be in her apartment in ten minutes. "I love you."

"I love you too. I'll text you before I go to sleep."

Chapter Thirty-Three

Lavender stood in the woods behind the Bay cottage.

No one knew she was there. Not Sage and Will, who she assumed were fast asleep. Not Gavin who was miles away in Chatham.

The first effigy had taken ages. She didn't have that luxury.

There was no unburning wood. The original effigy was long gone, ash on the wind hundreds of years ago. She couldn't unweave it like Laurel had done with her curse of Morana.

She could only rebuild and hope that was enough.

She worked silently and quickly, gathering fallen sticks, branches, some drying shrubs. She gathered it all into a pile near the dormant herb garden. There were still hints of life among the rosemary and lavender; those hardier stalks could appear alive for much longer than the leafy plants.

Lavender slowly sliced her finger and let her blood seep into the ground. It was a risky move, what with a chaos warlock wanting exactly that. But she felt alone. And the earth responded to blood. And this was her land. She might not live on it anymore, but she had taken care of it for years. It belonged to the Bays.

She stuck her finger in her mouth and sucked until the wound stopped. Then she turned to the wood in front of her.

It was time.

The sun rose slowly on Samhain morning.

Lavender hadn't slept.

She finished while the sky turned purply-blue with the new day, then went back to her apartment and paced, trying to tire herself out to no avail. Erie had done his best to help, attempting to herd her into her bedroom like she was a sheep and he was a working dog. But after she tripped over him a third time, he gave up and went to sleep under her bed.

Her stomach was in knots, her heart beat erratically, and all she could focus on was...

That four years ago, she'd been doing pretty well. Sage was out of high school and loving the farming thing. Rosemary and Verbena both had steady work. Laurel was bringing in money only occasionally but doing fine. The bakery was making money; her sisters were all doing well.

And she hadn't thought it was time to reach out to Gavin. To be with Gavin. Four years. She could have found him, easily it sounds like. Called, texted, emailed. Asked him if they could meet up one weekend. Talk about the past, see what the future might hold. But she'd been too scared still. Afraid that any small change would throw her family into chaos again.

She'd lost four years. She'd lost thirteen years.

She'd lost so much.

Lavender didn't want to lose anything else.

"Enough of that." She shook her hands out and headed to the shower. Then she got dressed and made the strongest pot of coffee she'd ever made on her home coffee maker, added lavender simple syrup and four tablespoons of sugar. It wasn't very seasonal, in fact, it tasted like spring incarnate, but she needed it. She needed the protection of her name, and hell, she really needed the sugar and caffeine.

She stirred her coffee slowly, keeping her eyes on the swirling liquid.

"Protect the Bay line, protect the Bay line, protect the Bay line," she whispered over and over again, perhaps the last small incantation she would do if Miloslav got his way. All the little magics that filled her day would be gone in an instant, whether or not she survived it. Life as she knew it, would be gone.

She opened her Bay sister group text and started the day.

LAVENDER: Everyone okay? Night went okay?

ROSEMARY: All good here! No sign of any Stochs on our property. Have you heard from Gavin?

LAVENDER: He's in Chatham still. Didn't want to go all the way to Chicago.

VERBENA: Luke and I are good. I'm going to finish the boundary between Boris and me this morning. Once it's done, we'll walk over to the cottage.

SAGE: This is Will. Sage is still sleeping. Up late (for her) trying to recreate some of the rituals she performed as a priestess of Nemesis. But nothing really worked. We're fine though. You can come over whenever.

LAVENDER: Has anyone heard from Laurel?

VERBENA: Last night she said she was going to try some unweaving. She might have stayed up late doing it.

LAVENDER: They didn't stay with one of you?

VERBENA: I think she and Owen wanted some time alone. Before.

Before. Before they maybe lost. Maybe died. Before it might be time to start over again, in a new time and a new place, strewn across the world from her sisters, separated from Gavin until something horrible and sad brought them together.

Hell, Lavender should have let herself have one last before.

She shook her head and looked back down at the text chain.

ROSEMARY: Lav, Asher and I will pick you up in an hour, okay? We can go over together.

LAVENDER: Good idea. I also have three cakes to carry so if you could both come up, that would be great.

VERBENA: You made three cakes? Are two for fun?

LAVENDER: Sadly, none of them are fun Samhain cakes. I'll have to go crazy on Yule to make up for it. I made four cakes. All unbinding. If something happens to them, I want to have some backups. I'm going to leave one here just in case.

VERBENA: I guess there is always the chance the Stochs all puke and we have to jam more down their throats until enough stays down.

ROSEMARY: Or someone just drops a cake. I don't care if the Stochs have to eat cake with dust or hair on it, but I would really rather not.

LAVENDER: Hence the multiple cakes. Okay. I'll see you in a bit Rosemary.

LAVENDER: Laurel check in when you can.

The Bay cottage felt different this Samhain.

Last year, it had been a wild celebration. Laurel had read everyone's cards, no exceptions. Lavender had made a fall feast—butternut squash roasted with cinnamon and sugar, sweet potato and pumpkin pies, homemade bread with pear jelly, and a slow-roasted beef tenderloin with balsamic vinegar, thyme, and an herbed butter rub. They'd had wine and laughed until midnight, carved pumpkins and handed out candy to neighborhood kids brave enough to ring the bell at the witch's house—meaning Laurel, of course. They'd dressed in black and cackled and everything was full of joy.

A somber blanket lay over the cottage today. No pumpkins ready to be carved, no feast being prepared in the kitchen.

Sage and Will were on the couch, talking quietly when they walked in.

"Happy Samhain," Sage said dryly. "Ready to kick the absolute shit out of Miloslav?"

"You sound ready." Lavender laughed, then pulled her sister into a hug. "Happy Samhain."

Rosemary rooted through her purse. "Will make sure Sage is taking these every day. Now that it's officially the dark time of the year, she's going to need a bit of a boost."

Will took the bottle from her and turned it over in his hands. "What is it? A tincture?"

"No, vitamin D supplements. She needs them more than most." Rosemary grinned devilishly. "The vitamin D you are providing her with doesn't have the same effect as sunlight."

"Rosemary, I swear to Nemesis. We are on death's doorstep waiting for a man whose soul I've killed at least four times, and you are making a dick joke?" Sage shook her head.

"If I'm not making a dick joke, the world has truly ended. And I thought you only killed him three times?"

"Apparently, I killed him in Raetia at some point! I didn't even get to see it!"

"Where the hell is Raetia?" Lavender asked.

"It was neighbors with the Roman Empire, and then part of the Roman Empire. If we make it through the night, I might need another slice of past-life bread so I can relive a couple more lives and watch myself murder Miloslav. It was so refreshing."

"Uh, let's hold off on that for a bit. I didn't love getting stabbed in the stomach," Will interjected.

Lavender burst out laughing.

What a family she had. An amazing family.

The door slammed open and Owen pushed through with his arms around Laurel.

"What happened?" Lavender shouted, running toward them.

"Morana." Owen grimaced, then walked Laurel to the couch and sat her down. She was pale but awake and breathing hard. "Tried to put her hands on Laurel when we were getting into the car. She came out of nowhere. She must have followed us last night and waited until our guard was down. I didn't think any of them knew where we lived."

"Why did she grab you?" Lavender picked up a blanket and handed it to Laurel.

"I think she was trying to drag me back into the Hedge World. We've still got a weird connection. Fuck, my heart is beating so fast."

"Take some deep breaths." Lavender walked into the kitchen and filled a glass with water, then brought it to her sister. "You're safe inside. We're here."

Laurel looked at Owen as she tried to steady her breath. "Are they on their way?"

Owen nodded.

"I'm sorry, is who on their way?" Sage asked.

"The Davies water witches. I met them at Aidan's wedding. We need them."

"We don't know them," Rosemary said slowly.

"I do. And they know Owen. And most of all, they really fucking hate warlocks who don't stay in their place." She threw a look at Will. "No offense."

"None taken. Never in a million years would I think I was more powerful than one of the Davies water witches." He paused. "Should I call my mom? And Cate?"

"No. They are too far away to help. I'm sure Owen's cousins will be the backup we need. If they can even get here. Plus, isn't Cate super pregnant? And she has children. She shouldn't...she shouldn't risk it."

Laurel pulled the blanket up to her chin. "Morgan'll come. Probably Millicent. Molly's in Illinois, I don't know if she can make it. Even if it's just Morgan. It'll help. They can...go by water. It's faster for them."

Lavender nodded. "If Morana is already trying to attack Laurel, I think we can assume Miloslav and company will be here sooner rather than later. I'm going to text Verbena and see what her ETA is."

She took a deep breath. This was it. The last day of the prophecy. They could do this. They could win this. They had to.

"I did it!" Verbena shrieked as she walked through the door. "I unbound Boris from Luke, Danny, and me!" Dutifully behind her, Luke and Danny walked in, smiling, but less exuberant.

"Holy shit. How do you know?"

"She did." Danny said quietly. "I felt it happen."

"We all did," Verbena continued. "It's hard to explain, but sort of like there was this weight on my chest, that I didn't know was there. It had been there since I was born. And now it's gone. Boris will never find us in another life. I feel amazing."

"I'm so proud of you." Lavender pulled Verbena into her arms. "You are amazing."

"Too bad all the Stochs aren't dead. Then we could have Verbena do that for all of us, and we'd be set." Sage raised her eyebrows.

"We can't kill three people," Lavender reminded.

"I'm still not one hundred percent sold on that. They are terrorizing us. Have tried to kill almost everyone in this house and have literally been biting us on the street. I don't think it would be a huge leap for a jury to believe they broke into our house and we killed them in self-defense. Asher? Thoughts? As a former police officer?"

"For that to work, every one of us would have to lie on the stand and say that your story is what happened, and not that there is some curse on your bloodline."

"I could never lie on the stand," Rosemary admitted. "I don't think any of us could, right? An oath is an oath, even if it's sworn on an object and not our souls."

"Damn. I forgot about that whole I swear to tell the truth bullshit." Sage scrunched up her face. "Maybe Miloslav will run at me with a weapon, and then I wouldn't have to lie. There has to be a witch practicing law in Massachusetts who would be able to lead the questions in the right way. Here's hoping."

"I'm...going to get some air," Lavender said quickly, then ducked into the kitchen and out the back door.

The effigy was still there. No animal had knocked it over during the hours she had left. It was small—much smaller than the one Katherine had made. And it was different. The first had been a woman, but a woman so filled with darkness and pain.

This was an offering to hope. To sisterly love. To soulmates.

"Whoa. You actually did it," Laurel breathed beside her. "You made an effigy."

"Please don't tell anyone else," Lavender said quietly. "I need...I need to have this ready to go if we need it."

Laurel nodded. "But make a promise. When you try to use it, I want to help."

"Laurel—"

"No. I started all of this looking for Owen in the Hedge World. You and I both died casting a curse. Maybe if we're doing it together, breaking the curse together, the power of it will spread between both of us. Plus, I've broken a curse. I'm your sister. Don't do it alone."

Lavender wrapped her arm around Laurel and sighed. "I won't."

They all took their separate posts.

Laurel and Owen climbed the stairs to her old bedroom. Laurel was going to check out the Hedge World for a minute, then go back to attempting to break the curse on her own. She'd been a bit off all day, almost like she had one foot in the real world and the other in the Hedge World. Her mind was more than distracted.

Verbena circled the interior of the house, looking for any gaps in her boundaries that needed to be filled. Luke and Danny sat on the back screened porch, making certain the Stochs weren't coming from Luke's land.

Asher and Rosemary had the front door, Asher in front, Rosemary behind him, ready to block any ill that might befall her.

Sage and Will sat in the parlor. They talked in low tones and by the look on Sage's face, Lavender was certain he was trying to convince her youngest sister not to go to prison today. Best of luck to him. The more Lavender learned about Sage's past lives, the more she thought that was a very real possibility.

And Lavender was alone. She sliced the cake and handed out pieces, which were eaten quickly and without question. She took her plate to the table and sat down, then pulled her phone out.

LAVENDER: In my apartment, there's an extra cake in the fridge. If you don't hear from me tomorrow, I put a key under my welcome mat. Wait until night, then get yourself a slice of cake in case Miloslav ever finds you and make him eat it. And please take Erie. I love you.

GAVIN: Please don't send me texts like that. What is happening right now?

LAVENDER: We're waiting. But I don't know. This feels real and scary.

GAVIN: Can I come?

LAVENDER: No. I don't think I could concentrate if I was worrying about you too. Almost everyone I love is in danger right now. I need you to be okay or I won't be able to handle it.

GAVIN: Text me the second you want me there. Okay?

LAVENDER: I will. Just remember the cake in the fridge, take a slice for Miloslav, and take care of Erie. Love you.

GAVIN: Love you, Moonbeam.

Lavender looked at the time, then slipped her phone into her pocket. Four thirty-one. It would be dark in less than an hour.

Miloslav was waiting for the cover of darkness. Add another layer to his chaos.

But witches didn't fear the dark. They'd lived in it for centuries.

"Hey," Owen interrupted her thoughts. "My cousins are on their way to help. Morgan and Maeve from Maine. Sea and storm. Millicent, the swamp witch, is coming from South Carolina. She has to hitchhike part of the way, but she can be very persuasive. Molly is coming from Illinois. I don't know if she'll make it, but if it's all gone sideways, she'll be there to help in the end."

"Thank you," Lavender answered. "I'm glad to know the Davies water witches will be supporting us."

"Always." He paused. "And they won't have to wait for the ferry. They can make the swim in no time."

Lavender rolled her neck and walked into the kitchen. She had another potion to prepare.

Chapter Thirty-Four

At eight-thirty, Lavender's anxiety crept down her throat and rested in her belly.

Where were they?

The smattering of trick-or-treaters who had been very surprised when Asher had opened the door and not a jolly Bay sister had gone home a while ago. The streets were too dark this late on Halloween, so those who were still out would be in town hitting up the houses that were closer together and well lit. They'd switched the porch light off a few minutes earlier to further dissuade anyone from coming to their house tonight.

"Do you think they are waiting until the veil is at its thinnest?" Sage muttered.

"I hope not." On Samhain, the veil was always thin, but times of transition—noon, sunrise, sunset...midnight—were even more fragile when it came to the barrier between the worlds.

They stayed on edge, peeking out windows and stretching their legs, waiting until the Stochs would finally appear.

At ten thirty-one, the air around them shifted, felt heavier, and crackled with magic.

"Fuck, he's here." Sage jumped to her feet and grabbed Will. She pressed a kiss against his mouth and said, "I love you."

"I love you too," Will answered.

"They're here!" Lavender shouted through the house. Keeping quiet seemed ridiculous. The Stochs knew they were there.

Asher wrapped his arm around Rosemary. "Stay close to me," he said.

"I will."

"Is the chaos magic going to seep into the house?" Lavender asked.

"I hope not. But they are pushing like hell on the boundaries right now." Verbena ran to the parlor window and quickly crossed her hands over it. "Shit. They've been studying."

"Boundary magic?"

"It's Ivan. He's trying to do his metal control to bypass the spell work I've laid down."

"Can you change the metal like you did before?" Rosemary asked. "Make it all plastic?"

"I can try." Verbena took a seat on the floor. "Keep your eyes open. It's hard to control everything in the house. I'm going to focus on big stuff."

Lavender dashed into the kitchen and grabbed a glass bowl, poured the contents she had been boiling into it, and then tossed the pan into a cabinet, dripping and all. Ivan might still be able to control the metal, but she'd give him an obstacle with the wooden door. She dipped two vials into the bowl, capped them, and stuck them into her pocket.

"Front door!" Verbena yelled. "I can't...it's too many things!" Asher barricaded his body in front of the door with Rosemary behind him holding onto his waist.

"It's going to bust open!" Rosemary shrieked. "I can feel it. Get behind something!"

Lavender ducked behind the chest in the dining room, where Luke was wrapped around Verbena. Danny upended the dining table and crouched behind it. Sage and Will jumped behind the couch, and Owen pulled Laurel into the kitchen, then lay on top of her on the ground.

The door exploded into pieces, splintering all over the parlor. The house was full of screams.

No. Their beautiful house.

Lavender pushed onto her hands and knees and looked at Luke and Danny. "With me, now." She sprinted to the kitchen, the two men close on her heels. She stopped at the kitchen counter in front of one of the cakes.

"Two handfuls each. I've got Morana. Luke take Miloslav, Danny take Ivan. You know who is who?"

"Yeah. We've met them." Luke grimaced. As distant cousins to the Stochs, this wasn't Luke and Danny's first time running into this family.

"They have to swallow it and hopefully keep it down." She turned back to the parlor. Asher and Rosemary had been knocked to the ground but were moving out of the way backward, like someone was coming toward them.

"Sage!" Lavender yelled. Her sister's attention snapped to her. "Protect Verbena." They'd all be screwed if someone knocked Verbena out, and her alchemy stopped working.

Sage nodded and darted to the dining room with Will close behind.

Lavender trained her eyes on the door. "When I say so, just run at the door. Grab them and get this into their mouths. If nothing else, we aren't going to be bound to them anymore. None of us. Got it?"

Luke and Danny nodded.

"Ready?" Lavender watched the spot on the front porch just in front of the threshold. Suddenly, the tip of a shadow was visible. "Now!" She took off running, through the kitchen and dining room, across the parlor and took two steps on the porch.

Morana came into view. Her brothers were there too, but she focused on Morana. Only Morana. The witch who'd started it all. The woman who'd tortured Laurel. Her baby sister.

She tackled her to the ground. They hit the stairs with a thud, and Lavender smacked her knee so hard it rang through her body, but before Morana could register what was going on, Lavender smashed the cake against her face. It went in her mouth, her nose, her eyes—Morana thrashed, but Lavender held on until she saw her throat bob as she swallowed.

"Down!" she shouted with glee, just as Morana threw her off and into the bushes. Lavender rolled into the darkness, then risked a look at the porch. Luke punched Miloslav twice in the stomach, then hit him in the face with the cake, so forcefully it knocked him off his feet. She watched Miloslav swallow, then kick out at Luke, who hit the porch. Danny headbutted Ivan in the face, who doubled over and held his forehead, just as Danny took a handful of cake and shoved it in his mouth.

"Sleep!" Miloslav yelled and in a second Luke and Danny crumpled to the ground. "What the fuck is in my mouth?" he shouted.

"Chocolate? Trying to choke us? Who knows." Morana climbed off the stairs.

Lavender didn't wait for them to find her. She jumped to her feet and sprinted around the side of the house as fast as she could. Her knee screamed in pain, but she ignored it. She would worry about her knee if they made it until morning. Her lungs burned as she went, but she had to get back into the Bay cottage. She needed to help her sisters.

The house was in chaos as she rounded into the backyard. She could hear everyone yelling, Sage above all. Lavender crept onto the screened porch but stayed in the shadows.

"Back for more? You tell your siblings about all the times I took you down?" Sage was moving toward him, keeping his eyes off Verbena. Will stood in front of her, blocking her from view.

"Nemesis is the one who killed me!" Miloslav shouted back. He had his hand up toward Rosemary and Asher. They weren't injured, but they looked stuck.

"Um, once? I'm pretty sure I took care of the rest of those untimely ends." Sage looked over all the Stochs. "Morana. Good to see you. Looking forward to punching you in the face again. Ivan. Wanna step out to the apple orchard?"

"Fuck off," Ivan grumbled. He scanned the room. "There's the one stopping me." He pointed to Verbena. Miloslav raised his hand just as Ivan rubbed his together.

"Stop!" Lavender shouted and burst into the kitchen. "I'm here. Leave her alone. And for the love of every god and goddess, do not destroy a house that witches have lived in for centuries, Ivan. No one would be able to stop the curses that rained on you with an action like that."

Ivan looked at Miloslav, who shrugged, then put his hands down.

They stood frozen for a moment, with Miloslav, Morana, and Ivan in the middle of the parlor. Verbena and Will crouched in the dining room, Lavender in the kitchen doorway, Sage standing opposite the Stochs, and Laurel and Owen on the stairs.

"Did you hurt Luke and Danny?" Verbena demanded.

"They're taking a little nap. Couldn't really hurt them, you know?

Bringing down a curse on my own blood? I'm not stupid. We protect our own."

"Let's come up with a truce," Lavender said slowly. "We just want this to stop. Sage doesn't want to kill you anymore."

"Don't speak for me," Sage growled. "I only want to kill him when he partakes in behavior that is deserving. You know. Simple things like murder and attempted rape."

"Good thing I haven't done any of those things this time," Miloslav said as he grinned. "Your little ethical heart isn't going to be able to handle it."

"Oh, trying to steal my magic is on the list. Biting my sisters on the street and beating the crap out of my soulmate sounds like pretty good motivation for you to come after me. I've always wanted to use a self-defense plea." Sage cracked her knuckles and rolled her neck.

"Stop it! Both of you." Lavender slowly walked between Sage and Miloslav. She couldn't watch. Couldn't watch Sage kill Miloslav and risk going to prison. Couldn't watch Miloslav win. She had to do something else.

She looked at Rosemary, the only sister convinced they would all make it out of this alive. She was behind Asher still, but she looked between Lavender and the lemon tree standing next to the window.

A tree.

Lavender had seen what Rosemary could do with a tree.

"Where's Erebus?" Sage asked. "Not hanging out at the moment?"

"I don't see Nemesis coming to your aid," Miloslav bit back.

Rosemary carefully turned her palms outward and closed her eyes. Slowly, the tree limbs grew and reached out, creaking slightly, but no one noticed over the arguing.

"Nemesis knows I can handle myself most of the time. Hell, she's only had to bail me out once. And what was the age difference in Rhamnous? Pretty sure I was sitting at about fifteen and you were close to forty. Right?"

"Doesn't matter," Miloslav scoffed.

"Loser is the only one who thinks that!"

That did it. He went from calmly bantering with Sage to all-out pissed. In a moment, Will fell to his knees behind Sage.

"Fuck!" Sage screamed and grabbed Will. "Stop hurting him!"

"If I can't hurt you, earth witch, I'm going to hurt the person who matters most to you." Miloslav flicked his wrist, and Will howled.

Sage jumped to her feet and rushed Miloslav, punching him in the face and breaking his concentration.

"Stop!" Lavender screamed, but her voice was drowned out by screams from all the Stochs. The lemon tree was now wrapped around the torsos of both Morana and Ivan, inching toward Miloslav.

"What the..." Miloslav muttered just as the branch tangled over him as well.

"Stop hurting Will," Rosemary commanded. "And don't fuck with my mind. I'm holding the tree back. It'll split the three of you in two."

"How you going to explain that to the police? Three half bodies in your living room?"

Verbena crawled from the dining room and grabbed Lavender's hand. "Wake up Luke and Danny." Verbena commanded Miloslav.

"Or what?" Ivan laughed. "Good little witches can't do anything bad."

Verbena looked at Lavender and ticked her eyebrow up.

"Maybe it's time we stopped being good."

Chapter Thirty-Five

Gavin turned his phone over in his hand rhythmically.

No texts from Lavender, no calls. Nothing from Rosemary either. Or Asher. The pit in his stomach was the size of the Grand Canyon.

He wanted to call or text...but what if they were hiding? What if Lavender forgot to turn her phone off, and his stupid text told Miloslav where she was?

His mind was awash with all the terrible what-ifs he could imagine.

What if she was already gone? What if Miloslav had already won and he never saw her again? He couldn't...he couldn't do that again. His time as Arthur had been a life less than half lived.

He needed Lavender.

He paced around the hotel room like a caged animal. He couldn't just stay here. Right? He had to go to her.

But Lavender said she didn't want him there.

Maybe...maybe he would just run down to The Muse and see if Luke was in. Or if any of the other employees there had heard from him. Yeah. That was more noncommittal.

He slid his boots and coat on, then dashed down the hall toward the front door.

"Hey! Why are you running?" The girl behind the front desk looked positively terrified.

"Oh. No reason. Thought I would speed down to The Muse and grab a drink before they closed."

She laughed. "Sir, it's a weekday in October. The Muse closed at ten-thirty. You've missed last call, I'm afraid. Everything's closed by now. The restaurants, the market. If you didn't get yourself some alcohol for your room, you're out of luck."

"Ah. Okay." He looked at the door nervously. "Maybe I'll just go for a walk then?"

"Suit yourself. It's cold and windy though. Maybe pop back to your room and grab a hat and gloves. Scarf too. And don't go on the beach. The waves can come up pretty high in this weather, and no one is relishing a night swim to save a tourist when it's this cold. If anyone even realizes you've gone in." She picked up her magazine and went back to reading.

"Good idea," he muttered, then walked back to his room. He grabbed his hat and gloves. He didn't have a scarf. But every moment that passed, he felt more uneasy. Something was wrong, really wrong. He needed to get to Lavender.

No car. No cabs. No bike.

Gavin would walk to the Bay cottage.

No. He would run.

He changed his clothes, put on the running gear he'd barely used since getting here. Ignored the woman at the desk who made some sort of comment as he walked by and pushed out into the cold autumn air.

Gavin took two minutes to stretch. He didn't want to waste any more time, but thirty-five wasn't twenty-five. If he pulled his calf in a mile, he'd be really pissed he hadn't taken the few moments to stop that from happening.

Then he turned toward the interior of the island and took off.

He might not have cared much about his running times before, but tonight it mattered. He would get to Lavender as quickly as possible.

The island was nearly pitch black once he crossed out of Solaris. Every once in a while, light spilled from someone's bedroom window, but for the most part, the small flashlight on Gavin's phone bobbing along in time as he ran was the only thing illuminating his path.

It felt foreboding but also appropriate.

He was running through the dark to get to Lavender. He'd run through anything to get to her.

Chapter Thirty-Six

The sound emitting from Ivan Stoch's mouth was akin to a horror movie. His howls were deep and low and nearly unnatural.

"What the fuck..." Miloslav mumbled. He grabbed his brother's arm and shook him, then pulled his arm back and stared at his hand.

Lavender wouldn't have believed it if she didn't watch it happen with her own eyes. Miloslav's hand wasn't...hand-shaped anymore. It was like watching ice cream slowly melt and lose its shape in the summer sun.

"As I said, please wake up Luke and Danny," Verbena reiterated.

"Do what she says!" Ivan screamed. "Now!" A gurgling sound from Morana joined her brother's screams. They both sagged against the branches of the lemon tree keeping them from falling to the floor.

"This is interesting," Miloslav said, inspecting his hand. "I didn't know house witches could affect reality."

Verbena huffed. "Nothing about reality getting shifted. The bones in your hand, Miloslav's shin, and Morana's feet are now made of jelly. As in a jellyfish."

His eyes narrowed. "An alchemist?"

"Wake up Luke and Danny. I'd love to test this out on more important parts of you, like your heart. Or your brain."

"Can't believe Luke landed an alchemist." Miloslav threw his good hand in the direction of the porch. They could hear Luke and Danny moving around. "I'd like my bones back."

"Luke? Danny? You okay?"

"Yes," they both called.

Verbena nodded at the Stochs and their bones were restored.

"Fascinating sister you have here," Miloslav said to Lavender. "The gloves are coming off of the Bay witches, I see." He smirked and, in a moment, Verbena hit the floor.

Lavender opened her mouth to scream, but her vision started to go cloudy. In the moments before it all went dark, she saw Sage jump on Miloslav, breaking through the branches and taking him to the ground.

The world was gone.

Her sisters, the cottage, even the Stochs—everything had disappeared. Lavender knew she must still be on the floor of the dining room. She knew that the Stochs were still there, that Sage was trying to beat Miloslav into submission.

But here, Lavender was alone in the dark.

It was almost like being hidden in the back of a closet under rows of winter coats. There were muffled noises and clangs that shook the ground, but everything felt so far away.

Lavender pawed around, patting her hands up and down her body.

She needed to break the curse. And she needed to do it before Sage killed anyone.

She knew Sage. She would throw her life away for all of them. She would do anything for her sisters.

But Lavender was the oldest. The protector. This was her role, what it actually meant, when she became their guardian. Not unlike Asher's role with Rosemary, Lavender's job was to protect her younger sisters. And there was a chaos warlock trying to destroy her family.

Lavender closed her eyes and focused. She had never tried this type of magic, but desperate times...

Witches were always more powerful when their feet were held against the flames.

Aunt June. Pull me out. Please. Get me out of this state. Let me fight. I need to fight.

She repeated it over and over again, calling to the ghost of her bloodline. Calling to the woman who had given them so much over the years. The warden of the Bay cottage.

Destroy them. June's voice rang clearly in her head.

Lavender blinked her eyes open but didn't move. She shifted her hand slightly and felt for the vials. They were still in her pocket.

She took stock of the room. Ivan and Morana were still wrapped up by the tree and looked close to unconscious. Sage grappled with Miloslav, while Luke tried to shake Verbena awake.

Laurel stayed on the stairs, looking at everything below. She locked eyes with Lavender and mouthed, "Go."

She ran. Maybe she should have slunk toward him, not given him a chance to counter her, but Lavender was too worried she would lose her nerve.

She hit Miloslav hard, knocking him off Sage and onto the ground. She scrambled to gain higher ground, kneeling on his arms as she unplugged the vial and dumped it over his face. He buckled and knocked her off her place, sending Lavender sliding across the floor.

He screamed as he clawed at his face, then dove toward her.

"Lavender!" She looked to the doorway in time to see Gavin rushing over the threshold. He grabbed Miloslav's shoulders, trying to pull him off Lavender.

"Get off her!" Gavin shouted. He pulled at his arms, but Miloslav threw an elbow back and connected with his nose, then looked back down at Lavender.

And in that moment, she knew she'd lost.

They'd lost. Gavin was here but...Verbena was unconscious, Rosemary was using all her strength to hold back Ivan and Morana, Sage was bleeding and—

"Finally," Miloslav hissed, grabbed her wrist, and bit into her forearm.

She still fought—fought with everything she had—Gavin came back, his face a bloodied mess, crawling over Miloslav like a wild animal.

The chaos warlock finally let go, his lips stained red once again.

It was done.

Gavin pushed past Miloslav and dove to her.

"Gavin," Lavender called, reaching up to her soulmate. "Your...your face."

"I'm okay. Your arm..." Gavin buried his face against Lavender's neck.

"It's all right. At least this time, I'm in your arms." She held on to Gavin with everything she had. As if she could stay with him just out of sheer force of will.

"You are supposed to be in Chatham," she finally said.

"I've been at the hotel. On Star Island." Gavin pulled back and pressed a kiss to her forehead. "Couldn't leave you again."

The room was oddly still, like they were all waiting for something to happen. The sisters hadn't dropped dead, which was a good sign. But all eyes were on Miloslav.

All the spells in the room loosened their hold. The lemon tree shrank back to its normal shape. Verbena stirred awake and Luke pulled her into his arms.

Would they be able to tell when he powered up? And what would losing her magic feel like?

"Told you to have him leave. Remember? Made a deal with you that Arthur wouldn't be a part of this if only he was gone. Now he's a witness," Miloslav said.

"Not the only witness." Asher sneered. "You going to kill all eleven of us?"

"Keep hiding behind your Guardian magic," Miloslav shot back. He brushed his hand over his face, then shook his head like he was trying to clear it of something. He groaned a little, rubbed his arm and his neck.

Finally. He was feeling the effects of Lavender's poison. He may not have gotten any in his mouth, but his eyes or nose would work too.

"What the...what the hell was in that?"

Lavender stayed silent.

"Tell me!" He shouted now, but she stayed by Gavin, wrapped in her soulmate's arms.

Miloslav fell to his hands and knees with a thud.

Gavin looked up from his place beside Lavender. "What did you give him?"

"Pain. It won't last long. But he's getting all the pain he's caused us. In this life. I couldn't figure out how to compound all the lives. That would have been a treat. But"—Lavender pushed herself to her feet with help from Gavin— "We have a minute now." She looked over her family. Rosemary looked exhausted, Verbena had her head in her hands, Sage looked like she'd gone five rounds in the ring. Laurel looked at Lavender and then her gaze flicked to the rest of the sisters.

Rosemary, Sage, and Verbena. Stop Ivan and Morana from following Lavender and me outside. Laurel's voice was in all their heads.

Lavender squeezed Gavin's hand. "Stay with me," she whispered, hoping the Stochs wouldn't notice.

Lavender looked at Laurel and nodded.

In a flash, Lavender and Laurel were dashing out of the living room with Gavin and Owen close behind. Morana and Ivan were screaming, but Lavender didn't turn around to see what was happening to them.

She needed to get to the effigy.

Maybe she still had enough time.

They skidded outside, stopping in front of the small effigy.

"No," Gavin said immediately. "You're not doing this again."

Lavender gave him a look, then turned to her sister. "Miloslav got my blood. Why isn't it over?"

Owen looked at Laurel, then back at Lavender, saying nothing, but conveying the opposite with his expression.

"It's not over," Laurel said quickly, grabbing Lavender's hand. "We're going to work together. This curse is strong. It needs more than one witch. We're going to break this curse together."

It wasn't over? But how? There were no other living Bays. Lavender had done her due diligence last May when Morana had begun terrorizing Laurel. Their lines all led to them or died out. There were no hidden Bays.

But Laurel clearly wasn't done fighting. So, she wouldn't be either.

Chapter Thirty-Seven

"Stop. It's still too dangerous," Gavin yelled. He pulled Lavender back to him. "You can't."

Lavender paused and looked back at him. "I might die in the next few minutes. Miloslav has all of our blood. And when I'm gone he might kill you too."

"You seem oddly calm about it," Gavin answered, bringing his hands up to cup her face.

"I'm a witch. I'm made of magic. I can cast curses, and I can break them. This is who I am. And I'm not dead yet. Maybe Miloslav isn't as powerful as we thought." She pressed her forehead against his. "I need to try."

Resignation washed over him.

This was who she was. Lavender was a witch, a protector, a bleeding heart who would save the world if she could. Would sacrifice everything for the greater good.

And if he didn't love her even more for all of that.

"I love you, Gavin Murphy. I could apologize for the rest of my life, but one last time, I'm sorry I wasted so many years away from you."

Gavin wrapped his arms around her and buried his face in her hair. "I'm sorry I left you when I panicked. Never again."

"Never."

She went up to her tiptoes and kissed him softly. His face was as bloodied as her arm, but they didn't care. One last kiss was always worth it.

Lavender turned away from him and looked past him.

"Um," she said slowly. "May I help you?"

Gavin turned and saw three unfamiliar women standing in the backyard against the house.

"You made it!" Owen yelled. He and Laurel rushed to the women, embracing all of them, including the absolutely terrifying one who looked like she'd crawled out of a swamp a few minutes ago.

"These are my cousins: Morgan, Millicent, and Maeve," Owen said, pointing to each of them.

"Molly is out front," Morgan added. "There was a very injured human there. She'll get him taken care of." She turned to Owen. "Are we too late?"

"No."

"Sort of," Lavender interrupted. "The chaos warlock got everything he needed. We don't know why we're still magical. He'll come into his powers soon, though. And no one should be near him when that happens."

"We'll take our chances." Morgan looked at Laurel and Lavender. "You two have something to complete, no? Why don't Owen and...that guy show us how we can help." Her eyes glinted for a moment, almost like they were flashing silver, and Gavin suddenly wasn't sure if it was safer to be with these women or the Stochs.

"I don't want to leave Lavender," Gavin said quickly.

"Go for a second. Make sure Rosemary, Verbena, and Sage are okay. Then come right back." She pressed a kiss to his jaw.

"One second," Gavin promised, then followed Owen.

Walking back into the Bay cottage was like walking into a disaster scene. The one sister, Molly, stayed on the front porch with Luke and Danny, but the other three followed Lavender and Gavin into the parlor, where Miloslav still writhed on the ground and Morana and Ivan were bound by Rosemary's tree.

"I don't think I can hold them much longer," Rosemary panted. "We need to do something else."

The scariest looking of the new witches, Millicent, stepped forward and looked at Morana. "What did this one do?"

"Tried to steal Laurel's powers. Tried to kill Laurel. Had Laurel burned as a witch in another life," Owen answered.

Millicent clucked her tongue. "Oh dear. You betrayed a sister in craft?"

"She cursed me over lifetimes in retribution!" Morana gasped.

"Well-deserved." Millicent looked over the bound witch as if she was searching for details, then smelled her like a lion smells its prey. "A hedge witch? Interesting. Laurel is one as well. You're a dark little bunch." She shook her head. "I could forgive it if all you did was kill her yourself. But dragging another witch out into the light? No, no. We cannot abide that sort of behavior. Especially one connected to the Davies. We'd lose our reputation." Millicent put her hands on Morana's head and hummed low.

Gavin's eyes went wide. He didn't know what she was doing but the air felt heavy with terror.

"Millicent." Owen's voice was sharp over everything else. "Leave it."

She stopped and looked at her cousin. "You want her to go unpunished? After all she did to your soulmate? You are too soft for this world, cousin."

"I'm not. I... Don't add her blood to your hands."

Millicent scoffed. "I wasn't going to kill her. Just put a little leash around her powers."

"What do you mean, a leash?" Sage asked.

"It's like a muzzle for a witch who can't be trusted around her kind. She'll still be able go into the Hedge World and practice divination. But no more spells or curses."

Owen looked over his shoulder toward the yard where Laurel and Lavender were.

"Do it."

Morana screamed. "No! Mercy! Mercy! Please! Do not take a witch's powers from her! You will be cursed in later lives!"

Millicent grinned. "I'm already cursed in later lives. Might as well do all I can in this one." She grabbed Morana's head and pressed their heads together.

Gavin couldn't watch.

Morana howled, and he could hear her feet smashing against the ground, and then silence.

"Go home," Millicent commanded.

"But. I can't. The ferry. My brothers."

"These warlocks are not who you should be working with." Gavin turned around to see Millicent helping Morana to her feet. "You need a coven. Do not fraternize with these types of warlocks—especially those who work with metal and chaos. You are a hedge witch. *Do not waste your life in the service of men.*" She said the last bit like an incantation, her voice rich with power.

Morana looked like she'd been slapped across the face. She stared at her brothers for a moment, Ivan still held in the branches by Rosemary, Miloslav on the floor, twitching but unconscious. Then she turned and walked out of the house and into the darkness.

Gavin shook his head and looked around. Rosemary was okay, if faltering a little. But with Morana gone, she was only holding Ivan. Verbena was on the front porch with Luke, Danny, and another new witch. And Sage and Will stood over a writhing Miloslav.

"I don't suppose you can muzzle the chaos warlock while he is still out cold?" Sage mused. "He'll have the full force of the Bay witches when he wakes."

Millicent furrowed her brow and looked over Miloslav. "He doesn't feel that powerful. And look—the garden witch is still using her powers, right?"

Like a shot, Miloslav jumped to his feet and ran at Sage. He knocked her to the ground, then looked back up wildly.

"Sleep," he commanded, driving every Davies witch to the ground, as well as Rosemary, Asher, and Will. Ivan shook off the branches and scrambled next to his brother.

Gavin stood his ground with Owen beside him. He looked at Sage, who was rubbing the back of her head. Verbena and the other witch on the front porch had slumped.

Miloslav had left the humans conscious. And Sage. He couldn't control Sage. But she didn't look good.

"Ivan," Miloslav said slowly and in a moment, there were knives hanging in the air around everyone still awake.

"Thank you. Now. Why on earth do I feel the same? I've gotten the blood of all five living, magical Bay witches. So. Who are they hiding?" He looked at Gavin and Owen.

"No one," Gavin answered.

"I swear it on my soul. There are no other living Bay witches who we know about. Their mother is dead. She had no magical siblings. There are no more Bays," Owen added.

Miloslav's face pinched. "That's impossible. I remember the curse work. It is sound." He looked around the room, while Gavin tried to think of a way he could get the hell out of there and back by Lavender's side.

But he couldn't. He needed to keep Miloslav here. And if he died doing it...it would be worth saving Lavender.

Suddenly Miloslav laughed. "Oh. How did I miss that? All fertile women, fucking their soulmates daily, no doubt. I didn't get all the blood today, did I?" He walked to Verbena on the front porch, crouched down and smelled her. "Not you."

Why was he smelling them?

Oh, shit. He said fertile. Was one of them pregnant? Was that messing with the spell?

Miloslav walked over to Rosemary and rolled her over before smelling her. "Not you either." He turned his head back to Owen and Gavin, then grinned.

"Oh. Someone smells upset. Is Daddy feeling protective already?" he mocked.

"Stay away from her," Owen bit.

"Aw, a sonofawitch thinks he can stand up to a chaos warlock? I doubt it."

"You're spread too thin," Owen said slowly walking toward Miloslav. "If you weren't, we'd all be asleep. You're holding eight people's minds. That's a lot of work, even for you. And Ivan," he continued. "You've got every knife in this house in perfect position. Wouldn't want to accidentally stab your brother. Or yourself."

"Sit down!" Miloslav boomed, and Owen hit the ground. He stomped past Owen. "I've had this spell work laid for hundreds of years, unable to complete the spell, and now I have it in my grasp. A *hedge* witch will not stop me."

Gavin acted. With every bit of strength he had, he pushed Miloslav toward Ivan and ran to the backyard.

If anything, he needed to warn them.

He felt a knife scrape against his arm, but he didn't stop. He heard Owen grunt and bodies hit the floor.

Gavin had to get to Lavender.

Chapter Thirty-Eight

"What do we do?" Laurel asked as they hurried to the effigy. It was loud in the house. Morana was screaming, other people were talking. They had no idea how long they had.

"I've been trying to figure it out. Burning it laid the curse. So not that. Maybe..." Lavender searched her mind. "The other elements. We aren't going to burn it. We could drown it but..." The closest small creek was at least a mile walk, and they'd have to bring the effigy.

"No. This is our land," Laurel began.

"We need to bury it."

Lavender ran to the shed and grabbed the two biggest shovels she could find, then she and Laurel hurried, digging as fast as they could. The effigy was smaller than the original, but it was still three feet tall. It wasn't a small hole they had to dig.

"Damn it, where are Owen and Gavin?" Laurel complained. "This would go a lot faster with them."

Lavender stopped for a moment and strained her ears. It was quiet inside, too quiet. Something had changed.

"Hurry," she spat out. She kept working but closed her eyes as she did. She focused on breaking the curse. She had spent days obsessed over laying it. Unmaking the curse had already begun.

The line of the Bay witches does not end tonight. I, Lavender Bay, Katherine Fortworth, the soul of both, command it unmade. I command it dissolved. I command the curse sink into the earth with this effigy. No shadows will fall onto this line, no witch or warlock will gain any powers from our blood. Our power is ours, and no one else's. We hold it in our hearts and souls, in every life until we are lain to a final rest.

Suddenly, she could hear Gavin.

"Protect Laurel!" he yelled, bounding toward them, then turning to stand between them and the house.

"What?" Lavender looked at her sister.

"Where's Owen?"

"Miloslav and Ivan are coming. Laurel, run into the woods. Now."

Lavender looked at Gavin, then her sister, whose lips were trembling.

Lavender wasn't sure what was going on, but she trusted Gavin. "Laurel, go. Get to Luke's house and behind his boundaries. It will give you some time."

Laurel looked back at the house, then nodded and disappeared into the darkness.

"Moonbeam, you have about thirty seconds to finish breaking the curse. And watch for flying knives."

"Grab a shovel and help," Lavender said. The hole was deep enough, but she needed help to bury it now. "No matter what happens, get it completely buried, okay?"

Gavin nodded and began working much faster than she or Laurel had.

"Where'd the new mommy go?" Miloslav yelled into the darkness.

Lavender felt her skin go cold.

Was Laurel pregnant? Holy shit...

This wasn't for nothing. She stopped shoveling dirt and stood between Miloslav and Gavin.

"Tell me where she is, Katherine!" Miloslav called.

"Fuck you, Jonas. You awful excuse for a brother." She looked at Ivan. "I feel sorry for you and Morana. What a terrible fate to be tied to this monster."

"Screw you," Ivan yelled back.

"If you think I have qualms about killing you because we used to be related," Miloslav began, "I don't." He turned to Ivan and nodded.

Everything slowed down, but she couldn't move. There was a knife, from her butcher block. She hadn't taken all her knives to her new apartment. Not that Sage cooked a lot, but she needed a knife. And it was coming toward her. Sailing through the air like a paper airplane. It registered slowly that the knife pushed into her shoulder and knocked her to the ground.

"Lavender!" Gavin howled. He dove to the ground beside her. "Fuck. No."

"I'm okay. I'm okay. Is...is it buried?" she panted.

"It's buried. I've got you. Shit, I need to take you to the hospital."

"No. I need to finish this."

Everything went dark. The whole world was suddenly thrust into a darkness so bleak Gavin could barely see Lavender right in front of him.

"I can't see you," Gavin said, panicking.

"I can't see you either."

"What's happening?"

Gavin squinted. In the distance, someone was glowing.

Laurel. Like the moon against a dark sky. An owl came out of nowhere and scratched Miloslav's face.

Gavin looked back to Lavender, who was glowing as well. She pushed herself out of his arms and stood.

The two witches turned toward the warlocks and spoke in unison.

"*The line of the Bays will not end under the work of a warlock. We unweave the curse laid by Katherine Fortworth. We call upon the goddesses and gods who watch over our line to bless our work. Llŷr, Idunn, Nemesis, Hestia, Demeter, Phoebe. We call on Bay witches of past and present. Holly Bay. June Bay. Eliza Bay. Alice Bay. Mary Bay. This evil has hung over our line and ends tonight. We break every strand of the curse. We dip the curse in oil. We light it on fire. The curse is no more. The curse is no more. The curse is no more.*"

Gavin looked on as three more glowing figures came from the house chanting,

"*The curse is no more. The curse is no more. The curse is no more.*"

They glowed so bright he thought the entire house might catch fire. The chanting didn't stop. They went on and on until the light became so bright it was like daylight. A thin black dust rose from each of the Bay sisters and joined into a cloud, then buried itself right where he had just finished burying the effigy.

The lights dimmed, and everyone magical—the Bay sisters and the Stoch warlocks—collapsed to the ground.

Chapter Thirty-Nine

Being stabbed in the shoulder hurt really badly.

But after that, everything was a blur.

She remembered saying the words, doing the spell...but it was like someone else was doing it. And almost as if it was all a dream. She could barely remember what she was saying. Also, they were all glowing? That had never happened before. And then...it was like there had been something stuck in Lavender's chest, and it was loosened. She coughed, as if she had some phlegm stuck that needed to get out of her body and watched as black dust flew out of her mouth.

"What the hell is happening?" Gavin muttered.

"It's the curse," Lavender managed weakly. "It's leaving our line." She fell to her knees.

"Lavender's been stabbed!" Gavin shouted now. "Help!"

Asher came running from the house, punched Ivan straight in the temple, and he crumpled to the ground. Sage turned to Miloslav and did the same, though he stayed on his feet.

"Fuck you," he shouted, trying to brush it off. "I can still fuck you all up. I'm still stronger."

"My sister has a knife wound," Sage seethed. "You think you have the upper hand?" She threw another punch, which he blocked, and then returned one to her shoulder.

Verbena pulled her phone out of her pocket, her fingers quickly moving across the screen. "Miloslav Stoch attacked nine witches tonight. He is a chaos warlock. He tried to take the power of an entire line of witches. Any earth witches out there interested? He has no power over any of you. Last seen on Star Island, Massachusetts." Verbena paused her typing. "I'm uploading your mug shot. The whole Back Hat Haberdashery knows now. You might want to get a head start. Most witches don't take well to warlocks trying to take their powers."

Miloslav looked around.

"Your choice," Sage began. "Run, or I won't hold back."

He scowled, then hurried into the darkness.

Asher was the next to pull out his phone. "This is Asher Evans, and I need an ambulance and police officers at 100 Gazer Lane. Lavender Bay has been stabbed by Ivan Stoch. He's currently unconscious. I subdued him after he attacked Lavender. He is breathing and has a strong pulse. His brother, Miloslav, fled the scene. Both have mug shots in the system." Asher sat down on Ivan's back. "I can keep him subdued until you get here. Thank you."

"I think we're going for a ride in an ambulance," Gavin whispered.

"We are. Have them look at everyone. You might have a broken nose. And Sage looked awful."

"I will."

"My arm hurts really bad."

"You were stabbed. And the knife it still in there."

"Oh shit. Someone needs to put away all the knives."

"On it," Sage called.

"I want to go to sleep."

"I'm pretty sure you are supposed to stay awake." Gavin rubbed her cheek.

"Keep her awake!" Asher yelled.

"I love you," Lavender said. She let her eyes flutter closed.

"Moonbeam, keep your eyes open."

"I can't..."

"Lavender Lily Bay. Do not close your eyes..."

The next thing Lavender knew, she was in a hospital bed with far more people than were allowed to be in the room there. She was bandaged up, had an IV full of painkillers and antibiotics, and was feeling...pretty high.

Within the week, Lavender was out of the hospital, Ivan had pled guilty to attacking her and at her request was transferred to serve time in Montana, and Morana and Miloslav had disappeared. While she didn't relish the thought of the two of them out in the world...the curse was broken. Her mind was shifting toward ease.

The Davies witches stayed for a while, populating all the empty bedrooms of the Bay cottage. It was a little bizarre, having a family of witches they didn't know well staying at the house, but Owen vouched for them. Plus, they'd all be together for a wedding at some point. Erie didn't care for all these strangers hanging around Lavender and mostly kept to her lap.

In bed, Lavender had a lot of time to think.

She had reversed a curse that she had created. The fear over the Stochs was over. Her sisters were safe. And she was with Gavin. Forever.

But...there was still no North American Witches' Council. As much as she had wanted to make it happen, she hadn't been able to. And now, she felt very done.

Done with big magic. Done with curses. Done with risking her and the people she loved's lives for the greater magical world. If someone else wanted to take it over, she would happily stand by their side. But for now, Lavender Bay was going to slip back into her life as a kitchen witch. Little recipes and spells to make the world a better place.

Once the cottage was put to rights and the guests were headed back to their corners of the country, a family dinner was in order. But with orders from the doctor to take it easy, Lavender was sitting at the table and not allowed to cook at all.

It was almost as bad as being stabbed.

Thankfully, Gavin took over everything.

He made a four-course meal—his carrot soup, an endive and blue cheese salad, a lobster risotto, and prime rib with roasted potatoes on a creamy pumpkin sauce—plus he followed Lavender's instructions and made her Samhain pumpkin cake, since they didn't get to have any on actual Samhain.

They celebrated like witches who had just broken a generational curse could—with wine (none for Laurel), good food, and lots of toasts.

"I still can't believe you are going to have a baby," Sage said offhandedly. "A baby. Holy shit. That is a big deal."

"No one is as shocked as we were." Laurel laughed. "I found out right after Verbena was bitten. I was a little more pukey than normal and decided a test was in order."

"Due date?" Rosemary asked.

"June seventeenth."

"Aw, a summer baby!" Rosemary cooed. "Here we go! The chapter of the Bay witches being single and wild is closing, and now we are going to be responsible!"

"Speak for yourself," Sage added.

They all laughed and cackled and enjoyed a very filling meal, and by ten Lavender was ready to go home.

Gavin packed her and the leftover cake into the car—he'd left the rest of the food to be divvied up by the family—and drove them back to Lavender's apartment.

"You doing okay? That was a lot," Gavin said quietly as he pulled out of the driveway.

"I'm tired. But yes, I am okay. You do not need to take me back to the hospital."

"You sure? Dr. Pavarati said to come back if anything felt weird."

"I don't feel weird. I just feel tired."

"Okay." Gavin snuck his hand to her side and took her hand. "Am I being overbearing?"

Lavender laughed. "You are being the right amount of bearing for a man who watched his girlfriend get stabbed less than eight days ago. I promise I'll tell you if we need to go back."

Lavender had lots of stitches, both internal and external, and a very, very sore deltoid. Thankfully, Ivan had hit her left shoulder and not her right. While she wasn't planning on suddenly becoming a competitive volleyball player, she didn't want her stirring arm compromised.

They pulled into the spot right in front of the apartment, where all the residents of Star Island had vowed not to park until Lavender had made a full recovery. She waited until Gavin came around and opened the door for her, then let him gently lead her from the car all the way up to the apartment.

Gavin opened the door for her, fed Erie while he mewed in complaint that his dinner with at least ninety-minutes later, and put away the leftover cake before following her into the bedroom.

"I miss having sex with you," Lavender complained as Gavin gingerly peeled off her sweater and shirt, then unclasped her bra, and put her into pajamas.

"I miss having sex with you too." He laughed.

"What if I lie really still?"

"Well, that sounds fun," he teased and pulled the covers back.

"It might be. We've never tried it."

"What if," Gavin began as he pulled off his shirt and pants and slid beside her in his boxers. "We are responsible adults and wait until Dr. Pavarati gives you the all clear for physical activity? And then we spend a few hours making up for lost weeks?"

"Fine." Lavender sighed, but smiled. Because Gavin propped up a pillow under her arm and kissed her cheeks, forehead, nose, chin, and lips. He turned her good arm over and ran his fingers over her skin again and again, and within moments Lavender had a deep relaxation settling in her chest. Something she hadn't felt in a very long time.

Because the curse had been lifted.

Because the ties had been severed.

Because her sisters were safe.

And because the love of her lives was beside her. And he wasn't going anywhere.

"I love you," she murmured.

"Love you too, Moonbeam."

Yule: 10 Years Later

The Bay cottage smelled like Yule. Cinnamon and nutmeg and sugary butter with added layers of roast beef and mushrooms, scalloped potatoes, cranberry mulled wine, and crisp pear salad.

Dinner was ready, and Lavender finished applying her mascara as quickly as she could. While she could depend on Rosemary, Laurel, and Sage to be late, Verbena's family wouldn't arrive a moment past four-thirty, as the invitation said.

"Best behavior, Mr. Erie," Lavender said as he curled his tail around her ankle. "Lots of nieces and nephews coming over. They will expect to give you a few pats. Then...you may hide wherever you like."

Lavender swore Erie rolled his eyes, but then dutifully pranced out to the parlor to await the aggressive cuddles all the kids would bestow.

"I've put out the charcuterie and the chips and dips. Juice boxes are on the lowest shelf of the fridge, all other cold drinks are in the cooler on the screened porch. Table looks amazing. But not as good as you." Gavin's voice went low at the end. "Is this dress new?"

"Mhmm," Lavender answered as she smoothed the mulberry velvet under her hands. It was floor length, three-quarter sleeved, and had a V in the back that showed off the entire length of her spine. She'd done her hair up in a braided bun, both beautiful and practical, and felt every inch a winter goddess.

"Damn." Gavin ran his hands over her shoulders. "Happy Yule. It's going to be a trick keeping my hands off you until everyone leaves. They'll leave early, though, right? Don't kids usually need to go to bed at some point? Earlier rather than later?"

Lavender laughed. "I'm sure they do, but it's Yule. I think we can expect everyone to stay until at least ten. All the beds and couches will contain sleeping nieces and nephews by the end of the night." She leaned her head back. "Give me a ravishing kiss and then I'll do my lipstick."

"Whatever you say," Gavin murmured and pressed his lips against hers just as the doorbell rang.

Gavin groaned against her mouth. "I'll get it."

"Thank you," Lavender giggled and went back to finishing her makeup. By the cacophony that immediately filled the house, she knew that not only Verbena, Luke, and their four kids were there, but Sage and Will as well. She hurried out to a flurry of hugs and presents being put under the Yule tree in the parlor.

"Merry Yule!" Lavender exclaimed, pulling Verbena into a hug. "How was this morning?" she asked, turning to the kids.

Luke and Verbena had two biological children, six-year-old Kit and five-year-old Amelia, as well as twelve-year-old Julie and nine-year-old Gabrielle, fire witch sisters they'd adopted three years ago. They still lived next door but now that the kids were getting older, Lavender was a little worried they would need to move into a bigger place. Or at the very least build a room for sonofawitch Kit to get a break from all the witchy stuff.

Two years after Gavin had come to Star Island, Sage and Will had moved to New Hampshire. Will got a job at the UNH library, and there was a small homesteading farm for sale twenty miles away. It felt like the perfect compromise to make both of their lives full. So, Sage Bay left Star Island.

But she was back for Yule, with a round belly and a nervous-looking soulmate.

"I fucking hate being pregnant," Sage moaned as she hugged Lavender. "One and done. Should have asked Laurel to surrogate for me. This sucks."

Lavender patted her back. "Sit down. I'll bring you a plate and something to drink. Want me to really boil some of the wine and burn all the alcohol off of it?"

She shook her head. "I'd rather have a juice box. And just put the bowl of potato chips and onion dip right next to me." Will followed her dutifully to the couch and moved the chips onto Sage's lap. As soon as they were in place, Julie collapsed next to her and took a handful. Erie jumped onto the couch and sandwiched himself between the two of them—a perfect place to sit and keep his tail from being stepped on.

"Good," Sage began. "Sit by me. You can tell me about all the cool fire magic shit you are doing."

Gavin took everyone's coats into their bedroom, and a moment later, Rosemary and Asher arrived with eight-year-old Hyacinth, seven-year-old Daisy, and five-year-old Forrest.

"Merriest of Yules!" Rosemary announced. "We are ready to celebrate! We've been accidentally growing mistletoe and holly all morning so preemptive apologies if anything strange happens." Hyacinth and Forrest both inherited their mother's garden magic, while Daisy was showing some early signs of being a Guardian like Asher. Last summer, she'd gotten between a swarm of bees and her little brother, and neither of them had gotten stung once.

"I love your outfits!" Lavender exclaimed. The girls were in matching green renaissance faire-style dresses with lace-up corsets, and Forrest had on his very own woodland elf get-up complete with bracers.

"Presents today!" Rosemary peeled off her coat to reveal a positively wench-like outfit complete with ample cleavage.

Lavender smiled. She was so happy Rosemary hadn't changed at all with motherhood.

The cousins shrieked with delight and ran around the house like little sprites filled with Yuletide cheer.

Fifteen minutes later, Owen came to the door with the four children, then raced back to the car to help Laurel.

"Come in, come in!" Lavender waved her four nieces in.

"Happy Yule, Lav!" Gwen called as she took Rhiannon's coat off. "Dad ran back to help Mom. She's not feeling great today."

"Is she okay?" Lavender asked, taking Nia and Anwyn's coats and looking over their heads.

Owen had his arm around Laurel's hips and was helping her up the stairs.

"You okay?" Lavender reiterated.

"Yes. Just terribly uncomfortable. But it's my own fault. I agreed, one more baby and maybe we get a boy. Or another girl! Who cares? Five is the magic Bay number. So of course I get two boys."

"Two boys?" Lavender exclaimed.

"Yup. Appointment yesterday. Two *big* boys. Both measuring over the eightieth percentile. Even though they are sharing real estate." Laurel waddled over to the couch and sat next to Sage.

"Oh, good. Now I feel a little better about my current condition," Sage said. "I look downright dainty next to you."

"Don't curse yourself. We Bay women have huge babies. My smallest was nine pounds."

"Bite your tongue. Rosie, wasn't Daisy only seven pounds?"

"Yes. But she was also three weeks early because of that weird storm that came through and made everyone go into labor. Hyacinth was nine-two. Forrest was nine-six."

"Kit was ten pounds!" Verbena called. "And Amelia was eight pounds fourteen ounces, but she was also technically a week early."

"Argh! Stop! No more talking about how my vagina is going to be destroyed." Sage leaned back and closed her eyes.

"I think that's my cue to get dinner on the table," Gavin said quietly in Lavender's ear.

"Please do." She laughed.

"Owen!" Laurel called. "Will you keep an eye on Gwen?" She turned to Lavender. "She's gotten in the water four times this month. She's having a hard time with the whole 'sea witches need to keep a low profile.' We're going to Maine for New Years'. She can get some good ocean time with Owen's cousins and hopefully a more understanding coast guard."

Looking over her nieces and nephews, Lavender had no regrets in their decision not to have children. She'd raised a family already. And she could still dote over plenty of babies. Her family was complete with Gavin, and the past decade had been filled with time for each other, finally. They'd spent a summer in Italy three years ago, traveled throughout northern Europe for their honeymoon, and even gone to Japan earlier this year. After years of putting everyone before herself, Lavender was finally enjoying all the things she had postponed.

"Dinner is ready!" Gavin called to the masses. "Grab a plate and fill up!"

After dinner was eaten and enjoyed, but before desserts were brought out, their family headed outside to give thanks for the season.

Lavender led the way, crunching through the thin layer of snow that had fallen earlier in the day but was now frozen over. A trail of people followed her—cottage witches and water witches and fire witches and Guardians and warlocks and sonofawitches and humans. The whole group that made up their beautiful family walked in relative silence to the bonfire Lavender and Gavin had set up in the morning. It was unlit, waiting for Julie and Gabrielle to light it.

They circled the dry wood, each breaking into their smaller families. Laurel with Owen, their four children, and her ever-expanding belly. Rosemary with Asher and their three children. Verbena with Luke and their four children. Sage with Will and her round tummy.

And Lavender with Gavin, the love of her lives and the perfect complement to her soul. She wound her hand in his and leaned against his shoulder.

"I love you," he whispered and pressed a kiss against her forehead.

"Love you too," she whispered back.

"All right, can we start?" Sage complained. "I already have to pee."

They all laughed and turned their heads to the sky, taking a long breath in unison, and began.

By midnight, the house was empty save Lavender and Gavin. The kitchen was clean, the leftovers either wrapped up and put away or in the cars of the rest of the family. The tornado of wrapping paper that had littered the parlor floor was stuffed into large black garbage bags. The table was cleared and wiped down, the floors swept.

And Lavender stood in the middle of the parlor, her mulberry dress still on, the twinkling lights from the Yule tree the only illumination.

"Finally," Gavin murmured as he came up behind her. His hands circled her waist and he teased her neck with a quick kiss. "As much as I've admired this dress all night long..." His fingers slid to the zipper.

Lavender giggled. "Take it off. Please. I'm ready to be alone with my soulmate on Yule."

"Longest night of the year. This year it truly was." He peeled her dress off, then waited for her to step out of it and tossed it onto the couch.

He smoothed his hands over her skin as she quickly unbuttoned his shirt. She never got tired of this. After ten years together, she still felt her heart thump against her chest as he slowly undressed her. She shivered when he ran his hands over her favorite spots. She couldn't believe how much she loved and adored this man.

Lavender pushed his shirt off his shoulders, made quick work of his belt and pants, and led him to the couch.

Climbed onto his lap.

Dug her hands into his hair as she moved over him.

Buried her face against his neck when she came.

Wrapped her legs around his hips when he flipped her to her back.

And smiled softly in the moments afterward with Gavin's head against her chest, his breath warm on her skin.

They picked up their discarded clothes and tossed them into the corner of their bedroom, before collapsing, side by side, into their bed.

"Come here," Gavin mumbled, pulling her to lie on his chest. "Happy Yule."

She smiled against his skin. "Happy Yule. Let's sleep all day tomorrow."

He grumbled an affirmative, his large hand splayed over her back.

"Love you, Moonbeam," he mumbled as his body settled into sleep.

"I love you," she answered, melting into his embrace.

The deep cold and quiet of the longest night of the year settled over the Bay cottage, their land, and all of Star Island. Two souls, lovers over hundreds of years, thousands of heartbreaks and joys and finally peace.

And in the moments before sleep took over, Lavender smiled against his skin.

They had gotten their happy, quiet life by the sea.

Thank you for reading! Did you enjoy? Please add your review because nothing helps an author more and encourages readers to take a chance on a book than a review.

And THANK YOU for reading Colleen Delaney's *The Witches of Star Island* series. Find more from Delaney at www.colleendelaney.com

Then, discover THE NIGHT'S CHOSEN, by City Owl Author, E. E. Hornburg. Turn the page for a sneak peek!

You can also sign up for the City Owl Press newsletter to receive notice of all book releases!

Sneak Peek of The Night's Chosen

BY E. E. HORNBURG

Eira never dreaded sunset. Or the Moon Festival. Or returning home. Or seeing the Oxarian royal family. She had always looked forward to those things. But not today. If only she could stop time.

No, not stop time, exactly. If she stopped time, Eira would never become queen.

She'd spent her life, all twenty-odd years of it, preparing to reign. She wanted to stop the *wedding*, something she should have been as prepared for as ruling Cresin.

Eira twirled the betrothal band around her wrist. The wedding was going to happen, regardless of what she wanted. With a deep exhale, she closed her eyes and sang, hoping to ease the storm brewing inside and instead focus on the peaceful magic bestowed on her by Luana's priestesses.

The song ignited the crescent moon tattoo on her chest, and as it glowed, stars formed and sparkled around her head. Swirls of darkness poured out of her fingers and mingled with the betrothal band. The tune and words were meant to sooth and calm the soul, make the singer become one with Luana and be as peaceful as the night sky. Yet it did little to ease the darkness, ice, and stars warring underneath Eira's skin.

Luana grant me peace...grant me grace...

The wedding was this week. Tonight, she and Alvis were going to perform the opening ceremony for the Moon Festival, ushering in Luana's season, where the nights became longer than the day. This year, it would also signify the start of the wedding celebrations. As the Chosens of Luana and

Ray, it was believed pieces of the souls of the god and goddess resided inside both she and Alvis, making them the closest to the deities their people would ever have. The two had been betrothed her entire life. Yet now the week arrived and she still wasn't ready.

A knock came at the door, breaking Eira's trance. With a wave of her arms, the stars and darkness vanished, and her tattoo faded. Taking a deep breath, she closed her robe and moved to the door, where the knocking was becoming incessant.

"Eira! Will you quit all your praying and let me in?" Rose's voice drifted from the other side of the door.

Her younger sister almost clubbed Eira in the eye with the velvet box she held as Eira pulled the door open.

"I'd imagine after a year of visiting temples, you'd have had enough of praying by now." Rose barreled into the room, leaning on her crutch, and dropped the box on the vanity with a thud.

"It was more necessary than usual today." Eira shut the door behind them and exhaled, pressing her lips together before placing her hands on her hips. "And maybe if I hadn't received dozens of letters from you and Father begging me to come home from those temples, I wouldn't need to pray so long this morning."

Rose waved Eira off. "It wasn't as though you hadn't planned on being home in time for the Moon Festival. We were simply reminding you."

She dropped her crutch and it clattered to the ground as she flopped onto the plush, deep blue bed, pale freckled arms outstretched. Her copper hair splayed out on the quilt like fiery waves.

Eira had only been home for a few days since her yearlong pilgrimage, and had a curious new fascination with Rose. In so many ways she was the same, but in spite of sending letters all year and seeing one another for the holy days, there was still something different Eira couldn't put her finger on. Rose had always been as fiery as her red hair and ready to speak her mind at any given chance. She never sat still for more than a moment. Yet now there was an air of unease and distance about her Eira didn't recognize. This was one of the reasons she was glad to be home, in spite of everything. She wanted to get to know her sister again.

"And it wasn't *dozens* of letters," Rose replied. "It's been a difficult year."

Eira crossed the room and sat on the bed next to Rose.

"I'm aware. It's not as though I was only sitting in temples praying the whole time. I went and visited as many of the villages that needed help as I could. They're recovering from the fires, but it's going to take a long time."

"I'm not only talking about the fire recovery." Rose propped herself on her elbows. "People have been...talking."

Eira shifted in her seat. "People talk often, Rose, whether I'm here or not."

"Last night after supper, Father and I overheard the Oxarian king and queen talking. It appears they have been concerned about your dedication to the betrothal."

"Oh?" Eira rubbed the band on her wrist again, as though it were squeezing her tighter with each moment.

"It's been five years since your original wedding date. While Father and Alvis have been more than happy to let you go off to university and travel the kingdoms, and your pilgrimage came at the perfect time after the forest fires so you could help the people while you traveled, King Rahim and Queen Shideh and other nobles from Oxare don't see it the same way."

They were smart. Of course they were. They'd raised Alvis, after all, and he was one of the most intelligent people she knew. Eira had been running for so long, and now there was nowhere else to go.

She straightened her shoulders and smiled. "Well, I'll have to prove them wrong, won't I? The whole opening ceremony for the Moon Festival is the commencement of the wedding celebrations. Once they see me there, they'll know I haven't changed my mind about the wedding."

Rose groaned and pushed into a sitting position. "It's not only them. There're other people, too. They're wondering why you haven't been around."

"That's ridiculous," Eira said through a clenched jaw. "Royals travel through their kingdoms all the time. Father did before he became king, and still does. Besides, after I get married, I'm going to be in Oxare with Alvis for half the year anyway."

"I know."

Rose's touch on her arm sent a wave of warm comfort through her, and Eira felt her shoulders relax. A hint at the closeness they once had.

"But you know how people are. Normally I wouldn't worry about it, and I've been defending you, especially with the guard, and you have so many who are loyal to you..."

Of course Rose defended her. It's what she'd been doing for her their entire lives. What they both had done for each other. No matter how many months Eira was away, she knew she never had to doubt Rose. Even when Eira doubted herself, if Rose was there, she knew all would be fine.

"But?" Eira prodded.

The hesitation in Rose's voice was enough to make Eira's concerns heighten.

"But it's not only gossip. Some members of the council eventually listened, and talked too. So did Queen Amelia." Rose grimaced at the idea of their stepmother. "You know how she is, though. I don't suspect any of the priestesses have gossiped, but you know how close High Priestess Nyx is to some of the council members. I don't want to concern you, but I'd be lying if I said I wasn't relieved you were coming home. This ceremony could be the start of your gaining back their trust."

The new complication brought more to consider, and Eira rubbed her temples to ease the faint throbbing that had started, and slid off the bed. While she respected High Priestess Nyx as the leader of Luana's temple, the two of them often disagreed in matters of theology and politics.

With Nyx having the ears of many councilmen, planting seeds of doubt, Eira was sure all eyes would be on her even more during the ceremony and wedding celebrations. Regardless, whatever doubts Eira had about herself or this marriage, she couldn't—and shouldn't—let it interfere with ascending the throne someday. Her people needed to have complete confidence in her.

She may not have been ready to be married to Alvis, but her desire to be queen never faltered.

The remnants of an afternoon snack sat on the vanity next to the velvet box, and Eira took a piece of apple, popped it into her mouth, and gobbled it. When she opened the box to reveal a silver and blue diadem, the stardust sprinkled on the metal twisting around diamonds made it sparkle on its own without needing any light from the room. Eira lifted it out and perched it onto her long dark hair.

It was one of Cresin's oldest antiques and had been worn by Luana's Chosen for hundreds of years. Eira didn't wear it often, but when she did, she found herself sitting straighter, with her shoulders back and head held high. When she wore it, she could imagine herself being a woman worthy to have it on her head and to live up to the legacy she'd been born into.

She could do this.

She had to do this.

People always said she looked like Queen Isadore—the first Chosen of Luana—and Luana herself. Not as though she ever had anything to compare herself to, other than paintings that followers of Goddess Efare created of what they supposed Luana and Isadore looked like. Legend said all of Luana's Chosen through the generations looked like Luana, and all Eira's life people claimed she had the closest likeness since Isadore, with pale—almost translucent—skin, blood-red lips, dark hair, and sky-blue eyes.

Each of the firstborn heiresses of the Cresin throne were the daughters and Chosen of Luana, as the firstborn heirs of Oxare were the sons and Chosen of Ray.

Rose grabbed her crutch and limped over to Eira. They stood side by side in front of the mirror, opposites at first glance, with Eira's gentleness and Rose's wild nature. On further inspection, the two sisters were perfect compliments to one another.

Rose groaned. "You're not even dressed yet and you already look perfect. It's not fair."

"Perhaps it would help if you changed out of your training leathers."

Rose had a unique and free beauty about her, but usually she was too busy beating the other members of the guard on the training grounds for many to notice.

Or at least, for Rose to notice others noticing her.

Another knock came at the door. The familiar melodic voice of Priestess Cynth came from behind it.

"Your Highness? The opening ceremony is supposed to start soon. We need to prepare you."

Eira's heart sank. Once Priestess Cynth and the ladies-in-waiting came into her chamber, it would be nonstop preparations, celebrations, and being surrounded by people until she was at the altar and at Alvis's side for their wedding at the end of the week. She'd have no peace. No personal space. No chance of stopping the wedding.

Outside her window, past the white rose tree which bloomed and grew up the wall no matter what the season, the songs of Luana's priestesses floated in the air. Part of Eira wished to join them. They didn't know how lucky they were. Free to worship, to make friends, and even to take whoever they wanted to bed whenever they liked.

She could do it. Be one of the priestesses. She'd been bestowed with the same powers, and studied Luana's ways the way they had been—even more so as the Chosen. She'd trained and studied longer than most priestesses, and was given more power at her dedication ceremony as a young woman than the others. Traveling to all of Luana's temples over the past year had shown her this, especially when she'd been in the oldest temple in the Paravian Mountains and her magic awoke there.

Cynth's own mother, who was a priestess there, welcomed Eira with open arms, and when she'd left, promised there would always be a place for Eira.

The town was small, and the mountains dangerous, with strange winged creatures terrorizing them. But she'd still go back in a heartbeat.

And priestesses weren't required to marry.

Eira turned and glanced at herself in the vanity mirror, with the stardust circled around her hair, looking like the midnight sky. She was a queen. Or at least, was going to be.

Queen. This was what she should be focused on. Becoming queen was what was important here.

"Are you all right?"

Her sister's touch on her shoulder brought Eira back to reality.

She blinked and forced a bright smile. "Of course. Why wouldn't I be?"

Rose cocked her head, with a raised brow. "It's a big week, and we've barely talked for months. It's not an odd question."

Priestess Cynth knocked again. "I'm sorry to disturb, Your Highness, but we do need to prepare. Sunset will not wait for us."

No. It would not.

Luana bless it.

Eira took a couple deep breaths, touching her thumb to each of her fingertips to calm herself.

Her pulse slowed to normal, and her muscles relaxed.

"Yes, please come in."

A flurry of women entered the chamber with dresses and cosmetics overflowing in their arms and excited chatter pouring out of their mouths like a waterfall, drowning out the priestesses' songs from outside. Lady Evony at the back of the group held glasses in one hand and a bottle of wine in the other. As the women went to work at removing Eira's robe, Evony, court's unofficial patron of festivities, passed out the glasses and poured the wine with extravagant flourishes and twirls, without spilling a single drop.

Whatever calmness had resided in Eira vanished. Her nerves fired off, her senses overloaded at the ruckus surrounding her. She barely registered the weight of the drink in her hand.

The ladies cheered when Evony raised a glass over her curly head of hair, and they all followed suit.

"To our royal highness, Princess Eira," Evony said, "her betrothed Prince Alvis, and the coming of Luana's season. Gods know all the fun happens in the night, after all."

The stardust in the ceremony gown Priestess Cynth held glimmered in her eyes as she looked over her shoulder at Evony.

"I wasn't aware you had the patience to wait for night for your type of fun," Cynth said.

Rose chuckled when Evony placed a hand over her heart and dropped her jaw.

"It's not my fault people beg for my company, no matter the time of day," Evony said.

Rose cleared her throat. "Less drinking, more helping." She stretched her permanently twisted ankle in front of Evony and wiggled it in a circle. "I can never get my straps tight enough."

Evony sighed before she finished off her wine, then set the glass on the table with a thud and cocked her voluptuous hip.

"Out of all my talents," she said, "this is the one I'm asked to do. Whoever said coming to Farren Castle was going to be glamorous never mentioned this."

"Yes, I'm sure the fish in Slania are much more glamorous," Rose said.

"It took months to get the smell out of my clothes." Evony took the straps from the pile of Rose's ceremonial clothes, and winked.

Within minutes, the white leather-like straps were wrapped around Rose's ankle, straightening and smoothing the limb. It had been a gift from their grandmother, who served Kutlaous, the god of nature, in Eral Forest. The straps were enchanted with Fae magic to give Rose the strength she needed to walk without a crutch for short periods. Such as evening ceremonies and balls.

Or as Rose preferred, on the training grounds and while patrolling the castle.

The white of the straps faded until they were invisible, showing off Rose's tattoo, dedicated to Aros, the god of war and hunting. When unbound by the straps, the tattoo appeared to be thorny rose vines etched into Rose's warped and twisted skin. When straightened by the straps, it was the sword of Aros, with white and red roses wrapped around the blade, like the roses outside each of their bedchamber windows, planted after their mother died. A symbol of Rose's dedication not only to her god, but to their bond as sisters and princesses.

Something stirred inside Eira each time she saw it.

The time spent preparing went by in a blur of cloth and perfumes and stardust. The sparkling gown clung to Eira like a second skin once it was pulled over her head and down her body. The skirt swirled around her legs and ankles in a silver river. The neckline, like all of her ceremonial gowns, dipped low and wide to expose her tattoo. A symbol to be showed off and admired, proving she belonged to Luana. It was a fashion Eira had grown used to after she'd received her tattoo.

When she was younger and first growing into her body, she'd felt exposed and shy. Now she was proud to show her dedication to Luana and kingdom. She enjoyed the power mixed with sensuality in her costumes.

Where there wasn't fabric, there were crystals and stardust stuck and painted to her arms, legs, and bosom. This day, it was a gown she could hide in. In this gown, she not only belonged to Luana, but *was* Luana. Goddess of the night, darkness, and winter. In this gown, she was supposed to welcome the changing of the seasons, where the daytime was shortened to make way for longer nights.

She was also supposed to greet her lover, Ray, god of the sun.

Eira could only imagine what Alvis's ceremony attire would look like.

Perhaps Eira could at least pretend to be Luana if she was dressed for the part, and be separate from herself.

Time moved too quickly, and before she knew it she was being escorted by Priestess Cynth out of her bedchamber and toward the great hall. All the attendees were waiting for them there. Her father, stepmother, Alvis and his family, and all of the lords and ladies of the kingdom. Her kingdom. The one she'd spent months helping to regain its bearings after flash forest fires burned through the villages, leaving only ashes in their wake. The one she'd been born in, and who believed in her through every step of her life.

Until she'd started running away five years ago.

Now she returned, and people were talking. Eira's cheeks burned as shame washed over her. She'd been foolish and immature all this time. So many others had it far worse than she did, and Alvis was a good man. One of the best she'd ever known. He was the perfect person to bring the kingdoms of Cresin and Oxare together the way Isadore and Sanson did all those centuries ago, when they were at war with one another.

Rose was at her side when they approached the great hall's door, and squeezed Eira's hand. She was out of her training leathers and wore a simple silver gown which resembled a long jacket with short sleeves. It was shorter in the front, revealing tight leggings, and billowed out in the back like a cloak. If it weren't for Rose's usual playful smile, she'd look regal.

"You'll be wonderful," Rose said.

She gave her sister a warm hug, then walked away and into the great hall, leaving Eira and Priestess Cynth alone. Eira pushed her shoulders back and straightened her diadem, but despite that her heart sank as it begged her to turn and run.

No, it was time she behaved like the future queen and Chosen they all pictured her to be.

Thank you for reading Colleen Delaney's *The Witches of Star Island* series, and be sure to find more from her at www.colleendelaney.com

Then, discover THE NIGHT'S CHOSEN, by City Owl Author, E. E. Hornburg.

Chosen of the Moon Goddess. Destined to rule. Fated to marry. A quest to save her family, kingdom, and heart.

For the past five years Princess Eira has run from her impending wedding. As much as she loves her goddess and kingdom, she's searched the kingdoms for another way to rule as queen someday while also choosing her own husband.

Yet, Eira's claim to the crown falls into jeopardy when her father, King Brennus, is poisoned and fated to a sleep of living death and Eira is next on the assassin's hit list – who happens to be her stepmother, Queen Amelia.

After Eira escapes Queen Amelia's clutches she journeys to the northern Paravian mountains in search of an enchanted cup to save her father.

Her quest is more than she anticipated with evading Queen Amelia's guards, traveling with the one man she shouldn't be with, and having to bargain with the ancient dragon guarding the enchanted cup.

She'll have to decide how to save her family and kingdom, even if it means sacrificing her heart and all she's wanted her whole life.

Please sign up for the City Owl Press newsletter for chances to win special subscriber-only contests and giveaways as well as receiving information on upcoming releases and special excerpts.

All reviews are **welcome** and **appreciated**. Please consider leaving one on your favorite social media and book buying sites.

Escape Your World. Get Lost in Ours! City Owl Press at www.cityowlpress.com.

Acknowledgments

To finish a series is a complicated feeling. Relief, despair, elation, and grief all mix together into a concoction of emotion that has pressed upon me for the last year, and, truthfully, I could barely get through an editing session without crying. In my defense, this last one was a pretty angsty story so tears were expected. But something that began so long ago has finally come to an end, and now it's time to say goodbye to the Bay sisters.

I have to begin by thanking my husband, because without him I would not be able to be an author. This is not a calling or career that pays many bills, and without him supporting both me and our children, these stories would have to be content as half-finished ideas entertaining me as I lay awake in the dark trying to fall asleep. So thank you, to my best friend and partner. To quote Ingrid Michealson, I love you more than I could ever promise.

To my kids: you were real troopers the last couple months. The final push to get this book out into the world was a big one, and some deadlines coinciding with the beginning of summer meant we didn't beach/pool/park as much as everyone wanted to. I plan to rectify that ASAP.

To my sisters: Thank you for listening to me complain when I got stuck and things were hard, especially because I wanted zero advice and only responses like "oh no!" You both are perfect. (My brothers are great too; they do not field writing woes.)

To my mom and dad: Thank you for supporting me and my dreams, even when those dreams were things like an English Lit major, a History/Philosophy double minor, and a concentration in Women's Studies. My dad may have said, "for the love of God, will you take a business class?" And this witchy daughter answered...no. I probably should have listened and taken at least one marketing class. Miss you, Dad.

To my writing friends: Jen, Abigail, Tova, Natalia, Charish, Desirée. Your friendship and community mean the world to me. I am so happy I met all of you. Thank you for your support throughout this entire series.

To the whole team at City Owl, but especially Tee Tate. Thank you for guiding me throughout this process and making these books the best versions of themselves. Tee, I have thoroughly enjoyed working with you over the years, and I will miss you! If I ever write that lightly outlined "Skáldi and Gundrun adjacent Viking story," I know who I am sending it to.

And now, the fun ones. Thank you to all the librarians who waited in line to get The Hedge Witch signed at ALA this summer! Thank you to everyone who came to Meet Me on North September 2025 and came to my table and bought all my books! Thank you to the AMAZING readers in the Dark Tomes and Tombstones book club (I love you all)!!!

In closing, I am one of five kids, so five has always been a magical number to me. It has been an absolute joy to write The Witches of Star Island. I thank you from the bottom of my heart for reading five whole books in this magical world. While I can't promise you'll see the Bay sisters again...I may have first draft in a folder somewhere where you can catch glimpses of them in the corner. I can safely promise I will write about magical women for the rest of my life.

Find the light, and draw a circle around it.

Goodbye, Star Island.

About the Author

COLLEEN DELANEY is an author, librarian, gardener, and occasional baker. She likes being outside in every season except winter, which she prefers to enjoy from a window. She currently lives on the shores of a Great Lake with her husband and four time-consuming children.

www.colleendelaney.com

instagram.com/colleendelaneywrites
x.com/cdelaneywriter
tiktok.com/@colleendelaneywrites
youtube.com/@ColleenDelaney
threads.com/@colleendelaneywrites

About the Publisher

City Owl Press is a cutting edge indie publishing company, bringing the world of romance and speculative fiction to discerning readers.

Escape Your World. Get Lost in Ours!

www.cityowlpress.com

facebook.com/CityOwlPress
x.com/cityowlpress
instagram.com/cityowlbooks
pinterest.com/cityowlpress
tiktok.com/@cityowlpress

www.ingramcontent.com/pod-product-compliance
Lightning Source LLC
Chambersburg PA
CBHW022013140826
49883CB00027B/130
9781648985836